WHISPER OF A WITCH

THE SAVANNAH COVEN SERIES

SUZA KATES

ICASM PRESS
SAVANNAH

Published by Icasm Publishing LLC
5710 Ogechee Rd. Suite 200 #278, Savannah, GA 31405
www.icasmpress.com

Library of Congress Cataloging-in-Publication Data

Kates, Suza
Whisper of a Witch / Suza Kates
    p. cm.

ISBN-13:978-0-9845929-0-6
ISBN-13:978-0-9845929-1-3 (ebook)
I. Title

Printed and bound in the United States of America

10 9 8 7 6 5 4 3 2 1

ACKNOWLEDGMENTS

There once was an idea about the thrill of magic and the camaraderie of sisters.

I would never have seen this series come to life without the help of others and would like to thank Brian McCann for his amazing talent in graphic design and Donna Wood, Julie Bruce, and Sheila Dickens for their writing advice and encouragement.

I also want to thank David, not only for his website design skills, but for his constant supply of patience and support.

While writing a book, I usually get a feeling of who I should dedicate it to by something in the story that reminds me of that person. It's often because they've taught me a lesson or influenced me at some point in my life. At the end of this one, I was still at a loss, and then I realized why. In this case, I wasn't reminded of any particular person.

So...

This book is for the ones who have been by my side for many, many years and have been a never-ending source of love and entertainment.

This one is for my cats.

PROLOGUE

The day was ordinary, a simple Saturday, though whether it was morning, noon, or dead of night varied depending on location. The event coincided with no particular marking on any type of calendar, almanac, or celestial chart. No equinox or solstice, and not any particular holiday.

But for nine women, the moment had arrived, though only one of them had known to expect it.

~

"Well, that's where you'll find her, alive and unharmed. Check it out if you don't believe me. She's living it up with her new boyfriend," Hayden told the police officer who viewed her through his narrowed, skeptical eyes.

"And you know this how?" he asked, slapping the file on the counter between them. The force had been scouring the area for days, following up any and every lead concerning the missing teenage girl. Her parents had money, and along with that came lots of strings for pulling.

Pressure was on big time, and their chief wanted any information brought straight to him, regardless of its source.

Hayden simply tossed her caramel hair over her shoulder and held her ground. She was used to this sort of reception.

The large man sighed. "Wait here. I'll let the sergeant know."

When he left, Hayden turned to the little, silver-haired lady beside her. "Okay, they'll take it from here. You should go now. They'll find her and get her away from him before anything happens." The older woman smiled in thanks, clutching the yellow handbag that perfectly matched her yellow shoes, and faded away into nonexistence.

"Who are you talking to?" the cop asked from behind.

"Oh, just myself." Hayden smiled, despite the look he gave her and the shake of his head. He was probably classifying her as "nutcase" right about now, but she was used to that, too.

You can come on back. Tell us what you know," he mumbled with little enthusiasm.

Hayden took one step then halted as knowledge bolted through her like the detonation of a nuclear warhead. It was so intense she had to rub her temples and the pain that lingered.

She'd always been so sensitive.

Shoving the notebook paper into the officer's hand, she retreated a step. "Here's the address, but I have to go."

"Wait. You said…"

"Just go to the address. She's there," Hayden tossed over her shoulder, hurrying across the lobby and bursting out into the bright San Francisco morning.

First she had to pack then book a flight.

She was needed elsewhere.

~

Slashing her way through the dense, tropical brush of the Philippines, Lucia held up a hand to halt the motion of the two men she'd hired to help carry her belongings. She had come to the hot, green paradise to locate Yamashita's gold, or at least a few coins, maybe some trinkets, as others had been lucky enough to do.

But she wouldn't have to count on or require any sort of luck. She had a unique gift and would have put the tale of lost treasure to bed once and for all if not for the punch of instinct to her gut that had her changing plans, virtually in mid-stride.

She re-tied her mass of black curls in a brown band and

heaved a frustrated sigh, eyeing the mountains with regret. As dawn streaked its way across the peaks, she made a silent vow to return. For now, she had somewhere else to be.

The pulls and nudges were nothing new, as Lucia had been born with an uncanny knack for finding things, whether lost or hidden. A force guided her, and she had learned long ago to trust it, to harness it. But this time the directive was laced with an undeniable and trembling urgency that shook her to the tips of her hiking boots. This one was different.

Biting out an order in her Spanish accent to begin back down the trail and toward camp, she took a swallow of water from the bottle hanging from a belt at her hips and trudged along in silence, both intrigued and anxious. She knew exactly where she was going and would set out immediately. No time to have a respite as she often did between excursions. She had to hurry.

No doubt about it, she thought, taking another swig.

This one was different.

~

Rubbing the flanks of an elephant that was heavy with the load of impending birth, Shauni murmured to the gentle animal and soothed its fear. The clean, liberating smell of nature danced through the grasses at the base of Cheyenne Mountain, and she lifted her face to the cool wind as it washed over her. One of the perks of being a biologist was the office view.

The zoo in Colorado Springs allowed its animals a more authentic environment than most, even manmade cliffs for goats to roam. Lions roared their dominance and monkeys laughed, the sounds blending with the cries of children as they stroked and marveled in the animal contact area. Here was peace. Here was the reward for long years of work and study.

Here was home.

And in a flash it all changed.

She patted the hind quarters of the elephant one more time. "You'll do fine, Priscilla. Maybe a girl this time." She walked away, already outlining the resignation letter in her head.

I don't know what's happening or why, but I'm going to miss this place and my job. She scanned the happy faces and contented animals, her own little extended family. *I'll miss them, too.*

~

Paige, a soldier recently discharged from duty, was taking a long-awaited road trip across the States. She had no family to visit, her friends were few and scattered, so with a load of free time dropped in her lap, she'd opted for a vacation.

She relished the idea of peace and beauty. Time to think. All things that would be a welcome change from what she'd seen and done over the last several years.

Hydrangeas would be blooming soon in North Carolina, and she'd always wanted to tour the gardens of Biltmore as they opened their eyes to look for spring. Room service in a grand hotel and glimpses of life at its most luxurious. That would do the trick.

Catching a glimpse of herself in the rearview mirror, Paige studied the white blonde hair as it shagged across her forehead and noticed the hardness around her sea-blue eyes, a fierce edge of defense that had started years ago and had only increased as time and humanity continued their education, teaching her that the world was often more cruel than ever expected.

Paige huffed out a breath. She really needed some time off.

She tried to envision a quiet walk among dew-kissed flowers, but the image exploded and was swiftly replaced by a picture of an entirely different place.

I-20 was already leading her East, but she knew she wouldn't be taking the route as previously planned. There would be another exit, and she waited for the green signs to announce its arrival.

Veering onto the ramp she checked the mirror one more time but was looking behind her now and couldn't say why. She felt as if she were being followed, though that made no sense at all.

Cranking up the sound of the hard and fast song on the radio, she tapped her fingers on the wheel. Sharp eyes focused on the road as she accelerated.

And headed south.

~

"Don't ask me why. I just have to drop out." Kylie tore through her dorm room like an angry cleaning crew, tossing her favorite and cutest clothes into a large suitcase the color of sour apple bubble gum. It barely closed, even when she sat on it, but finally she heard the latch click.

Spying a large cardboard box on top of her roommate's bookshelves she climbed up and knocked it to the floor. *Screw it. I'm taking everything.* The rest of her clothes, makeup, and shoes went flying in. She would worry about wrinkles later.

"The semester is almost over. This is stupid," complained the boy she'd been dating, though she used the word "dating" loosely. When the first joke of their date-night movie had flown over his head, Kylie realized he was no descendant of Einstein. He was, however, a brother in the most popular fraternity on campus, and she had been in the mood for some social climbing.

Unfortunately, the higher the ladder, the lower the IQs. Or so it seemed.

The fact was, Kylie was gorgeous as well as brilliant, therefore, a fish out of every kind of water. She never seemed to fit in.

"I don't have time to explain. Will you help me take this all down to my car?" she pleaded, batting the lashes over her big, hazel eyes. Might as well test her powers.

"Whatever," he said but hauled the box out despite his disappointment.

She trailed after him, pulling her heavy suitcase on its wheels with a prayer they would hold up under the weight but stopped and shrieked when she spied a pair of red strappy heels on top of the refrigerator. They'd been left there to dry after she'd had to clean the mud off from a keg party hosted in a field.

Whisking them off the fridge, she hugged them to her chest. "Thank you, God. I almost forgot the Guccis."

~

Post-Newtonian parameters were essential tools for testing general relativity. The problem was the results only added more information that firmly debunked the theory of telekinesis.

But it's still bullshit. Slamming the cover closed on her latest journal, which she preferred over computer files, Viv rubbed the bridge of her nose as she often did when stressed.

The notebook was a personal ritual and a type of creature comfort with its soft leather, aged to look older than it was. It also served to keep her research private.

Oh, she performed above and beyond for the company she worked for as a physicist, but had no qualms about using the lab for her own experiments when the work day was done. And the research notes always went home with her. No need for anyone to wonder over her after-hours obsession.

Her pomegranate flavored green tea had cooled, so with a lift of her hand, she simultaneously pulled open the microwave door and floated the cup inside. Thirty seconds should do it.

Viv rarely used her power for simple tasks, as that spoke of laziness, but at the moment, she didn't care. She needed to understand what she could do before telling anyone and didn't want to end up in a government cage, knowing all too well they existed.

The microwave beeped three times, but the only sound she heard was the rush of voices and light, if light could be heard, then well, this is what it would sound like. A hum and trill, like an otherworldly instrument unknown to human ears.

When it subsided, she breathed in and out in an attempt to calm herself, and once succeeded, she said only, "Okay then," and rose to dispose of the tea and wash the cup. It was her favorite, a jade green that faded into olive with striations resembling layers of earth.

She would take it with her.

~

Thanking her lucky stars that she had taken the PRN position, which meant "as needed" in the medical world, Willyn looked at her schedule and was glad she only had one more shift scheduled. She would work tomorrow then explain to her nursing manager that she would be unavailable for a while.

Then she would have to tell her son. He was old enough to understand they were moving away and young enough to throw a fit. How she and her equally calm husband had managed to produce a temperamental child was a mystery.

But she couldn't discount the stress of the last two years. Mason's death had been hard on them both.

They would only take what was essential. He would outgrow most of his winter clothes by the time they were needed again, so those could go to the church.

The church.

Willyn chewed on her bottom lip, realizing she couldn't tell her religious family the truth. It was beyond explanation, and well... they just wouldn't understand.

She would have to talk to her pastor, though. She'd schedule an appointment for the day she was planning to leave. They could meet in his office, where she'd shed more than a few tears, and she would thank him for all his help. She would hug him and his wife, since they had been honorary parents to her, grandparents to her child, and had supported and cared for her during the harshest hours of her life.

Then she would smile at them and lie through her teeth.

~

Claudia swung through the front door of her parents' home calling for her father. He was sitting where she'd expected, cozy in his recliner and engrossed in a book, something historical, she was sure. After all, she had developed her love for the past's secrets at his well-educated knee.

"Where's the fire?" he asked, peering over the top of his glasses.

She clasped her hands together and beamed. "I have to go somewhere. I've already gotten approval for you to cover the rest of the semester for me, and everything is all laid out. You only have to show up and look scholarly."

The chair moaned as he lowered the foot rest. "Dare I ask why?"

"You can ask, but I have no answers to suit. I just have a… feeling." Claudia practically jiggled in her excitement, and her father, knowing her as well as he did, recognized the arrival of something bigger than them both.

"Alright. When do I start?"

She rushed over to plant a smacking kiss on his bearded cheek. "I have a seven-thirty tomorrow. And, Dad," she added, "I think I might finally get an answer to the why."

Her father sighed. He had guessed as much, and the fact thrilled him as much as it terrified. "You'll stay for dinner, of course."

~

In her yard, where she nurtured tender, young blossoms and made plans for a layout of new flower beds, Anna stilled suddenly and cast aside her gardening tools. She stood to find a man moving toward her, his brow marred with a wrinkle of concern.

Anna raised her eyes to meet his, the same brilliant blue as her own, and in response to the question there, she nodded. "It's time, and we need to prepare. The others are coming."

1

After a quick stop at a gas station featuring hot dogs, egg rolls, and the most amazing selection of espresso drinks she'd ever seen outside of coffee shops, Shauni Miller was back behind the wheel. With one ridiculously large cup of Sumatran Bold in her hand.

The stop had been out of necessity, since even hybrids could go only so far without needing a fill-up. Born of neo-hippie parents, one Irish, one Scot, and a natural born animal-lover raised to be an environmentalist, Shauni wouldn't be surprised if her blood actually ran green. Well, green with swirls of caffeine.

The little silver car had been a graduation present to herself, once she'd landed a job that would pay for it, and now, as it purred its way quietly down the highway, Shauni's body seemed to hum along in tune, excitement building with every roll of the odometer.

Savannah. Twenty miles.

Pressing a button to eject a Simon and Garfunkel CD, she slipped Nellie Furtado's in its place for a little funk and soul. Jangling nerves clashed with hope, so the music fit her mood. She did feel like a bird who didn't know where to roost. Something was waiting for her, of that she was sure, but the full scope of it was still unclear.

This was where Shauni had to be. This time and this place. It had come to her as clearly as a voice in her ear or scripture in her hands, though nothing as easily defined. The only way to describe it was…a knowing. Truth and clarity from somewhere so deep inside it may well have come from an alternate universe or past life, but it belonged to her and only her and couldn't be denied.

Shauni would miss the life she was leaving behind in Colorado; it had been challenging and contented, albeit a bit lonely. She could count the number of serious relationships she'd had on one hand. If she were a three-toed sloth.

Shauni had a secret, and even the most solid relationships had yet to survive it.

There had been few romantic affairs, and the men she'd actually allowed herself to love had ultimately faded away from or stormed out of her life. The rare times she had dared to let down her defenses and share her true self with a love interest, they'd reacted in one of three ways. Angry denial. Silent apprehension.

Or they'd thought she was crazy.

Beside her in the front passenger seat a cat curled on a fuzzy blanket and slept as if traveling cross-country were an everyday occurrence. Just like Shauni, its hair was jet black and shone in the sun that poured through the window. If the animal's eyes had been open, they would have flashed the pure green of emeralds, again in reflection of the woman who owned her, though neither Shauni nor her cat would feel comfortable with the idea that one of them owned the other. And she was well aware of her cat's feelings on the matter.

You see, Shauni Miller talked to animals. Not such an extraordinary habit, unless you counted the fact that they frequently talked back and by way of telepathy. Some had called her a whisperer, but no one had ever truly understood the extent of her gift. It was better that way.

She had been communicating with other species since long before mastering her own mother tongue, and because of her comfort with the special ability, she wasn't as surprised by the summoning, for lack of a better word, as she might otherwise have been.

Taking the appropriate exit, Shauni sat forward in her seat, mesmerized by the lush beauty of the city. It had been green and humid since the eastern edge of Texas, but nothing had prepared her for the romantic intrigue of Savannah. Postcards didn't do it justice, except there were no majestic mountain ranges here. Not even the smaller, green versions she'd appreciated while driving through Alabama. Savannah was flat, flat, flat.

But gorgeous.

"Cuileann, wake up." She stroked the cat until it stretched all four legs out and shook. A twenty minute nap and felines acted as if they'd slept the sleep of Rip van Winkle.

Spring was fully upon the city and the surrounding lands, and the fragrant air and increasing evidence of life were a welcome change. Shauni rolled down the window to breathe in the scent of rebirth and reveled in it. The thaw wouldn't come to Colorado for another couple of months, so maybe there were a few additional perks to moving south.

The promise of early flowers was a novelty, and warm, moist air a new concept, but what really revved her vital force were the stirrings she could sense under water and rock. Behind every leaf and blade of grass. And deep within waters still or flowing.

The animals were waking up.

A bird in flight caught her eye, and she knew by the mission in its mind that somewhere eggs had broken open, waiting for their mother to return with a wiggling worm. Caterpillars searched for dill and other welcoming herbs that would make the proper home for a chrysalis. And snakes. Yes, she even loved snakes. They would be sliding out from winter hibernation to draw energy from the sun and haunt the marshes once again. People strolling along the sidewalks of the town would be amazed at the number of living things they walked or drove past on a daily basis.

Shauni's heart filled with excitement at the prospect of how many new species she would find in the coastal plain. The aquatic biodiversity alone was glory in itself.

She wondered how a swamp rabbit would speak.

Taking a quick detour through the downtown historic area, she was awed by block after block of live oaks with moss so thick it was a wonder the branches held up. The arms of the trees twisted into amazing shapes, giving each their own distinct personality, and she imagined they spoke to each other late at night.

It would take a while to learn her way around. Every other street had a huge park, similar to the last with benches and lamp posts, and she could imagine walking in circles, unaware she had recently been in that very spot.

No hardship there. Hours could easily be lost amongst the charm and history of this town. She passed tall buildings of red brick and some built of stone, gray or cream, and all of them spoke of times gone by, proudly displaying elegant details of the past. What triumph and tragedy the old walls must have witnessed. Dogwoods of white or pale pink decorated the avenues as tourists pointed at them from the trolley-style buses.

With a promise to herself that she would return for a day of exploring, Shauni steered herself back in the right direction. She was getting closer to her final destination, and she could almost feel it throbbing a heartbeat as it emitted a beckoning light, gold and shimmering.

The road led her back out of the down town area as she followed signs for Skidaway Island. When she finally pulled up to the gate of an upscale community, she experienced her first inkling of doubt and bit her bottom lip.

Cuileann lifted her head with mild interest, then decided there was still nothing worth her attention and nestled back into the blanket.

Shauni wasn't sure how to get through the gates preventing her entrance, since she had no sticker for her car, and a guard was heading her way. As she poked her head out, a smile broke over his face. "You must be heading to the St. Germaine residence. I've instructions to let you pass."

Shauni nodded and offered a tremulous grin. She wasn't sure if she were deceiving him or not, but felt this was probably the workings of the mysterious force that had called to her and guided her this far.

The place was a paradise. There was a golf course dotted with people wearing uniforms of short skirts or collared shirts, depending on their sex, and a multitude of tennis courts outside a sports center of deep brown wood. Ponds and lakes spurted with fountains, swimming pools stretched long and blue, large enough to challenge Olympians, and the general mood was one of contentment. Luxury and privilege painted every scene.

And again the mysterious oaks.

Shauni let her instincts take her toward the water and pulled into the driveway of a house that backed up to a brown sweep of river. It was two stories of lemon frosting, fronted by large white columns and curving stairs that led up to the front door from both sides. "Wow. A palace," she breathed in awe.

She was out of the car and ogling a multi-car garage when a cultured voice, smooth and warm as velvet, called out to her. "You must be the next arrival." Long legs carried a red-headed goddess down the steps. The woman wore a coral dress, sleeveless and above the knee, and had her flaming hair pulled into a ponytail that fell straight as rain to her waist. She extended a hand adorned with a single stone, tiger's eye, which matched the one hanging from her neck. "I'm Claudia. You must be..."

Shauni thrust out her hand, feeling underdressed in her cargo pants and tee shirt. "Shauni. I'm from Colorado." She wasn't sure why she'd tacked that piece of info on. This Claudia evidently knew more than she did.

"You have questions, like we do, but all I can tell you is yes, you are in the right place." Her eyes curved with her smile, and upon closer inspection, Shauni could see that they were olive in color and flecked with gold.

It took a second, but Shauni brought herself back around to what Claudia had said. "We?"

"Yes, Paige and I. She's not the welcome wagon type, I'm afraid, but one of us all the same."

"One of us," Shauni parroted, her flat tone indicating her confusion. "What would we be then, the us? Why are we here?"

Claudia lifted a creamy shoulder. "I'm not sure, but have a feeling we'll know soon enough. Where's your cat?" she asked, peeking over Shauni's shoulder.

"She's sleeping in...wait. How did you know I had a cat?"

"Simple inductive reasoning. Every other woman who's passed through had a cat. I have a cat, and so does Paige. It makes sense really, but not so much overall."

Claudia looked away as if lost in thought. Her manner of speech was fluid and wove from one topic to another in a winding manner. She was intelligent, most definitely, but also whimsical.

"What do you do?" Shauni asked.

"Straight to the point, aren't you? You go first. What do you do?"

"I'm a... I mean, I was a biologist."

Claudia laughed. "Oh, I thought you meant...never mind. I'm a history professor, but like you, I'm not sure when I'll be returning to that." She quirked one side of her mouth. "Such is life. Now, let's get your things."

Shauni threw her duffle bag over her shoulder and let Cuileann sleep undisturbed while Claudia took a smaller bag and passed by the passenger side to take a peek at the feline. "Lovely girl you have there, black as midnight, like you." She glimpsed up to Shauni and closed her eyes as she hugged the bag tightly. "You usually wear your hair in a plait, ever since you accidentally trailed it through donkey dung."

"What? How do you..."

"You must have your hair bands in here somewhere. It's just a little trick I can do."

Shauni knew then that she would have more in common with the women here than a mysterious summoning, but she wasn't ready to share her own details just yet and opted to keep her ability to herself.

"Why don't you give us a hand?" Claudia said, directing the question to someone else. Shauni turned to see a blonde padding across the lawn, her approach silent and undetectable. She moved with the fluidity and confidence of an athlete. Around a stunning face was hair so light it would be described as tow-headed if seen on children. It brushed her shoulders and had the look of being razor-cut. Jagged bangs accented eyes of aqua marine.

Great. First the Goddess, now a super-model, Shauni thought, though the bland, arrogant expressions of divas on the runway paled in comparison to the fierceness of this woman. A silk, ivory tank top fell just shy of the waist of her low-hung and very snug jeans of the same color, giving a glimpse of severely toned abs. She was sexy, no doubt, but...tough, was the word that leaped to mind.

"Hey. What else you got?" she asked with a nod to Shauni's silver car.

"Just a couple more bags. I appreciate the help. Paige, is it?"

"Yeah." She offered nothing more and passed by to lean into

the trunk.

Claudia edged closer to Shauni as they walked. "Don't take it personally. She's just a hard shell."

"Oh."

The interior design of the house was as opulent as its exterior, but the décor was modern with Asian flair, dark wood and plants in exotic containers. A man came to greet her, a wide smile on his mocha face. The remnants of his hair circled the lower part of his head, leaving a shiny oval on top. "I'll take your bags," he said. "Please call me Joe, and welcome to Savannah."

"Thank you, Joe, but I don't mind carrying them." Shauni wasn't used to being waited on, and the concept of a servant made her feel guilty, though the wages earned in this home probably dwarfed her own. "Which room is mine?"

The man laughed. "Not here. I'll be taking you out to the house by boat. Plenty of room and your things will stay dry, I assure you."

"Boat?" Shauni glanced at Claudia as Paige skirted around them to follow Joe out back with more luggage. "We're going somewhere else?"

"Yep. An island, well, another island, but it will be a little different. A barrier island, but don't ask me what that means." Claudia patted her shoulder. "Don't worry. This is meant to be. Can't you feel it? Aren't you excited?"

"I'm not sure what I am, to be honest. It's a lot to take..." Shauni's words trailed off as the cry for help stabbed into her brain. The downside of being able to speak to animals is that she could also hear their pain. Intrusions into her mind didn't occur often, thank Jude, because she would have been suicidal by the age of five if she picked up on the needs of every creature that was sad, neglected, or hungry.

When it did happen, however, it was usually for a reason. She dropped her duffel. "I have to go."

"Go where? You're not leaving are you?" Claudia rushed after her, since Shauni was already out the door and darting down the front steps. "Do you want me to come with you?"

"No, no. I'll be back. I just have to take care of something." She jumped into the car, startling Cuileann from her dreams and receiving a glare in return. "Sorry to wake you but someone needs us."

It's not a wolf this time, is it? I won't be making that mistake again.

The cat didn't vocalize the words, but Shauni heard her just the same. "No." She tried not to drive too fast through the neighborhood with children playing in a few of the yards and the occasional group of women walking in twos or threes, as females were wont to do. "Not a wolf but in the same family. *Canis lupus familiaris*, and it's only a baby."

Cuileann huffed a dismissive breath out of her nose and laid her head back down. *Why can't you just say puppy?*

2

Shauni couldn't repress the smile tugging at her lips when she looked over at the odd couple curled up together. The little black dog with a white patch on his chest was being thoroughly groomed by Cuileann. Despite the cat's hesitancy earlier, she had jumped into full rescue mode once the little guy's situation was understood.

As young animals often did, the puppy was sending out images and emotions with only the occasional string of words, but Shauni had gathered enough information to know he had hurt his leg. Once he started limping, the people who owned him decided they didn't need the hassle or the medical bill and solved the problem by doing what any rational and humane person would.

They dumped him out on a desolate country road.

After a quick call to information for an address, Shauni followed the directions on her GPS and pulled up to the front of an old colonial style home. Someone with an eye for design had painted it sage green with navy shutters to match the sign hanging out front that dated the building to circa 1876 and told passers-by of its value to the historical society.

A larger, wooden sign hung above the porch steps as she passed under and had words carved into it designating the building a veterinary clinic. Leaving a worried Cuileann in the car, Shauni bundled the puppy in her arms and pushed through the door. The blond, ponytailed girl behind the counter was busy with a man and his leashed Doberman, but Shauni felt they would sympathize and forgive an interruption. "I'm sorry," she said, making brief eye contact with both of them, "but this puppy is injured. Is there any way the vet can take a look at him?"

As expected, the man with the fierce dog pursed his lips with concern, and the girl disappeared to the back.

"Sorry," Shauni said again as she and the man waited.

"No problem. We're just finishing up." He rubbed the puppy under its chin. "I hope he's not hurting too badly."

Shauni kissed the top of the little black head but made no comment.

"Follow me." The counter attendant was back and came out a side door to show Shauni the way. They went down a hallway and into a room with a six on the door. "Dr. Black will be right with you."

"Dr. Black," Shauni said to herself. "Sounds ominous."

The door swung open again. Shauni might have been worried about her flippant statement being overheard, that is, if a single thought had managed to stay put in her head. The man standing across the examination table from her in faded blue jeans and a white shirt rolled up to his elbows had momentarily caused her to forget where she was or why she was there in the first place. For a nanosecond, she even forgot her own name.

"What's going on, big guy?" he asked, homing in on the injured animal and paying little notice to Shauni. "What happened?" he asked her, still not looking up as he ran his hands gently over the puppy in what was probably a well-rehearsed routine for a vet, feeling for broken bones and...well, Shauni had no idea what else he could tell by his touch.

"I'm not sure. I found him near the woods. Abandoned, I

think."

The vet made a sound of annoyance but continued probing. She felt as if she should be paying attention to the puppy's reactions, but all she could focus on were long, attractive fingers and the muscles flexing in the good doctor's forearm as he performed his assessment. When he skimmed closer to the puppy's hindquarters, she regained her senses and blurted, "Careful. It's his back, right leg."

"Is he favoring it? Limping?"

"I picked him right up, so I couldn't say."

"So, what makes you think it's that leg?"

She had to think quickly. "Uh, I noticed him licking it on the ride over." *Good save*, she thought to herself.

After another minute, Dr. Black stood and put his hands on his hips, a wrinkle of contemplation between his eyes. "I think you're right, but we should still run some tests and x-ray that leg."

When he finally looked up at Shauni, she sensed as much as saw him do a double-take with his serious gray eyes. *Score one for team female.*

He performed a quick recovery. "Do you plan to keep him?"

Shauni tore her gaze away from his firm lips and looked instead to the trembling dog on the table. Innocent brown eyes stared back, and like a single domino performing its duty to keep the line moving, a bond formed and cemented between them, where none had been a mere hour before.

She would need to come up with a suitable name. "Of course. He's mine now."

"Good. If you'd like to wait out front, I'll take him back and get started. Donna can get you a drink, if you'd like." The vet's eyes raked over her before he left with his newest patient, and Shauni swallowed hard.

A bubble of energy fizzled and died, leaving her to wonder what the fates had in mind by bringing her here today. There had been a connection, raw attraction between her and the tall man with dark blonde hair. That click and sigh that made her chest flutter with curiosity. How would it feel to have those hands stroking and searching for her weak spots?

And his eyes, swirling thunderclouds when he had learned of the animal neglect and possible abuse. Fury and reprisal on his mind, yet competent, tender hands when holding the injured pup. He was definitely one of her kind.

Still in a daze, Shauni found her way to the lobby and sat in a wicker chair with yellow cushions where she pretended to watch the show about Amazonian wildlife. She took the bottled water from the young girl, she now knew was Donna, and let the coolness salve her throat.

She sighed and leaned back, amazed and speculative about all the new people, and pets, she'd met since coming into the city. Savannah was supposed to be a place of secrets and surprises, but this was out of control.

Shauni closed her eyes and waited. It had been a hell of a day.

~

Adjusting the x-ray machine and the dog as needed, Michael Black shot the films he would need. He didn't call a tech for assistance, as he could handle the puppy himself and needed some time to get it together. He found himself gazing into space and losing his train of thought when the woman he'd just met resurfaced in his mind.

Ridiculous words like Renaissance and Gerhartz popped into his head when he remembered the sweep of raven hair and eyes flashing green fire. Then there were the curves she couldn't hide with the khaki cargo pants and simple v-neck shirt that conjured comparisons to swimsuit models. She would be a stunner in any time period.

And that was the problem.

He would probably get past the shiny exterior only to reveal a cunning temptress at the heart. He'd dated beautiful women before, and most recently, one that had kicked him in the face as she walked out the door and on to greener, as in the color of dollar bills, pastures.

Who could blame her? When things are repeatedly handed over to someone because of their looks, that person learns to expect nothing less. It's not solely their fault for being fashioned into shallow, manipulative trophies. But after his last experience with a Lady-of-Shalott-meets-Demi-Moore beauty, Michael had laid down some hard rules for himself. Look first. Look again. Then, maybe take a leap.

He wouldn't be kicked twice.

With his resolve firmly entrenched again, Michael scanned the films and found the fracture. Not much of one, but enough to cause pain with walking. Now that he knew for sure what he was dealing with, he gave the dog a dose of medication and wrapped the leg. Opening a side door, he asked the tech to finish the cast before heading back out. He had steeled himself and felt steady enough to speak with the enchantress.

The classification was appropriate. He imagined a man could get lost in those eyes, tempted to fulfill her every need. Once behind the front counter, he rolled his shoulders in preparation and located the paperwork she'd filled out. "Ms. Miller?"

Shauni stood and came over.

"The dog does have a fracture, but we're applying a cast now. I gave him some medicine to ease the pain. He should heal quickly, given his age, but I want to keep him here overnight to see how he does." Michael patted his pockets before realizing his glasses were hooked in the collar of his shirt. He slipped them on and gave Shauni a stony look. "How will you be paying for this?"

He should let Donna handle the transaction, but male ego

was rearing up unexpectedly. He could handle this. Handle her. Despite the itch to reach out and see if her hair was as silky as it looked.

His gruff voice and expression put Shauni's back up. Why was he looking at her like that? "I have a card. I just relocated, so that will be simplest."

She watched him scan her paperwork again then he asked, "Can we reach you at this number?"

"Yes. It's my cell phone. I assume it will have some reception where I'm going, but just in case, I'll call and check in tomorrow." She felt herself frowning at the prickly vibe radiating from the man behind the counter.

"Have you ever owned a pet before? If not, we have some pamphlets on..."

The cool, condescending tone lit a fuse. "I have a master's degree in biology with a concentration in animal behavior. I'll be fine." She waited as he swiped her card. "No offense, but do you talk to all your customers this way, or is it just me?"

He managed to look annoyed and ashamed at the same time. "No...I'm just put out by the dog's abandonment. It happens more than you know. Some people should be...Well, I'll keep that particular idea to myself."

Shauni felt herself grin. He was doing a pretty bad job of hiding his irritation, and she was glad to know the reason. She would probably agree with whatever he'd been about to say. Those who harmed the helpless and defenseless made even a pacifist like her wish for swift retribution.

Michael returned the card and laid out a receipt for her signature. Since he would probably never see her again after today, he decided to smooth over the rough edges he'd created. "I'm Michael by the way, Michael Black." He offered his hand with an apologetic look on his handsome face.

Relieved but suspicious of the fluctuating temperament, Shauni took his hand, then jumped and pulled back, as he did, when the contact shocked them both. "Must be some static in here," she said, shaking her fingers.

"Must be." He handed her a yellow copy of the bill and told her the office would contact her the next day. "We'll let you know how, let's see...how 'Puppy Miller' is doing." The smile that broke over his face surely made the angels weep, and Shauni felt her bones transform into a semi-solid.

The man should have to have a carrying permit for those dimples.

Still grinning, he said, "Animal behavior, huh? Maybe you can tell me why the cat I just treated decided to take a chunk out of my arm. Never saw it coming, either." He raised a hand to wave as an older lady passed by holding a large gray cat in its carrier. "See you next time, Mrs. Templeton." Then under his breath, "You, too, Adonis."

Shauni heard the cat's thought loud and clear. *Try sticking that thing up your own butt some time.*

"Ah..." Coughing to cover a laugh, Shauni backed away from the counter and the man who was making her head spin. "Maybe next time. Thanks for everything." She turned to leave, but couldn't resist one last look over her shoulder. He was still watching. "Good-bye, Dr. Black."

Sliding behind the wheel, she reassured Cuileann regarding the puppy's welfare and turned the ignition with a glow on her face. "Good news. I think I found us a vet."

~

Tiny particles of water flurried in the air by the time she returned to the house, not quite rain but enough to dampen her hair. Lights were on in the house. Though the sun had yet to fall over the horizon, a dense fog had ridden in with the wet to darken the skies.

Someone materialized at the yellow edge of the headlight

beams and waved Shauni back toward the garages. Based on the stature, the figure seemed female, but was wearing a blue raincoat with the hood pulled up to shield her from the cool moisture. She pointed to an open door, and Shauni pulled in.

With her bags already on the boat, Shauni had only to open the door to Cuileann's pet carrier and let her in. *As long as this is only temporary*, the feline projected. *Crossing water is bad enough, but I don't want this cage to become Ms. Cuileann's Locker.*

"I would never let that happen," Shauni told her with a pat to her sleek, black rump before sliding the metal bar securely into place. She climbed out and locked her car as the woman ran up to her and slid the hood off to reveal sunny blonde hair falling in waves to her shoulders.

"I'm used to the South, but these mists are like being tricked into taking a shower." She tousled her curls. "So much for the straightening iron." She smiled and Shauni was treated to her second set of beguiling dimples for the day. "Yours looks great, just a little sleek, but that's the style now anyway."

The woman's genuine disposition was a balm to Shauni's frazzled nerves, and she smiled back. "I'm Shauni, and this is Cuileann," she said, hefting the carrier slightly.

"Willyn." At Shauni's puzzled look, she clarified. "Willyn. It's spelled funny, but pronounced like willow except, you say in instead of oh. My cat's inside, hating her cage as much as all the others."

"Yeah, we all have cats. What's that about?" Shauni followed her around to the back door of the house.

"What's any of this about? Nobody knows anything, or if they do, they're not talking."

They entered together and found themselves in a spacious, modern kitchen that was still warm and inviting. Claudia, Paige, and another woman were seated at the table with steaming mugs.

"What's your poison?" Claudia asked. "Coffee, tea, or... what's that stuff again?" she said the last to a woman whose long hair reminded Shauni of caramel. It fell in soft layers to her shoulder blades.

"Canjee," she answered before turning to Shauni. "It's an acquired taste. Hot drink with carrots, mustard seed, and..."

"Chili powder," Shauni finished. "Ooh, I'd love some."

The woman's warm smile reached her eyes and told Shauni they had both found a kindred spirit.

"Whatever you're having, we need to get moving. The sun's about to set, and I'm ready to get this thing going," Paige announced, sipping her drink out of a dainty cup painted with flowers, yet still pulling off the tough-as-nails aura.

Shauni accepted the glass from Claudia who then proceeded to make introductions. "Shauni, you and Willyn have obviously met out in this lovely weather, and the woman bearing Canjee is Hayden."

"Welcome to the club," Shauni told Hayden with a smirk." The club of WTF," she added, drawing smiles from everyone, even Paige. "Sorry if I held us up, but I had to take care of a last minute emergency."

"I just arrived myself," Willyn tossed in, "so you were right on time."

"Then let's throw these bad boys into some styrofoam cups and head out," Paige said, instigating the jumble of movement and murmurs that often accompanied packs of women preparing for any kind of departure.

With five cat carriers added to the mix, it bordered on controlled chaos.

Willyn disappeared for several minutes and returned with a small boy sleeping in her arms, his light blonde head resting on her shoulder. Seeing Shauni's surprise, she whispered, "This is Tadd." The light shining from her eyes and smile was proof enough that she held her son, and Shauni saw the ladylike blonde in a new light. The bravery it must have taken to bring a child into this unknown was astonishing. Strength of steel hid behind those dreamy blue eyes.

As if sensing their intent to travel, Joe appeared at the back door. "Can I offer anyone a windbreaker? The breeze across the water is a bit nippy. There are towels on board, but the crossing won't take long."

Feeling a generalized urgency now, the group refused the offer of jackets and wound through the backyard on a path of flagstones to the dock. A fairly large white boat, Shauni had no idea what kind, bobbed in the water as the tempestuous evening stirred the water. They each passed a cat to someone already boarded then followed suit one at a time.

Though a cabin below deck offered warmth and protection from the wet air, the women all stayed up top, allowing the cold air to pinken their cheeks as they searched the dark land mass for any hint of what was to come. Against the dying light behind it, the island could be made out on occasion, whenever the wind cleared away enough of the fog. Its silhouette was long and flat, a black pancake on the horizon.

A hush had fallen. Even Joe remained quiet, and the thump-shush of the hull hitting riotous waves was the only sound. It remained so until Claudia gasped and pointed. "I saw it. There's a house rising from the trees."

As they drew closer, the texture of the island could be made out and was densely populated with trees. They all blended into a lush forest, but again the monstrous oaks were present with their moss drapery.

The boat docked and Joe tied it down as the cat-pass was performed in reverse. When Willyn moved to the edge with Tadd, still sleeping in his mother's firm grip, Paige opened up her arms to receive the precious bundle.

Shauni was surprised by the tenderness on Paige's face but even more so when Willyn handed over her son without hesitation.

The women all walked to the beach to stand side by side beneath the moonlight. Thrusting peaks of a house could be made out above the trees, and considering the size of the old hardwoods surrounding it, Shauni wondered if castle might be a more apt description.

No one moved, even when lightning slashed in the distance and drummed its thunder across the water. Shauni was the first to hike her bag to her shoulder and take a step toward the path. "Come on," she told the others. "I think we're home."

3

High above an osprey cried out its glory of flight while searching, no doubt, for an evening meal. The women followed a path through the thick forest, keeping in sight the jutting roof of the house and windows glowing warm in the night. All around them the woods were alive, frogs called and leaped, looking for mates yet trying to stay hidden from the hungry eyes of predators.

Life and death, renewal and decay. Here on the island, the unavoidable cycle continued, and the splash in water caused Shauni to wonder if the sound had been one of discovery or escape. She didn't care to listen more closely to find out. For once, she was being pulled by a stronger force.

Once they reached a clearing, the house came into full view. It couldn't truthfully be described as a castle, but the size and architecture whispered of those ancient dwellings. Aged stonework made up most of the rambling structure, but the upper portions of arched or rounded additions had wood-shingled siding, brown or green, though Shauni couldn't be sure in the dark.

"It's huge," Hayden stated in awe, giving voice to what they were all thinking.

Beneath the arched roof of the porch, one half of a massive front door swung open to reveal a gorgeous young girl, woman, Shauni realized when she stepped into the light, with flowing golden curls, unbound and whipping in the breeze as she came to the edge of the steps. "Finally! We've been waiting for you."

She angled herself out of the way of the door and waved an impatient hand. "Come on, come on." She bounced on her toes and rubbed her arms, bared in a tight tee shirt over red shorts. "When did it get so cold? I thought Savannah was always warm."

Claudia was the first to move this time, but stopped to ask, "You said we. Exactly how many of us are there going to be?"

The girl rolled her eyes to the side in thought. "Anna said you'd be the last, and besides her there are three of us so...nine total." She ran her hand over the golden silk of Tadd's hair. "Make that nine and a half."

"Thank God." This from Paige who was looking more disgruntled than ever as she blew her white-blonde bangs out of her eyes. "I'm not sure how much more female bonding I can take."

"Don't mind her," Claudia said. "She's only travel-grumpy."

They passed into a foyer wide enough for the six of them to stand shoulder to shoulder and then some. The flooring was stone but smooth from either design or use, and a glittering chandelier hung at least eight feet above their heads.

"I almost forgot. I'm Kylie, and I'll get all your names later, but first, go ahead and pick out your rooms. The others and I have already claimed ours, but according to Anna, you should still find one that's just your style."

"Who is this Anna, and how can she be sure of that?" Paige asked.

Lifting her shoulders in a careless and unaffected manner, Kylie replied. "I don't know, but she was right. I couldn't have decorated my room any better. Oh, Anna lives here. She's been expecting us."

"Is that an elevator?" Willyn asked walking over to peer through the square glass.

"It is." Kylie was bouncing again. "It comes in handy if you have to haul things up to the third floor. That's where my room is, and let me tell you, the view is sick."

"I'm sorry? Did you say sick?" Claudia had been stroking her long, red ponytail and drooling over the antiques when she caught the last.

Shauni laughed and nudged her new friend with an elbow. "Don't worry, that means good. Cool."

"Oh." She opened up a huge smile. "Then let's go. I can't wait to see the bedrooms."

"Me either." Willyn had already pushed the elevator button.

Caught up in the frivolity, Hayden dropped her bag, but held onto her cat, still in its carrier. "Let's leave our things and start at the top then work down. I'm letting Daisy out to stretch first thing, then will probably have to take her outside."

"I have to assume cats are allowed, since we all just happen to have one?" Shauni said.

"Ms. Anna loves cats and fully expects them to have the run of the house." Joe had come in behind them, having just arrived in a truck with the rest of their belongings. "You ladies have any questions, the Attingers will be happy to help you out." He pushed a button on a box affixed to the wall and spoke into it when a female voice asked, "That you, Joe?"

"Yep. Just dropping off the last of our guests. You call if you need anything." Joe nodded at them. "Good night ladies, and blessed be."

They all waved with a couple of warm wishes for him to have a good night thrown in. Everyone had liked Joe.

"Blessed be? How odd," Willyn said.

Shauni joined her as the elevator door swung open. "Must be a local expression. Looks like there's room for two at a time."

"Go ahead. I'll find the stairs." Hayden lifted her head and smiled to cover her worry. She'd heard people use the expression before, and not only in the South. Why that would trip a wire in her system, she wasn't sure, but a tingle was revolving in her chest. "You two coming with?" she asked Claudia and Paige.

"Sure," Paige replied. "Let's beat them to the top."

~

After they had each planted their flag in a bedroom of choice and Willyn had tucked her son into an adjoining room, miraculously decorated for a young boy, the women assembled below in the grand hall. This time they all walked down the wide stairs and marveled over the ornate woodwork of the home. Raised panel wainscoting and banisters in delicious mahogany, works of art that spanned centuries, and an eclectic mix of furniture provided a comfortable yet classic quality.

Shauni felt like a pauper turned princess, especially trailing around the walkway that looked down into the hall. She'd chosen a room there on the second level, third actually, if you counted the above-ground basement as the first. The lovely Ms. Attinger had explained the need for such in Savannah, given the water table, particularly on an island.

The Attingers were a couple in their sixties and had been caring for the home and its occupants for almost forty years, having met in their youth while serving Anna's grandparents. The mysterious Anna, Shauni thought, who she and the crew she'd come over with had yet to meet.

"I thought I would be the one running late, since I had to travel the longest path, but instead, I got here first," an exotic woman called from the green velvet couch where she lay reading a book. She shot them a playful wink. "And so, I chose the best room for myself."

"I thought I got the best room," Claudia said.

Shauni and Hayden replied in unison, "Me, too," then grinned at each other.

Kylie plopped down in the style of chair that was probably

named after some king, pulling her long yellow hair into a sloppy bundle on the back of her head. "I told you. Anna said we would each find the perfect room. Take Doc over there," she added, nodding to a petite black-haired woman just entering the room. "Hers is nice and neat, mod décor and a mix of cultures, just like her."

Shauni's eyebrows flew up, and she looked to see if the woman had been offended.

As the woman moved closer, her Asian eyes twinkled with humor. "I don't know why I like you," she said to Kylie in a dry tone.

"Because I'm your antithesis, and you find me fascinating, just as I do you," the younger woman shot back with a devilish smile.

"True dat," the woman on the couch said with a thick foreign accent, making the expression sound even stranger than it already did to Shauni's Coloradoan ears. "That's what you say, yes?"

"No," Kylie said with a crinkled nose. "That's Savannah all the way."

"I can't differentiate between your American colloquialisms," the woman said rising.

Shauni had heard of people sashaying, had possibly attempted it a time or two herself, but watching the dark-eyed woman move as she did now, Shauni realized she was witnessing a work of art in action. Here was a master of female persuasion.

"My name is Lucia Ruiz. My home is in Spain, but I am rarely there," she said to them. "And now I am here."

"I hope you don't mind my saying," Claudia spoke with a finger placed on her chin," but your English is exceptional."

Lucia flashed a feline smile. "The best money can buy."

"Hmm."

Shauni was becoming used to the sound Claudia made

whenever she was taking something into consideration. The goddess-slash-history-professor was always storing away tidbits of information in that steel trap resting on her shoulders.

"I'm Vivienne Sakurai, and I'm from Chicago." Despite a sensible haircut with angled bangs and no nonsense black rimmed glasses, the Japanese woman was ethereal. A small build, delicate features, and golden skin. "But please call me Viv."

"Thank goodness." This came from Willyn, and everyone laughed. "I mean…"

"It's fine," Viv told her, waving away the sweet blonde's concern with a toss of her hand. "My very Caucasian mother's grandmother was a Vivienne, and my father is Sakurai. Together it's a mouthful." Her speech was so evenly paced and free of cadence, Shauni was beginning to understand what Kylie had meant before about Viv's bedroom. Everything about her was friendly, but … structured.

Noticing Cuileann coming down the stairs, Shauni tilted her head to ponder. "Do any of you think it's strange that we all let our cats out together to roam the house, and none of us worried that they might fight?"

"I know. It seemed to be one of those things we just took for granted, without even discussing it." Hayden came to stand beside her. "Look. Even our cats like each other. We must have known each other in another lifetime."

Shauni's eyes lifted in a smile as she watched Cuileann come nose to curious nose with another black cat, though this one had splotches of orange in her coat. The tortoiseshell danced back with a high pitched noise that sounded more like a dove's coo than a cat's meow.

"Daisy's sweet but a little neurotic," Hayden explained with a laugh.

Lucia glided over to stand with them, her eyes open wide with humor. "My cat is a flower, too," she told Hayden. "My beautiful Iris. Named for the Greek Goddess of the rainbow who rode the colored ribbons to the heavens and back to earth again and again. She was a traveler, like me." She gestured to a solid black Persian who stopped grooming her paw as if aware she was under discussion. The cat's blue eyes were startling against her sleek ebony hair.

"Wow. Where did she get those eyes?" Shauni asked.

"Where did any of us get the things we have?" Lucia returned, and the look on her face said she was talking about more than physical traits.

"So you have a power, too," Hayden whispered. "I was wondering if we were ever going to talk about it."

"Talk about what?" Kylie called from her chair.

"Oh, the usual back fence gossip. Extraordinary gifts and cats named after flowers," Hayden replied, moving to sit on the couch Lucia had vacated.

"Mine, too. Sassy is sleeping in our room."

"I believe you have a cat named Sassy, since that so fits your personality," Viv told the beaming blonde, who was probably the youngest of them all. "But how is that a flower name?"

"Hello," Kylie said slowly with a roll of her deep hazel eyes. "I thought you were supposed to be the brilliant scientist."

"Oh, I get it," Shauni threw in. "Sassafras." When Viv nodded as if chastising herself for not making the connection, Shauni explained, "Don't feel bad. I'm a biologist."

"Physicist," Viv said.

"Ugh. You can keep that. The string theory hurts my brain." Shauni glanced over to where Paige sat in a separate seating area. "How about you, Paige. We've all shared something."

"Claudia and Willyn haven't."

"Oh, lighten up already," Claudia told her, wrinkling her brow. "Fine. I teach history, that oh-so-sophisticated fellow at the top of the stairs is Mr. Rowan von Ashbi, and when I touch things I can sense their past." She threw a glare at Paige.

"Happy?"

"Jubilant," Paige said, flinging one long leg over the arm of the stuffed chair.

"Ashbi, like ash trees," Shauni translated, and I'll wait until later to ask about that other little detail of yours.

Always one to make the peace, Willyn put a hand on Claudia's shoulder to soothe. "Your Ashbi is handsome, with his dark gray stripes and white chest."

"His feet are white, too," Claudia said with pride.

"Great." Paige rose and cocked a hip out. "We're all aware that we have things in common, including the fact that some unseen and unknown force pulled us all here at the same time, but what the hell is it, and why us?" She stalked toward the group. "I'm a good fighter and my damn cat's name is Tiger."

Claudia lifted one doubtful brow and waited.

"Fine," Paige said, heaving out a great breath of submission. "It's Tiger-Lily." Her aqua-marine eyes were even more angry than normal. "And that still explains nothing."

Willyn opened her mouth to speak, but paused and looked down at the stone floor. All of the women stilled and listened. They sensed.

Shauni grasped Hayden's arm just above the elbow when she felt a low but very distinctive vibration. It was more like a hum and came from the floor, the walls, possibly the ceiling. It was all around them, and judging by the others' faces, they felt it, too. "What is that?" she whispered.

A new voice spoke gently but with the authority of one who was well acquainted with privilege and position. "What you're all feeling is the power of the nine."

They turned to find another had joined them. Sable brown hair fell around her shoulders and brilliant blue eyes held warmth and welcome above a serene smile. "You'll get used to it, so that you probably won't even notice. And it only occurs when we're all together." Her lips spread into a playful grin.

"Just wait until we link."

"Cool," Kylie said. "Hey, Anna."

Shauni remained where she was but zeroed in on the elegant woman, still very young to be so comfortable wearing the unseen but almost palpable cloak of power. "Link?"

"You know why we're here?" Paige asked. "Because I'm ready for some…"

"Answers," Anna finished for her. "Yes, I know." She stepped back and swept a hand toward a door in the back of the room. An invitation. "And I have some."

4

Falling into a single file line, the women walked silently through the arched doorway and into another large room. No one made comment regarding the fact that cats were streaming in from every direction to slide in alongside them.

Shauni immediately noticed the change in atmosphere and saw that some of the others did as well. Claudia trailed her fingers over the stone wall and closed her eyes briefly before they sprung back open in surprise and pleasure.

"What did you see?" Shauni asked.

"It was different, hazy and gilded at the edges. This place is protected. It's sacred." She folded the hand that had touched the wall into a fist as if holding onto a secret.

Shauni didn't need Claudia's gift to realize they had entered a much older portion of the house, probably the original structure, around which everything else had been built. The walls were no longer painted and trimmed in wood. They were of ancient rock and mortar and supported a high, pointed roof with wooden beams intersecting each other. The design held her attention, and after scanning the length of it as it stretched from point to point, she realized what she was looking at. "A pentagram?"

Anna turned to face her and said, "It wasn't built for invocation, but as a long-revered symbol of the Goddess." Her blues eyes lifted. "That and as the Greeks were well aware, it employs golden section mathematics."

"As in, the golden ratio?" Viv, the physicist, asked before explaining to the others with a smile. "That means because it's pretty."

Willyn studied the work above, then tossed a worried look to Shauni. Whatever she was thinking, she kept to herself, but she fingered something beneath her shirt, and Shauni realized it was a motion she'd seen before. It was the movement of a Christian grasping their cross or crucifix for comfort, and here they were under a gigantic pentagram. *Oh boy*.

The dome-like architecture was overwhelming simply due to its age and the feats that had been accomplished in its creation. There were no windows, but a stone dais waited on the far side of the room with a fire blazing in its hearth. Four extravagant chairs were positioned at the edges, informally, suggesting relaxation more than ceremony. The platform was only a couple of feet above ground level, but its height declared it a place of importance.

The middle of the area was clear of furniture, though tables lined the perimeter. Light fixtures hung from the ceiling on chains. Round and intricately carved, the circles of wood and wrought iron held actual candles to provide illumination. Together with the fire, they created a fluid, golden glow.

Anna walked up to stand on the dais. "I can't tell you how long I've waited for this and how happy I am to finally meet all of you. I'm sure you've anticipated our gathering as much as I have."

The beautiful brunette spoke with such sincerity that Shauni wished she could return the sentiment, but she had no idea what Anna was talking about. "I'm sorry, Anna. You've been a gracious host, but I have to be honest. Everything that's happened since I felt the urge to travel here has been a surprise to me. I haven't anticipated anything." She apologized with her eyes and shook her head. "I never expected this."

"Me either," Claudia said.

For once, Paige was right in line. "No. No idea what you're talking about."

Anna looked puzzled. "No premonitions or visions?" She clasped her hands when they all shook their heads. "You aren't aware of the prophecy?"

"No, nothing," Lucia replied with her heavy Spanish melody. "All we know is we have powers and cats."

"And that we all felt a sort of calling to come here now." Hayden seemed more uneasy than many of the others, twisting her caramel-colored hair with one hand.

Anna put a hand to her chest. "Good, at least you know your strengths. The rest I can fill in."

"And what is the power of the nine?" Kylie asked. "Why did the room buzz?"

Anna lifted her hands with palms open, sweeping them outward to encompass them all. "Because we have always been destined to come together. It is our coven that was granted the power to defeat the Amara and prevent the summoning of the dark."

"Coven," Willyn gasped. "What are you saying?" She pulled a chain from beneath her shirt and began rubbing a cross.

Shauni had called that one.

Anna blinked once. Then again. "Please tell me you know you're witches."

Willyn shook her head with a quiet gasp then looked at the floor. The others glanced around at each other, and Lucia burst out, "*Brujas*? Witches. *Mi dios*. My priest would drown me in holy water."

The erratic switching between Spanish and English was so amusing Shauni almost forgot to be stunned at the fact she was a witch. However, she, unlike a few of the others, didn't doubt it for a second.

Anna moved to one of the chairs and sat, emitting a groan

of half pain, half humor. "So much for my special gift. I never saw this coming."

The door opened behind them, bringing a brief reprieve for the group that was still in various stages of shock and wonder. A man strode forward. His aristocratic features along with the brown hair and blue eyes told Shauni he was most likely a relation of Anna's. The ease in which he walked into a humming room of witches said a little more.

Regaining her composure as she stood again, Anna gestured to the man, the loose material of the peasant blouse she wore swinging with the movement. Shauni realized now that the simple white top with black jeans didn't carry any echo of pointed hats or broomsticks. Anna was still an enigma.

"My brother, Quinn, will be helping us prepare," Anna said then added in a deadpan voice, "Though I doubt he understands just how much he'll be needed."

The handsome Quinn nodded to the collection of women, thinking to himself that he'd never imagined they would all be so, what was the word, oh yeah...hot. He looked at his sister and frowned. "Meaning what?"

Sighing she brought her hands together with the tips of her fingers pointing up under her chin. "That doesn't matter." She turned back to the women. "You are all here because you chose to accept the calling. I have been raised knowing this day would come, and while I have the gift of foresight, I am also aware that the magical world likes to keep its secrets. If we were to be given everything easily, there would be no need for trial. Or our gifts, for that matter."

"I hate to sound repetitive," Viv said, pushing her glasses up harder, "but what are you talking about?"

"I see I'll have to start from the beginning. You should have the full story before making any decisions about your involvement." Anna rubbed her palms over her thighs while nerves she hadn't anticipated were running their course. How far back should she go? "All I ask is that you hear me out. Your intuition has brought you this far. If you don't trust me, at least trust in yourselves."

When no one made any moves or bolted for the door, Anna drew a breath and told her story in a voice as soft and wise as starlight. "This is not the first gathering of witches this island has seen. It's happened before, three hundred years ago, except then there were only three."

"Three witches. Three hundred years ago," Claudia mused. "Now there are nine." She lifted perceptive olive eyes to Anna. "Any reason for the increase?"

Smart little witch, Anna thought. "Yes, the odds we're up against are stronger, and so must we be. The source of the corruption my ancestors fought was always destined to come back again." She braced herself. It was now or never. "The demon they fought was born in the eighteenth-century, the hows and whys of his birth I'll save for another time. He caused a great deal of destruction in his short life, until he was vanquished, and thankfully never allowed to realize his full power. That would have resulted in apocalypse, at least locally, then farther out as his strength improved."

"Whoa. Demon as in demon?" Kylie asked, with the first hint of doubt crossing her face.

"Yes. He is called Bastraal, and simply put, it's time for his resurrection." Anna allowed the women to consider what she'd told them.

Hayden, of caramel hair and golden eyes, stepped forward. "Your ancestors were the witches? That's how you know about all of this, right? They passed it down to you?"

"They passed down the story, of course, but it's more than that. The three of them were sisters. One was an oracle or seer, and was given the secret of a great prophecy. One that was to come to fruition...well...now." Anna's rosy lips quirked up on one side. "I inherited the magic, the legend, and as you all can tell, the jackpot. I happen to be the St. Germaine witch born just in time for the big showdown."

"Do you really need us? I came because I do trust my instincts, but this is beyond comprehension." Willyn's face had gone white, and Shauni sympathized.

"The prophecy foretold of the nine. The only ones who have the capability to fight and destroy Bastraal and the Amara."

In a firm yet soothing tone, Anna continued. "I understand that this may be difficult, for some of you more than others, but I ask you to look inside yourselves for your own answer. The craft is by no means a strict master, in fact, it encourages personal choice and responsibility. You must each come to this of your own free will, or we are finished before we have begun."

With arms crossed over her chest, Paige shot a question out of the stillness. "What is the Amara?" She looked ready for a fight.

"In short, they are a group of people, some more than human, who follow the lead of a witch who lost her way a long time ago. The word 'amara' is Sanskrit. It means deathless." Anna kept the explanation simple, unsure how much they could absorb in one night. There was much they would need to learn about the enemy they faced, but there would be time. Time enough. "Ronja has great power, but she chooses to follow a different path."

Anna's face grew tense. "I won't lie to you. You will each be called upon to fight for what you hold dear. Truth, light, family. Our time together will test your virtue and resolve as well as your ability to use your powers to defeat the Amara and prevent them from bringing the demon back. If any one of us fails…" She left the warning hanging in the air, the unspoken words more alarming than the worry on her face.

A wave of dread formed and rolled through Shauni's stomach. She didn't like the idea of fighting anything or anyone. For Jude's sake, her parents were hippies and owned an organic farm in Colorado. She had been raised to promote peace. Now she was being told it was her destiny to do battle with the bad guys? The very idea was oil to her water.

Questions began to roll, some in raised voices, until Anna held up her hands in a halting motion. "There is no sense in moving forward until we know where we stand now, each of us. You are already familiar with your gift, whether or not you recognize it as such." She cast a meaningful eye at Shauni and a few others in the room. "Some of you are well aware of the scope of your power. As it applies to you specifically."

Hayden raised her hand. "What do you mean specifically?"

"Each of you has a, shall we say…a specialty." Anna smiled now and lifted her right arm in a movement so sinuous it drew every expectant eye in the room to her open palm. It began to shimmer as she spoke. "But there is more for you to discover. Deep wells of power that are yours by right."

A tiny spark of gold popped in the glowing light of her hand then grew slowly until the form of a flower could be made out, small, but blossoming. At completion, it was a rose, casting out a sweet smell that could only be described as euphoria.

Shauni breathed in the heady scent she knew was pure joy while the others gasped and smiled in wonder.

But Anna wasn't finished yet.

Trembling and pulsing, the rose began to shift, elongating and separating. A steady thrum of beats could be made out, increasing in speed until individual sounds merged into one. The object was surrounded by light as it ascended into the air, floating above them all. With a quick dart it flew over their heads, racing to and fro from corner to beam, a flash of gold now blending with the jeweled tones of emerald and deep dark purple until it slowed and came to a stop by landing where it knew it belonged. Like all creatures it was called to a place of understanding and comfort.

The small but vibrant hummingbird landed on Shauni's

shoulder.

"Beautiful," Willyn whispered beside her. "So...beautiful."

Even Shauni was amazed, and with no words to express what she was feeling, could only stare at the diminutive proof of magic as it looked straight back at her.

"You see," Anna said softly, bringing their attention back to her. "This is what sleeps within all of you. It has been waiting for you, for this congregation, and for the time of prophecy. It is the lifeblood of the earth, embedded in its very soil and growing into all that feeds upon its bounty. Some study the source, and it is called many names, but only a blessed few are gifted with true control of the energy that surrounds us."

"It's magic. That's what you mean," said Kylie, looking even younger with her face lit in wonder.

Anna nodded, "That is the easiest way to describe it, since the word 'magic' allows for many things."

"If we can do what you did, and we each have something of our own, what does that make us?" Willyn asked with worry tightening her sweet face. "I've always known I was different, and I had to believe it was a blessing from God. So, I used it the best way I knew. I could never waste something so precious. I became a nurse." With that she eased over to Quinn and laid a hand on his arm where a deep purple bruise colored his skin. When her delicate fingers withdrew, his flesh was clear and unmarred. "Hope you don't mind," Willyn whispered to him.

"Not at all," he told her with a conspiratorial wink.

She looked up to Anna. "I guess what I'm asking is, if I'm really a witch, does it mean I'm part of something...unholy?"

Anna answered Willyn's question with kindness in her eyes. "You are the essence of all that is good in this world. Never doubt yourself or your beliefs." She caught the attention of Lucia and Hayden. "It doesn't matter what you call yourselves. What matters is who you are and the choices you make."

"The choice to stay here. To learn from you?" Claudia called out.

"That and much more. You will each face a challenge. A trial. Your character and strength will be tested, not only by our nemesis, but also by the forces that grant us our abilities."

Anna waited as the hushed women looked at her. Their postures and expressions ranged from trepidation to resentment, each struggling to comprehend her role, her destiny in what was being described to them. "You will be asked to face the darkness that shows itself in the form of monsters, men, and shadows. The unseen foe that shakes the ground or an individual's sanity, whichever it chooses for that day's entertainment. Every culture knows it and fears it."

"Wait," Paige said, her tone furious. "Then why does it fall to us to take care of it? I just came back from war. It would have been nice to know someone a few hundred years back had signed me up for another one."

Anna's face changed, and roiling pewter clouds appeared behind her as the rafters above shook with her fury. The candles that had seemed romantic now quivered in the darkness that fell on the room. "If you choose to leave, go with the knowledge that you most likely sentence us all to death."

Paige's eyes went wide with alarm, an expression Shauni never expected from the fierce woman. She'd probably never pissed off a witch before.

Realizing she had overstepped, Paige nodded her understanding. "I'm not going anywhere. Just a little angry over here, but I shouldn't have directed it at you."

The apology and conflicting emotions emanating from Paige seemed to quell the riot in both Anna and the others. Warm yellow light returned amidst sighs of relief and second thoughts. There was no longer any doubt this was real.

"What do we do now?" Claudia asked. She was apparently taking all of this in stride. "You said we would all learn to wield what was inside us, and that we would each face our own challenge." She looked around at the others. "I don't know about all of you, but I want to be ready. I want to start preparing now." Refocusing on Anna, she asked, "How will we know when it's our time?"

Anna shrugged. "Like I said before, magic likes its secrets and will only give us what we need when we need it. I don't know the order of your trials, it will be revealed in time, as the power deems. There are pieces to this puzzle that even I haven't found yet. Things I won't be allowed to know at all."

Moving with grace across the dais, she bent to retrieve something from a stand between two of the chairs. She turned back with a chalice, silver and encrusted with precious stones of sapphire, garnet, and amethyst. A large round disc was on the front side as she carried it. From its swirling pattern and opalescence, Shauni guessed it to be moonstone. Usually found in necklaces and bracelets, it was a mineral worn for protection from harm. She had some herself.

"If you feel you are ready." Anna paused for effect. "I can tell you the first."

Claudia and Viv both cried out in the affirmative.

Willyn held her tongue, obviously unsure. She had a son to think of on top of everything else.

A few said, "Yes," quietly, and the rest, including Shauni, nodded solemnly.

"Actually, you already know." Anna's lips curved with mischief. "You see, magic does the choosing." She once again held up an open palm. "And it has made its choice." She slowly pivoted until the vivid blue of her eyes rested on one witch in particular.

One by one, the gazes of the women followed.

They were all looking at the miraculous hummingbird still sitting on Shauni's shoulder.

They were all looking at her.

5

It became clear the following morning that they would need another coffee maker to supply an adequate caffeine fix for the many now living under Anna's roof. And judging by the number of bleary eyes and grumpy dispositions, Shauni wasn't the only one who'd had a fitful night of sleep. Considering the revelations they'd had in the past twenty-four hours, tossing and turning was a given.

Shauni grudgingly left the third pot brewing when she and Hayden were told to join the others on the first level. They trudged down the stairs, following Claudia until they came to a stop in a long hallway. There was an open door halfway down, and the sounds of female delight flowed from within.

"What's got them so worked up?" Hayden asked before being overcome by a huge yawn.

Claudia moved to the doorway to look in then laughed and went in. With curiosity perking her sour mood, Shauni peeked in to find what looked like a sultan's treasure room. Bolts of fabric ran along the wall on one side with rolls and rolls of trim. Baskets of glimmering stones, buttons, and other detailing items sat on a table.

"I thought this was a basement," Hayden said to Anna, who was standing near them inspecting satin the color of sapphires.

She glanced up. "It is. Garage on the other side of the hall and storage through that door there. We did some rearranging to make this our own dress shop, so to speak."

"Why do we need dresses?" Hayden asked, a leery wrinkle in the middle of her forehead.

"Just a type of ritual. Symbolism." They all jumped when Kylie squealed in the back corner. Anna smiled and faced Hayden and Shauni again. "Just look around and find your favorite. Nothing's going to bite you. Oh, and today it needs to be satin."

Since Claudia was already stroking a ream of coral with a loving hand and Kylie had a bolt of yellow clutched protectively in her arms, Shauni and Hayden decided to join Paige, who looked as equally uncomfortable with the frills as they felt. "I like dressing like a girl, especially if it's something that will make a man my slave, but I don't usually do dresses," she told them with a stubborn lift of her chin.

"I like my earth tones," Shauni sympathized, "but I don't see any khaki." Her statement brought a quick and sharp smile to Paige's full lips.

"Yeah. I might feel better if there were some Army green I could drape myself in."

Anna glided up to them and placed a hand on Paige's elbow to gently but firmly turn her around for inspection. She finally stopped and met Paige's stubborn gaze. "There's more to you than you give yourself credit for. Your ability is a jewel in your crown, but it doesn't define you."

Stepping between them, Anna walked past, her hands skimming over the various linens until she stopped and said with triumph, "Perfect." She pulled out a stunning roll of turquoise satin and held it out to Paige. "Your eyes are like the Caribbean waters, so this will do well."

Still doubtful, Paige held it up against her chest and looked to Shauni and Hayden for their opinion. Hayden nodded while Shauni simply murmured, "Oh, yeah."

With a shrug that couldn't quite disguise the pleasure she

was feeling, Paige lifted one side of her mouth in a grin. "Sure. Okay." Then she narrowed her eyes on them. "Now your turn, and don't think you're getting out of this."

"Well, I like that pink over there, all soft and feminine, but I don't think it's my color," Hayden said and pointed.

Shauni assessed the pale pink, almost a pearlescent color, and thought her friend might be right. She couldn't envision it next to her hair, so light brown it was on the verge of being red, but Paige had already retrieved it to hold up next to Hayden's face.

And then Shauni melted inside. The light material punctuated the glow of Hayden's hair and eyes. She was angelic, the embodiment of life.

"Your eyes are golden," Paige said in awe.

Hayden blushed. "No, just brown."

"She's right," Shauni said, stepping forward and shaking her finger when she saw Hayden's intention. "Don't you dare put that down." She laid a hand on Hayden's and reached the other out for Paige, who took it without question. The three of them stood there with sentimental smiles and tears brimming. "These are your colors."

"Now we have to find yours," Hayden said.

"Uh-huh," Paige wiped an eye. "And figure out why the hell we're crying over fabric choices. It's not like we're getting married."

"No, but it is like we're being inducted. Into a sisterhood." Hayden looked to Shauni before squeezing her hand then slipping back. "Now for Shauni, and I think I know just the one."

"I thought I was supposed to pick it," Shauni called as Hayden slipped around the wall of material and disappeared.

Paige crossed her arms across her chest, but with a satisfied smirk instead of the normal defensive posture. "I bet I know what she's getting, and if I'm right, you have to accept it."

Shauni eyed the woman who was starting to warm up to her, despite all the female bonding she claimed to despise. "You're on."

"There was a green back there, the color of summer grass."

They both waited for Hayden to show, and when she did, Paige whooped and slapped Shauni on the shoulder.

Taking the roll with a smile, Shauni said, "Summer grass. It's beautiful."

"It is, and it matches your eyes," Hayden agreed. "But I was thinking emerald."

With their selections made, the trio joined the others who were stripping down to panties and bras. Spying Kylie's thong, Paige grumbled, "What now?"

"We have to be fitted," Viv explained. The Asian woman was holding up a ream of deep violet that suited her, subdued but with a hint of underlying passion.

Giggles and hoots exploded, and Shauni looked to see Willyn and Lucia doubled over. The wholesome blonde held a creamy satin color as her choice, and the luscious brunette clutched a bold red. Lucia's chocolate eyes sparkled as she laughed. "The angel and the devil, no?"

Anna crooked a finger for Paige to come over and allow Mrs. Attinger to start measuring. Holding her hands up in question, Paige spoke to the older woman whose silver-blonde hair was cut like a pixie's. "What? No mice and birds to do the work?"

Mrs. Attinger, in her sixties and positively lovely, replied, "I'm afraid I'm allergic." The lift of her brow as she studied Paige told them all the tiny woman could give as good as she got.

She fit right in.

"Nice," Hayden said close to Shauni's ear.

Looking around at the faces she was already becoming attached to, Shauni felt a little tremor in her heart that burst into a shower of warmth. Yes, she thought to herself as the laughter and teasing continued, it is nice.

~

With its more than adequate seating, central location, and massive fireplace, the grand hall had been designated as the official witch's hangout. Willyn had gone for a walk to explore the island with Lucia and Paige while Anna was helping Viv learn the library filing system. There were so many books, a rolling ladder was needed to access the upper shelves, and Shauni couldn't wait to dive in herself. She'd heard tell of a *National Geographic* collection dating back to the first edition, but indulgence would have to wait on another day.

For now, she needed a good brood.

She was the first chosen to face one of the prophesied challenges and perform appropriately, thereby dealing the Amara a defeat and pleasing the all-knowing magic spirits. Or something along those lines. Yet, here she sat, petting Cuileann, who was sleeping in a ball by her side on the couch.

Shauni didn't have the first clue about what she should be doing to prepare. Lives were at stake, if not those of the entire world, at least a good deal of it. However much a demon would be able to destroy if it set its mind to it.

Sorceress. Demons. The deathless.

How was a biologist and novice witch supposed to defeat such things? She huffed out a breath.

Would you stop worrying so loudly? I'm trying to sleep, and at the risk of sounding infantile, I was here first. Cuileann opened one green eye to pin on Shauni.

"Well, excuse me. I'd think you might be a little more concerned. If something happens to me, who's going to make your food just the way you like? Try explaining to anyone else about oatmeal and tuna."

Cuileann lifted her head to give Shauni's arm a rough lick.

You'll do fine. It will come to you.

"What will? And when?" Shauni continued stroking, the presence of her cat and the happy purr a comforting familiarity.

It's not for me to know, but you.

"Now you sound like Anna."

Of course. She's a wise woman.

Shauni grunted. "So modest."

"Who are you talking to?" Kylie asked, coming down the broad stairs with Claudia and Hayden a few feet behind.

"My cat. Just war planning."

Kylie came over to pet Cuileann. "And who is this?"she asked with a coo.

"Her name's Cuileann," Shauni supplied with a smile for her favorite feline.

Kylie's face dropped. "You named your cat Cuileann? That can't be right. Don't you know the rules?"

Shauni was in a rare mood, anxious and jagged with self-doubt. She gathered herself, reminding her well-controlled id that Kylie was still young and impetuous. Translation. She was mouthy. "Actually, I wasn't aware of any rule at the time, but regardless, Cuileann is a plant name. It's Gaelic, meaning defender, but it's also a name for holly."

Kylie wrinkled her brow. "Yeah, okay, it just doesn't sound normal."

"Like any of this is normal," Claudia chimed in, sidling up to Shauni in support. "Be nice, Kylie. It is what it is, meaning it's the way it should be. It's not for you to question." Her river-green eyes flashed with warning.

"I am being nice, and don't lecture me. You're not my teacher."

Sensing the groundwork for a squabble, and knowing she would feel guilty over being the cause, Shauni jumped back in. "Besides, I didn't give her the name. She told me what it was."

All heads in the room swiveled to her. The other women

looked at her as if she'd turned into a Leprechaun. Not that the possibility should be discounted after all they had learned since coming here. After all, witches were known for turning enemies into unfortunate beings. If you believed in dark fairy tales.

And Shauni was beginning to.

"You mean, you just knew what she should be called. Like the rest of us did." Even Hayden, her usual ally, had raised a skeptical brow.

Shauni swallowed hard. She'd been hiding her secret most of her life but had no choice with the group here. Honesty was imperative between the nine. "No. She told me. From behind the mesh of her cage door in the shelter, she said, 'Here. I'm the one you want.' Then she told me her name."

She waited as four faces stared at her in shock, a couple of them darting their eyes to one another. They all remained silent, except for the girl who never could. "What, she like, moved her lips and spoke to you in English?" Kylie asked with only a hint of sarcasm.

The disbelief in her tone made Shauni's eyes shine, a far more dangerous light than that in Claudia's only moments before. "She didn't have to move her lips, but I heard her just the same." She took a step toward the younger girl. "In Gaelic."

Kylie glanced at the others. As if afraid of losing face, she lifted her nose and challenged Shauni. "Prove it."

Normally of even temper, Shauni fought to control the sweep of anger that danced through her veins. Her protective nature itched to put Kylie in her place. Insults directed at her were one thing.

But nobody looked down their nose at her cat.

"Fine. Where's Sassy?"

"Why do you need her?" Kylie asked.

"Because she knows you best, and it's the only way to prove what I'm saying." Shauni looked away, trying to hide the hurt and disappointment. She still didn't know everyone else's special powers, but would never question their honesty. If they couldn't trust each other, what was the point in any of this?

Looking chagrined, Kylie reached out to stroke a shiny black tress of Shauni's hair that had strayed over the front of her shoulder. "I'm sorry. You shouldn't have to prove anything to me. To us." She offered a hesitant smile. "We're sisters now."

Shauni was transparent, as usual. Her emotions always ran across her face like a silent movie at the Bijou.

"Cuileann is a beautiful name," Kylie continued before lifting up on her toes. "Will you still show me what you can do?" She jogged halfway up the stairs and called her cat's name one time in a sing-song voice. As if bred from the same stock as the girl she was partnered with, the cat came bouncing down the stairs, taking two steps at a time. Her long golden hair was groomed to perfection, and her movements were spunky but graceful. Shauni had never seen a person and their pet more evenly matched.

Holding her cat and stroking it, Kylie came across the room to Shauni. "Okay. Ready."

Shaking her head and sighing, Shauni looked into the cat's yellow eyes. "Hello, Sassy. Could you tell me something about Kylie? Something secret I couldn't possibly know."

Sassy looked up at Kylie then back. After a brief lull of silence, Shauni chuckled and scratched the cat behind one ear. "Oh my."

"What?" Kylie looked more excited than concerned. "What did she say?"

"Why don't I tell you in private?"

"No way," Claudia said, hands on her hips. "Kylie opened this bag of catnip."

"Pfft. Whatever," Kylie replied, but smiled at Claudia in a way that smoothed over any cracks left from the hard words before.

"Well," Shauni began, stopping to clear her throat. "She told me to remind you that all men were named, 'Oh, yes.'"

With her face flooding the color of strawberry ice cream, Kylie put her cat down. "Thanks, Sassy. You can go back to whatever you were doing." The golden cat looked up at Shauni and lifted her head in acknowledgment then bounded away.

Hayden and Claudia rolled with laughter. "Call someone the wrong name?" Claudia asked.

"At just the right time?" Hayden added.

The humor was infectious, and Shauni couldn't keep her own at bay any longer. She patted Kylie on the shoulder when the young blonde buried her face in her hands. "Don't worry. We all have something."

Yes, you do. Cuileann rubbed against Shauni's leg, making sure her human remembered there was plenty of dirty laundry to go around. "I'm glad you can't speak to anyone but me," Shauni told the cat, bending to run a hand along the sleek black.

I'll take it to the grave.

Before Shauni could shoot back a response, her phone went off like a salsa bomb in her pocket. She loved Latin music.

The number was local, which probably meant the vet's office calling about the puppy. She'd forgotten to speak with Anna about it, though she was sure the addition of one more would be no problem. Any objections would come from the feline population of the house.

Shauni answered and the voice on the line, deep and rich, like dark chocolate, sent heat rushing through her limbs until it settled and clutched inside her chest. "Dr. Black, I'm surprised to hear from you. I mean, I assumed Donna would call."

"I wanted to let you know the puppy did well and can be picked up any time."

"Great. I'll come by later." Shauni cradled the phone, imagining stormy gray eyes and the way his blonde hair fell carelessly across his forehead. She remembered the current of sensuality that had coursed through her when their hands had touched and wondered if he'd felt the same.

"Actually," he said, "I was hoping I could take you to lunch and make up for my rudeness yesterday."

Shauni's heart *thunked* one time, squeezed and let go. "Do you always take your patients to lunch?"

"No. Restaurants don't usually serve dog food." After Shauni's laugh, he continued, "I don't do this, ever. But...I'm making an exception. If you feel uncomfortable having lunch with your vet, I'd be happy to refer you to another."

Shauni did a sedate but joyful dance. He'd rather give her up as a client than lose a single lunch date that might not even work out? Her mother would tell her it was an indication of quality goods. She could almost hear the voice she'd grown up with. Follow your heart as long as your head and gut decide to stroll along with it.

Ordinarily, she would take that advice, but there were too many extreme circumstances wreaking havoc on her life at the moment. What was the protocol for telling a guy the kind of details Shauni would eventually have to share? Second date? Third?

She could just see it. After dinner but before coffee and dessert. *Do you take cream and sugar? Oh, and by the way, I communicate with animals, but only telepathically. They don't actually speak. How? Well, as it turns out, I also happen to be a witch.*

No, there was absolutely no way she could date someone now. Not a good time. Not a priority.

"I was hoping to see more of the city," she heard herself say.

And like sand at high tide, priorities shifted.

"Good. Why don't you meet me here at the clinic, and you can pick up Puppy Miller when we're done."

"I still haven't thought of a name, but I know..." Shauni cut herself off and crushed her hand over the mouthpiece. Claudia and Hayden were teasing Kylie relentlessly with repeated orgasmic cries of, "Oh, yes! Oh, yes!"

Shauni dashed for the powder room, keeping her palm over the phone until the door was closed tight behind her. She blew out a breath and spoke calmly into her little silver phone. "I'll see you at eleven-thirty."

6

"Shauni. Could I have a word with you before you go?" Anna gestured for Shauni to join her in the silver elevator. Shauni was mildly embarrassed to have been caught pacing, though Anna probably didn't realize the butterflies in her stomach were due to a man.

What am I thinking? Shauni laughed at herself silently. *The woman's a prophetess. She probably already knows where Michael will take me for lunch. Maybe she can give me a sneak peek inside Dr. Hottie's head.*

They rode to the fourth floor of the mansion where Anna's bedroom and sitting area were located. An elegant loveseat of peacock blue sat beneath the windows, allowing a view of the area behind the mansion. Swaying trees and wild patches of flowers dotted the landscape in the distance. The back yard had been reined in with landscaping and a large garden area lined with paths. Anna loved her greenery.

The walls of Anna's room were a light brown, and the furniture here ran to dark wood, a lovely contrast against the blue running throughout the room as accent. Several framed watercolors graced the walls, and Shauni recognized them as local scenes. She walked closer to one of a nearby beach and lighthouse, the sea a beckoning, sapphire jewel in the background. "This is amazing." She turned to Anna. "A local artist?"

"You could say that."

Anna's sudden and unusual blush told Shauni she was talking to the painter now. "Oh, Anna. They're really good. Do you sell them?"

"No. I keep them for myself or give them as gifts. I don't think they're quality enough to sell."

"Well, think again," Shauni said.

"At any rate," Anna dismissed the subject of her artwork. "I wanted to talk to you about something else. I had a vision last night, after the meeting, and I wanted you to be the first to know." She motioned for Shauni to sit on the loveseat before joining her there. "I had the feeling I should take a look, which is my way of saying meditate. I find the relaxed state allows better reception." Anna quirked a smile at her own joke.

"I take it your vision involves me and my part in the prophecy?" Shauni asked.

"Absolutely. The message itself was clear, though the meaning is foggy. I find the spirit world enjoys confounding us mortals with its little riddles."

Shauni repositioned herself, anxious about what Anna had discovered. "What's the message?"

In a matter-of-fact tone Anna said, "The whisperer shall dive through the darkness to reach the light, but first will lead them all."

Shauni waited for more. When none came, she asked, "That's all?" then frowned. "Pretty vague."

"As I said...foggy, but that's how it is more often than not. I thought you should at least have it to mull over." Anna looked out over her gardens. A robin landed atop a trellis she knew would be covered in miniature pink roses come summer. "I wish I could help you more, Shauni."

"You have, and I know you'll continue to do whatever you can." Shauni sighed. "I hate to imagine what they mean by the darkness, but I'm sure it has to do with the Amara."

"Or with you." Anna's gaze was once again directed at Shauni.

"Keep an open mind. There may be many interpretations."

"Thanks," Shauni said with a dry smile. "It feels like I'm back in honors lit, trying to decipher Shakespeare."

Laughing, Anna rose, their tete-a-tete concluded. "Nothing as bad as all that."

~

The veterinary clinic was bustling when Shauni arrived, but Donna led her to the back, assuring her they were just clearing out the last couple of morning appointments.

As soon as Shauni saw the nameless black and white puppy and its pleading brown eyes, she was grateful Anna had approved another addition to the brood. As they'd left Anna's room, she'd told Shauni to think of it as her own home, since the house and its sanctity had always been intended for the coven.

With a small cast on his leg and food in his belly, the dog was far more energetic than before and trembled with excitement when Shauni stuck her fingers through the cage to scratch the white patch on his throat and chest. "You are adorable, aren't you?"

He licked her fingers, and though his puppy-speak was still coming at her in jumbled waves, one emotion was impossible to miss. The little guy loved her.

A door opened on the opposite side of the room. "Ready? We can walk from here, and since you're new to Savannah, I thought you might enjoy a mini-tour." Dr. Michael Black was wearing a pair of jeans, dark denim this time, and a light gray button-up, again rolled to the elbows. Shauni swallowed to wet her throat, gone dry at the crisp but ruggedly handsome sight of him. He was a cross between professor and survival guide. Brains and brawn tied up in one tasty package.

He gave her a lop-sided grin. "I can show you a few ghost

hangouts along the way, if you believe in that kind of thing."

Shauni felt it prudent not to respond. Instead she picked up her purse and said, "A walk sounds good."

She wouldn't have believed Savannah could be any more picturesque, but the view from a sidewalk in the historic district was even better than the one from her car. The leisurely pace gave her time to pick out a crepe myrtle or redbud among the ever-present oaks and smell something that might be waffle-cakes on the air already scented sweet with spring.

With their steps in casual sync, they walked to the soundtrack of light traffic and tittering birds. "Do you have any requests?"

"Hmm?" Shauni tore her eyes from a specialty store stocked with French designs. There was a surprise around every corner in the older portion of the city. And loads of charm. She would have to organize a shopping trip.

"For lunch?" Michael stuffed his hands in his pockets. "Any restrictions or favorites?"

"Well, I am a vegetarian, but meat is the only no-no. I'm good with eggs, milk, and other by-products."

"Ah," Michael said, side-stepping to allow a jogger to pass. "I'll keep that in mind, and I know a place that has a good variety with non-meat options. I think you'll like it. Is it the treatment of the livestock?"

"That's part of it," Shauni said. What could she tell him? Once you had a conversation with a pig, seeing them laid out on your dinner plate was a bit disconcerting.

Michael put his hand on her back to guide her over a break in the cement. "I'm going out on a limb and guessing you're an animal activist, too."

"Is that a problem?" She hoped not. Really, really hoped not.

"Nope. Since I'm a card carrying member of the ASPCA and HSUS, I think we'll be able to skip that particular issue. As long as you don't throw raw meat on anyone."

He smiled, and Shauni was dazzled all over again.

She nodded and began, "So...'

"So..." Michael said at the same time. He laughed and cleared his throat. "There's plenty to do in Savannah. We cater to all types of deviancy." She rolled her eyes at him before waving a hand for him to continue.

"Such as?"

"I'm sure there are some clubs, but I haven't done that scene in a while."

"Don't worry. I put those boots away years ago."

He gave her one check mark on the positive side. "We seem to have pubs around every corner."

"Now you're trying to appeal to the Irish in me, but the other half is pure Scot, so what do you have to tempt it with?" She was enjoying the banter, and its underlying flirtation. A strong, handsome man and a perfect day.

"Let's see. Ghost tours and enough history to fill ten text books. Art galleries and museums. Then we have a military base. It might have a museum, too."

Shauni held up a hand. "No, thanks. I try not to think about war, past or current." When he gave her a look, she said, "I'm not anti-military or anything. I respect and support our troops, I just abhor violence. It's a vicious cycle, and I don't understand why things can't be worked out peacefully."

Michael weighed his words carefully. "I'm sure that's what most people want, but it's not always feasible."

"Even if it is, political gain and world dominion seem to muck it all up." Shauni felt her shoulders getting tense. "I'm sorry. I guess I'm a cynic."

"Not a cynic, maybe a little idealistic."

Shauni laughed short and tight. "Don't hold back. Tell me what you think."

"You can always count on that." Michael gave her a wink. "Looks like we got lucky." He veered toward a table for two, wrought iron painted white and outside a bakery that smelled like salvation.

"A bakery?" she asked as he pulled out her chair. Here was a true southern gentleman, and her feminist heart actually found it a pleasant change from the hit or miss dating pool she'd grown accustomed to.

"Trust me. They have great subs. And salads," he added, nodding to acknowledge the waiter who'd lifted a hand in greeting. "John's a little blue today."

"Who?"

"John. The server. He, uh…looks a little upset." Michael took the menus from the silver clip on top of the napkin holder and handed her one. Focusing on the lunch specials, though he knew them all by heart, he silently upbraided himself for almost giving himself away.

He didn't want to say anything that might throw a hitch in their lunch. He was already nervous enough, damn those mesmerizing eyes of hers, and it was a feeling he wasn't used to. He attributed it to the fact he was naturally suspicious of beautiful women, especially ones who looked like they'd just walked off Mount Olympus.

Still, there was just something about her. Natural and easy.

After they'd ordered, he decided to ask the question that had been plaguing him since he'd first seen her. "How long are you here for? You said you'd just come to the area."

Sipping her diet soda as a stalling tactic, Shauni let her mind race for an answer that wouldn't open up more lines of questioning. But there wasn't one. "I'm not sure. I'm working on… a project and don't know how long it will take."

"For work? I imagine the ecosystem here is a world away from what you're used to out West." Michael's eyes roamed over her face, and she squirmed under the scrutiny.

"It's more of a personal growth exercise."

"Personal growth," he echoed, lines forming on his forehead.

Hearing him say it made it sound excruciatingly pathetic,

but she didn't want to lie, and there was no way she was telling him the truth. Maybe she could get by with a modified version. "I'm staying with a friend. She and I are working on the same project, and it's easier doing it together." There. That made more sense. Shauni offered him a sweet smile.

"Yeah." Michael smiled back. She was a terrible liar. "You'll need to bring the puppy back in two weeks. Let me take a look at the leg again."

Shauni flinched when the clinical tone entered his voice. It was the same as the first time they'd met, a frigid curtain just rolled down between them, except today she knew the cause. "Michael," she began hesitantly, "I can't really discuss it. Not yet. But I...when you called..." she looked down at the napkin in her lap where she was twisting it into a tight roll.

It was important she say it right. A glimmer in her mind told her so. Michael was important. She met his stare. "I'm glad you called."

He studied the sweep of her heart-shaped face, noticed the slightest quiver of her lip. Where lies had swirled in her eyes only moments before, truth now held steady. She was hiding something, he could sense it. But still. He reached across the table and laid his hand down, palm up waiting for hers.

When she slowly wrapped her fingers in his, Michael let the warmth flow between them and tried to ignore the streak of lust that shot straight to his loins or the single word that pounded in his brain. *Mine*.

By the shift in Shauni's eyes, he knew she'd felt it too. Her pupils dilated, and it took every drop of his self-control to keep from dragging her out of the chair and to the nearest dark corner. Hell, he told himself, he might just take her in broad daylight, laying claim once and for all.

Calm down before you scare her away. Not to mention Mother's reaction when I'm arrested for public indecency. Michael was both relieved and irritated when John showed up to take their order, and Shauni pulled her hand away.

Shauni picked a salad at random, blurting out the first name she saw. Her thoughts had scattered when she and Michael touched, leaving only a burning clarity behind. She wanted his hands on her. Now. And the sexy mouth that always kicked up on one side wouldn't be bad either. She crossed her legs, much too aware of the virile male sitting across the table from her.

Reaching for her drink, she relished the cool trickle of condensation down the outside that soothed her hand and gave her another sensation to focus on. Anything besides her reaction to him.

She asked about his clinic and where he'd gone to school, making small talk and avoiding any contact. Then she asked about his family, delighting in the stories of his genteel mother who lived for the social scene and her relationship with her mother-in-law. Michael's paternal grandmother still lived in a cabin out in the woods, used holistic medicine, and took great pleasure in haranguing Michael's mother, though he swore they actually liked each other.

His affection for his grandmother was apparent, and Shauni glimpsed a picture of him as a young boy, spending summer days with the older woman as she taught him about natural remedies and the wildlife that roamed freely near her home. She had been a great influence on Michael, and Shauni had to believe that was a good thing. She thought she'd like to meet his grandmother.

I know what you seek.

Shauni tensed, listening for the small voice to whisper again. She nodded as the waiter took her plate, smiling for Michael and hoping he couldn't tell she was listening to someone else. Or something else. She offered to split the check, but gave in when Michael waved her off with a wink.

Rising together they walked a few feet when Shauni knew she had to break away and try to find the voice again. "I think

I'll walk around town for a while before I pick up the puppy."
She flashed a flirtatious smile. "If that's okay with you. I'm sure
you need to get back to work." She hated leaving him earlier
than planned but felt an irresistible pull to find the source of
the message. She was sure it had something to do with the
coven. Most animals didn't speak with such obscurity. It was
as if a haze had surrounded the words. Something was off.

"I do need to get back." Michael frowned. "If you get lost, call
me, and I'll come pick you up." Any hope of finding out how her
lips felt beneath his was shot down, and Michael fought a surge
of disappointment. "I'll see you later then."

Shauni recognized Michael's changing mood and experienced
a selfish little thrill. He regretted the end of their time together
as much as she did. "I had a wonderful time." She stepped in and
pressed a kiss to his mouth, chaste enough to be appropriate
for a first date, but still sending a tingle down to her toes.

His square jaw relaxed a bit when she looked at him again,
and the storminess had returned to his eyes. She didn't have to
be psychic to know what he was thinking.

I know what you seek.

Shauni knew she had to go now. "I'll see you soon," she said,
backing up a few steps in the direction of the voice. Michael was
headed the other way, and she tossed a wave before turning to
start down the sidewalk, her inner ear tuned in to listen.

She didn't have to go far before the message came again
from right above her head. She looked up to see a small brown
bird staring intently at her. *Follow me. I know what you seek.*

It leaped from the branch it had been perched on and soared
across the street. Shauni hurried to the corner and waited for
the white flashing hand to tell her it was safe to walk. The bird
waited on the top corner of a building, allowing her to catch up
before it darted away again.

Shauni and the feathered courier played the game for
several blocks until the bird finally came to rest on a tall brick

wall. Skirting around the end, she saw that it enclosed a large cemetery and made her way to the nearest opening. People with cameras filled the area, taking photos of headstones, many broken or tilted. Across the expanse she saw the wall she'd just come around, its interior side lined with markers that should have been resting at the heads of burial plots.

That was a mystery for another day.

The bird had settled on top of a headstone, tilting its head at her as if wondering why she hadn't figured it all out yet. "Is this what I seek?" She asked it out loud as she came to stand beside it. "This grave?"

As if in answer, it fluttered up and landed on another stone a few yards away. *I know what you seek.*

"Can you tell me anything else?" Shauni stayed where she was, waiting for a reply. This time, the voice that entered her mind was clear of the haze, and she sensed it belonged strictly to the bird with no help from any spiritual force.

That's all I know. That's all it said. With that, the small brown animal streaked up and over the wall, leaving her to investigate the various memorials and ponder the meaning of the hallowed ground.

When nothing else came to her, Shauni simply stood in the middle of the graveyard. Gentle breezes blew and tourists milled around the place of burial, reading their guidebooks and smiling for pictures. Shauni decided to pick up a book herself and try to find more information about the cemetery. She would take it back to the others and tell them about the strange incident.

Hopefully this place would mean something to Anna.

7

Click-click-click-whump. Click-click-click-whump. A leg in a cast was no match for the vitality of a puppy. The bundle of quaking energy darted across the stone floor toward the women gathered in the grand hall. Viv, Willyn, and Anna were watching a movie but promptly broke out of their Hollywood-induced daze to greet the newest family member.

Shauni hadn't seen Michael at the clinic, since he'd been caught up in an emergency. It had been a reprieve in a way. Her emotions were a jumbled mess, and her physical response to him was a new ingredient added to the mix. An extremely combustible ingredient.

Anna paused the flick and scooped up the puppy for a cuddle after it came to an abrupt halt in front of the green velvet couch. "Look at you." She hugged her cheek to his and kissed his tiny black head. "I bet you need something to eat."

She passed him off to Viv and headed toward the kitchen.

Softening in a way none of them had witnessed before, Viv baby-talked and tickled the little black dog before putting him back down to investigate. "What can I say," she said, cleaning her glasses of puppy smudge, "there's just something about a baby."

"Glad you guys approve, but I'm not so sure how the cats will respond," Shauni said before lifting her head in the direction of the flat screen television. "I didn't know that was back there."

One of Anna's many paintings had been moved aside on a sliding panel to expose the colossal television.

"We didn't either," Willyn tossed over her shoulder from where she was bent down calling the dog. "Anna walked in with a DVD, hit a remote, and there you go."

Once again the puppy raced across the floor, only to put on its brakes at the last minute.

When Anna returned with a bright red bowl of food, Shauni asked her, "Remember the place I told you I found the puppy?"

"Sure."

"Would that still be considered part of Skidaway Island?"

Anna considered for a moment and nodded. "What made you think of that?"

"Put the food down, and you'll see." She and the others watched as a blur of black hurdled toward the dish as fast as three legs and a cast could carry him before sliding to a stop inches from the treat.

Shauni laughed and walked over to stroke her new pet as it gobbled and munched. "That's the one alright. Puppy Miller officially has a name." She looked up at Anna. "We'll call him Skid."

"A well deserved moniker," Anna said. "His food and bed are in the kitchen. Joe found the kind you requested, and, um, a little bit more." She grinned at Shauni's questioning look. "He likes dogs and felt sorry for the pup being so outnumbered by felines. Got him a few toys."

"As long as there are some chewies that will keep him occupied and away from my shoes." The last came from Kylie as she strode in wearing a sports bra and shorts, all her golden curls up in a twist. She too had to give Skid a rub and scratch. "What a cutie."

Just then, Quinn walked in and couldn't quite stop his jaw from dropping when he saw Kylie in her outfit. Recovering quickly, he fixed his eyes on his sister instead. "Anna, let me know when you're ready. I've got some work to do, so I'll be upstairs."

He made it to the bottom of the stairs before turning back to Kylie with his lips tight. "Could you not walk around the house dressed like that? We do have several men who either work or live here. You're not in a college dorm anymore."

"Quinn," Anna hissed, clearly taken aback by her brother's harsh words.

Kylie took the towel she was dabbing on her neck and tossed it over her shoulder, the movement quick and heavy with annoyance. "That's okay, Anna. I'll be more cautious in the future. Wouldn't want to make anyone uncomfortable." She glided across the room and passed Quinn where he still stood to saunter up the steps, giving him an unobstructed view of her assets.

Without looking back to the others, Quinn reversed himself and walked back across the room. "I think I'll take the elevator."

Once he was gone, the usually composed Anna threw her hands up. "What just happened?"

Shauni and Willyn gave each other knowing looks. "Does he get like that often?" Shauni asked.

"No. Never. Maybe he's just concerned." Eyes the color of sapphires filled with secrets and wells of knowledge as Anna looked at Shauni. "We need to have a meeting tonight. If you'll tell everyone to be ready, their dresses should arrive this afternoon."

"Wait. We need to wear our dresses?" Willyn wrung her hands. "Already?"

"We have much to do, but first, we must be assured we have the blessing." Softening her features, Anna reassured Willyn, who still struggled with the idea of witches and magic more than any of them. "You are more ready than you know, sweet mother. Stronger as well."

Tucking her light blonde waves behind her ears, Willyn

watched Anna sweep out of the room. The puppy, as if sensing her need for comfort, hobbled over to sit beside her foot. With the sudden exhaustion of the young, Skid dropped his head across Willyn's shoe and closed his eyes. She bent to lay a hand on the puppy's hindquarters, then closed her eyes as well.

Where Willyn's palm met the dog's black pelt, the air seemed to thicken and shift like heat rising from asphalt. Shauni blinked to clear her eyes, but it was gone. Willyn was standing straight again, sliding her foot gently out from under the sleeping Skid.

"You should take him back to the vet soon. He won't have to wear the cast long."

Shauni hadn't been seeing things. "You healed him," she said without question.

Willyn curved her lips in a sad smile. "Just a little push." She sat on the couch and tapped the button to resume the movie, a romantic comedy, though she seemed to have lost her happy mood.

"Thanks for that. He's already feeling a little better." Shauni would leave her friend to the movie, and give her some space. They both had to push through their remaining doubts.

She would go upstairs and pass the word. All witches to the magic room, and come prepared. For what, Shauni couldn't guess. Thoughts battered around in her head about what would be required of her and the sort of test she would be given. When, where, and how would she know?

Of course, she had to be the first. So much for the luck of her Irish heritage shining down.

Then there was the new info passed to her from the spirit world via her feathered friend. She would need to tell everyone about it but found herself lacking the necessary motivation and energy at the moment.

She ran her hand along the rich mahogany of the banister. The movie sounded from below her now, witty dialogue from perky characters. Willyn watched the screen in a daze. Skid slept on.

And Shauni took one step closer to her fate.

~

Lying back on her bed and the exquisite hand-crocheted, ivory throw that covered it, Shauni looked around the room. She still couldn't get over how it suited her tastes. The walls were painted a pale green set off nicely by the cream-colored furniture with Victorian curves. There were two windows, festooned with curtains the color of pine needles. A floral carpet spanned most of the floor, its leaves the same verdant color as the drapery.

It had an old world cottage feel. Cozy yet elegant.

A rap on the door had her jolting from the pleasant idea of a trip to somewhere overseas when this was all over. She was optimistic at the heart of it all. She planned to live.

"Come in," she called, throwing her legs over the side of the mattress to sit up.

Claudia poked her head around the corner and wiggled arched brows. Her straight as a board hair was loose and shimmered like liquid fire. The professor's olive-colored eyes were full of mischief. "Ready for the big night?"

"Whoopee," Shauni said, twirling a finger.

Shutting the door, Claudia joined her on the bed, piling into the middle and sitting Indian style. "Come on. You can do better than that. It's the first time we'll all come together with full knowledge of who we are. What we're meant to do."

"About that. I'm still not clear on where we go next. What exactly we, more to the point, I need to do. I have no timetable, no plan, and no real weapons." She bit her bottom lip. "Not that I want to use them anyway."

Claudia wiped the playful grin off her face and put on the

teacher's mask. She recognized fear when she saw it. Shauni was the first of them. They had all been thrown into a kettle and shaken about, but she was actually supposed to make sense of prophecies and power and win a battle against an unknown foe.

Shauni was carrying a great burden into unexplored territory.

Claudia ran a finger down her friend's arm and tapped it on the back of her hand. "You're not alone, you know. We've known each other less than a week, but we're a unit now."

Shauni stared at the wall. "Thanks, but you can't help me. Not really. I know you'll back me up and support me, but essentially, I am alone. Only I can find my path."

Claudia pursed her lips. "That sounds like Anna." The redhead angled herself so that the two of them were face to face. "Shauni, I have to tell you. I see unique qualities in every member of our coven." She shook her head. "Now there's a word that takes getting used to."

In a serious tone, she continued. "But despite Paige's ferocity, Willyn's ability to repair damaged flesh, and even Anna's amazing mastery of the craft, to be frank, I think you are the best choice. Magic knew what it was doing."

"Why?" Shauni's eyes abruptly filled with unspent tears.

Sympathy and respect steeled Claudia's lovely features. "Because you're worried to the point of crying. Because you saved a broken-legged puppy, stood up to Paige, and immediately forgave Kylie when she cut you so deep with her doubt." She put a hand under Shauni's chin when her head started to bow, bringing bright green eyes up to meet olive. "Because you're the steady one."

The two of them hugged, and Shauni let loose a sigh as if it had been pent up for a hundred years. "I guess I'll do what I can. Fate must know a little something, so I'll give it the benefit of the doubt."

They pulled away from each other when a firmer knock sounded on the door. Together they chorused, "Come in," and laughed at their timing.

Mrs. Attinger swung in. She was dressed in head-to-toe black and was holding fabric in the same color. Her other hand held Shauni's dress, covered in clear plastic for its protection. "Here's your outfit now. Ms. Claudia, I left yours in your bedroom."

"Oh." Claudia clapped her hands together and leaped up. "I'm going to go get ready." She spied the black draped over the older lady's arm. "But what's that?"

"Your robes, of course. It's an initiation of sorts. A graduation to a higher level. You'll wear your black robes over your dresses."

Claudia's face fell. "Then why the gorgeous dresses if we're just covering them up?"

"Ritual is important. These were sewn over thirty years ago."

"Well then," Claudia quipped. "Something old, something new."

"Yes." Mrs. Attinger stepped back out to let Claudia pass. With a wink and a wave to Shauni, the housekeeper said, "Hurry now, the sun is setting."

Indeed it was. The sky above the trees had changed from airy blue to indigo, and the moon was surely on the rise. Shauni imagined herself walking out there, over the forest floor as starlight filtered through leaves. She would hear the wildlife, its glory and strife, but deeper still, another sound. Beneath the scurrying paws and moaning winds, the flow and bubble of life, there beat another pulse.

It throbbed and whispered. Older. Wiser.

And from it Shauni would hear...something else.

Something else.

Bolting from the bed, Shauni surged across the room, out the door, and headed upstairs. Dresses and such could wait. She needed to have that talk with Anna. Now.

Night had fallen across the island as the nine women assembled in the back of the house. All were silent, due to nerves and a sense of respect. One by one they filed through the door and instinctively formed a wide circle around the altar in the center of the great room.

Though the air outside was pleasant with the promise of spring, a fire danced quietly in the stone hearth. Candles once again hung above to light the domed room. The natural illumination of flame cast a mystical aura over their faces, and for the first time, all in robes of black, gathered around a large stone table, they looked and felt like the witches they were.

Cats sat in front of their humans, as quiet and solemn as monks. For once, Shauni could hear none of their thoughts. Not even Cuileann. She wondered if she were subconsciously blocking them, or if the sanctity of the room and its inhabitants overrode individual talents.

Once they were all in position, Anna lit a single white candle and spoke.

"Welcome, sisters. Our work here tonight will be twofold. Our induction into this sacred coven will serve as both ritual and education. I'm sure the Goddess will approve any breach of protocol, as we come together to accept and serve the light, the truth, the balance."

A lock slid closed on the door they had entered, and Quinn crossed the ancient floor with a chest in his hands. He set it on the white marble altar and picked up a small, silver bowl as Anna lit another candle. As a new flame hissed to life, Shauni noticed it was one of four candles situated on the corners of the table.

"We receive Quinn, though not of this coven, as an honorary witch and offer our blessings and protection while within our circle." Anna inclined her head, and her brother began walking around them in a clockwise fashion, the bowl in his hands.

Anna's voice rang out. "We cleanse this ritual space by representing the four elements and calling forth their blessings."

When Quinn drew closer, Shauni could see a small pile of brown dirt in the silver dish and understood. He carried earth.

As Anna spoke poetic words, she lit each of the candles, and Quinn repeated his path around the room with each of the bowls. Water in one then a feather for air, and finally, a clear liquid that caught and burned. Fire.

Calling to the spirits of the four quarters, Anna lifted her arms.

Shauni looked at the faces around her. Claudia and Viv, both radiant with expectation, stood next to each other. The tall redhead and petite Asian were worlds apart in appearance, yet of the same heart. They not only accepted destiny but embraced it.

Willyn stood across from Shauni, pale blonde hair free and waving to her shoulders, powder blues eyes clouded with worry and something that looked like guilt. Was she wearing her cross beneath the pagan garb?

The Spanish beauty, Lucia, stood with Hayden, both women looking stern but relaxed. They had conquered any reservations and were ready for the task at hand. Suddenly Shauni knew. She could trust them with her life.

Kylie's face, yellow in the candlelight, was full of youth and vitality, a glaring contrast to the woman next to her. Paige, in her usual stance, appeared ready for battle, and though surrounded by her coven, she still stood alone.

"We will invoke the Goddess as one and bring her into our circle," Anna told them, "but first we will evoke or bring out the witch." She smiled. "That is, the witch who waits in each of you."

A thrill spurted through Shauni. Despite her fear, it felt right. It was her fate, and if she were honest with herself, it was also her duty. She had been granted a gift, and along with privilege came responsibility. If she could help prevent harm to innocents, she would use every tool at her command.

They were directed to repeat the words after Anna, and in voices ranging from quivering to bold, they spoke together in single harmony, filling the rounded room with swift and sparkling sound.

I am one with the universe.

I am no thing and everything.

I am the stars and the moon, the seas and storms, the breath of life.

As their chant spiraled toward the heavens, Shauni's skin began to warm, her blood to sing, and the breadth of the universe opened inside her. Here was the truth Anna had spoken of, vibrant life and continuity with every particle existing within the earth and beyond. Here was knowledge and love.

And it was glorious.

Anna turned to find Quinn. With no words needed, he strode to the altar and produced a key from his pocket. It fit the lock on the chest, and with an ease that belied the box's age, it clicked and opened fluidly. With great care, Quinn lifted black pouches from inside and laid them in a straight line along the length of the marble surface before taking the empty chest away.

"There have been no rules set forth to guide me in this practice, yet through tales of old and hereditary teachings, I know we must each choose for ourselves." Stepping back from the altar, Anna aligned herself evenly with the rest of them in the circle. "There is no direction or order. We should simply be in this moment and act as we believe."

Silence reigned for the space of three heartbeats.

Then Kylie crossed the center of the circle and with no hesitation, chose one of the pouches, and returned to her previous position.

It was both revelation and comfort when Willyn did the

same. No falter in her step or shake in her hand.

Next Claudia, Paige, and Anna, who fell into equal rank with the rest of them. She was guided now by the same force as the others. She acted without question, trusting and sure.

Shauni felt a pull and knew it was her turn. Her hand followed an invisible line of energy that led it to one particular pouch. She took it, leaving the last three for Viv, Hayden, and Lucia, who each followed suit.

Together, they opened the mysterious gifts. From inside the pouches slid silver chains fashioned in antique styling, amulets dangling from each. Shauni held hers up and saw a design of silver weave, connecting eight small stones perched on the perimeter. Each stone glistened in a different color, a representation of the other women in her coven. They were all connected to the larger center stone, a glistening green as deep and pure as the forest. As the rest of the witches were connected to Shauni.

She and the others had blindly chosen their amulets, led by something greater than simple sight.

Anna lifted her necklace, a bright blue stone glinting at the heart of it, and fastened it around her neck. The coven did the same, each with her own amulet. Their hands worked the ties of their cloaks, spreading the black material to expose the brilliant gowns beneath.

Kylie's yellow amulet gleamed above her gown of the same. Viv in violet, Lucia in crimson, and each gemstone seemed to throb when laid against the flesh of its true owner.

"These amulets were created ages ago, at the time of the prophecy, when darkness was locked away by the last coven called to protect and defend. Through these talismans we are linked. They will hold us together, even when we are apart." Anna paused. "Three centuries have passed, and the demon stirs once again." She held the ties of her cloak in her hands, preparing to shed the shadow and free the radiance beneath.

"We will face those that call Bastraal from the depths. We will face the beast himself if need be. And we will prevail."

In one great rush cloaks dropped to the floor, revealing the witches in their gowns, shining jewels each and glowing furiously with the power that radiated and hummed around the women.

"Breathe in the magic of the air that swirls around you, hear the great force of water as it streams through your veins, feel the earth quake beneath your blessed feet, and surrender to the fire of your own creation." With her eyes glistening with love and victory, Anna opened her arms. "Welcome to providence, my sisters. We are the blessed. We are the chosen. We are those who will serve as instruments of prophecy."

She lowered her arms but lifted her head with pride as blue flames burst from behind her before striking through the air like lightning. "We are the Savannah Coven."

~

Somewhere on the mainland, Ronja was holding her lover between her legs when a shaft of light pierced her spirit and shook it to the core. Her nails, already painted sangria red, sank into the man's skin to draw true blood.

The pain only urged him on, as it was something he knew Ronja often enjoyed inflicting.

"Harder," she spat next to his ear. "Harder. Drive it out of me."

She pushed herself and focused, tightening muscles to bring on the orgasm that would open the door to the shadow world. She needed the dark now more than ever. The prophecy had begun. They were here, together, and their unity was a blight on her soul.

Only a glimpse of magnificent evil would soothe the burns inflicted by the light.

When Ronja and her man were spent, breathing heavily and shining with perspiration, she threw off the black satin sheet to sit on the side of the bed. Her skin was paler than normal and her long, tawny hair was in disarray. The normally stone blue eyes now burned like coals.

"Ronja," the man rubbed her back.

"Don't touch me," she said before casting a small spell and slapping his face without moving. "You saw this, didn't you? You saw and didn't tell me."

"I had hoped to be wrong." He risked another stroke on the curve of her hip. "I only wanted to protect you."

The laughter that gurgled in her throat mocked him. "You know very well I need no man's protection. But it is all a moot point now." She turned her smoldering eyes on him. "You must not hold anything from me again. All of our training and preparation is at an end. They are here."

Ronja stood and walked to an old armoire, one she had acquired some years before, and opened it to retrieve a robe that shone like quicksilver. She tossed her blonde hair over the collar and faced the man again, the material still open in the front to reveal toned muscles and firm breasts. "We have to get to work." With a snap of her fingers, lanterns burst with bright flames to fill the room with light. "The battle has begun, and I mean to strike first."

8

"Wow. And can I just say again, wow." Claudia retrieved a cup from the kitchen cabinet. "I'm usually a little more eloquent with the verbiage, but I think the word suffices." She visibly shivered then broke out a smile. "I just tingle all over."

Shauni and the other women had all converged on Anna's kitchen after the ceremony, feeling charged and hungry. There was an oversized island in the cooking area, gray granite in the shape of a crescent, allowing several of them to sit on the stools. The black wrought iron seating offered high backs for support and burgundy cushions for comfort. Shauni sat with Hayden, Viv, Willyn, and Kylie while the rest of them stood or leaned against the countertops. Again Anna had chosen granite, but the lighter swirls were picked up by the ivory cabinetry and the great arch of stonework that went across the ceiling from one end to the other. The same masonry was repeated in a wall that held yet another fireplace, though smaller, and what looked like a pizza oven.

Bursts of color could be found throughout. Red tulips in crystal vases, a farm sink in shiny cobalt, and the lights hanging from above were narrow glass pyramids of ruby, yellow, and blue. It was as if a medieval castle had gotten a very modern overhaul, and the taste suited Anna, who was currently searching the pantry. She looked out of place holding a box of graham crackers while still in her sapphire dress. "I need a snack and would love some coffee to go with it, but I'll be up all night if I have some."

"Got any decaf?" Hayden asked.

"Ooh! I almost forgot, what with all the dresses and excitement. I got us a present." Kylie held up both pointer fingers. "Wait right here." In a flurry of gold satin, she was gone in a flash.

Viv chuckled. "That girl has boundless energy."

"Hmph." Hayden made the noise and glanced at Viv. "Says the brainiac who reads and types away on her keyboard until all hours of the night." At Viv's questioning look, she added, "I was walking past last night and heard you. Couldn't sleep."

From her position near the refrigerator, Paige fingered her new amulet and the turquoise stone at its center. "That would be the witching hour, right, Anna? Midnight?"

"That's debatable." Anna put the box in the middle of the island for everyone to have access. "There are some who still believe the thirty minutes before and after midnight constitute that hour, with the white magic holding power before and black magic after. Others refer to planetary hours, which are rarely sixty minutes long, and offer a calculation to help one determine the exact time."

"But that's not what you believe," Claudia said, being careful not to spill any of the powdered coffee mix on her coral dress. It was now a cherished memento of the night she truly accepted the craft.

Anna inclined her head. "Very observant, Professor. I subscribe to the notion that the darkest hours of the night, usually midnight to three in the morning, are collectively the witching hour. That's when supernatural creatures are rumored to be at their peak. It all depends on the practitioner and the time that works for them."

"Supernatural creatures," Willyn murmured next to Shauni. "Like us."

Anna heard her. "Yes, like us. Finding your peak time is largely a personal choice, but many find the stillness and shadows of the witching hour to be theirs, when the rest of the world sleeps and nature is easier to hear, to commune with."

"I believe I'll try dawn," Willyn replied. "I've always found strength in renewal and the promise of light.

 Making her away around the island, Anna came to Willyn and placed both hands on her shoulders as Willyn swiveled the seat to face her. "You will find your way," Anna told her. "Of that I have no doubt." She placed a soft kiss on Willyn's forehead. "Blessed be, little sister."

Before Shauni had a chance to gauge Willyn's reaction, Kylie burst back into the room with a box in her arms. "It's the biggest they had and still won't quite hold enough for all of us at once, but it's still better than the coffee pot."

Clapping her hands together, Claudia beamed. "Kylie, I forgive you for any previous annoyances. You are my new best friend." She moved to help the younger girl open the cardboard.

"What is it?" Viv asked.

Looking up at her in response, Kylie laughed. "Don't worry. I got some tea flavors for you and Hayden. I'm not sure there's room in here for all the varieties I bought, but we'll think of something."

"I'm sure we will," Anna said, arms crossed over her chest, "but you still haven't told us what it is."

Kylie only grinned and carried a black and silver machine to the corner, set it on the counter, and plugged it in. "Toss me something strong," she told Claudia, who was eagerly tearing into a smaller box that had come along with the appliance. Then she asked Anna, "You like bold coffee, don't you?"

Anna's eyes lit up as she realized what they had. "I do. Decaf, please."

"Got you covered," Kylie assured her. She held up a little cup for the room to see. "You wanna' talk about some magic? This is *truly* the greatest invention since sliced bread." After filling a plastic container and affixing it to the side of the machine, she opened a compartment and slipped the cup inside. When she closed it and hit a button, the room waited in silent expectation. Soon a brown stream ran into the waiting mug.

Taking it black, Anna accepted the drink and sipped. "Mmm. Joy in the little things." She smiled at Kylie. "This was very considerate of you. I, for one, love it."

"Me, too." Claudia tossed her flowing red hair back over her shoulder and hugged Kylie.

Paige drew closer to peer at the coffee machine. "Nice." She turned to face the others. "As much as I like it, I'm more in the mood for something else. I want a beer."

Seeing the caged energy in the other woman, Shauni felt her own start a push for freedom. "I'm with you. I've got something pinging around inside of me. I need to get out into the night, smell the salt air, feel the warmth." She laughed. "I don't know what's come over me."

"You've had your first taste of what's to come. A power you never knew, and now, with all of us together, it's bound to be quite a rush." Anna tilted her head. "I admit, I'm used to it, but there's a difference with the coven finally united. A vital force that's been unleashed." She lifted one sable brow to Paige. "But there's no law that says witches can't have fun. Go. Live. It's what we do, as well as what we fight for."

Running her hands down the turquoise satin, Paige said, "First I need to put this away."

Shauni slid off the stool. "Wait for me. I'm in."

"I'm coming," Kylie said, doing a little jig. "I've been legal for three months."

Claudia, Viv, and Anna all looked at each other. "I remember those days," Claudia said. "When I turned twenty-one, I closed down the bar and puked on myself on the way home."

"I never did overindulge." Viv blew her angled bangs away

from her long gray eyes. "But I have to work this out of my system, too. There's no way I'll be able to sit still and research tonight. First, though, I have a very important question." She turned to Shauni. "What are you wearing?"

~

Declaring they had nothing appropriate for a night out on the town, Viv and Shauni both turned to their new sisters for help. Due to similarities in height, Viv raided Kylie's closet while Shauni dug through Claudia's. And that redheaded goddess, in Shauni's opinion, sure didn't dress like a teacher.

Shauni emerged with a pair of low-rise black pants and leather Victorian style boots laced up to her ankles. The shimmery white top scooped down but remained chaste in front. The back, however, left little to the imagination, and Shauni promptly decided to wear her hair down.

Viv and Kylie both came out in playful dresses, suitable for Sunday tea or work, depending on how they were accessorized. Pairing the fitted, short skirts with mile high heels, their petite figures and killer legs turned the duo into serious head-turning material. Kylie was the golden girl next door, curls tumbling everywhere. Viv, cheekbones to die for and lovely Asian eyes, was exotic and alluring.

Paige was the only other one not in a skirt. Gray cargo pants fell over black boots that looked like military issue, but with a tight black shirt and model good looks, she still managed to ooze sex appeal.

The four of them waited downstairs for Lucia, who was still primping. Anna had begged off, saying she only wanted a good book and her bed. Willyn had also opted to stay behind, wanting to be near her son. She needed to recharge, she'd told Shauni, and evidently, the little blonde, blue-eyed boy, who looked just like his mother, was the best way for her to do that.

Though happy to donate clothing, Claudia had headed straight for the library and its history section, claiming she'd held herself back long enough. Meanwhile, Hayden was upstairs performing a ritual of her own. Wine, candles, and bubble bath.

At last, Lucia appeared at the top of the stairs. The black dress showcased an amazing body that Shauni just knew had perfectly proportionate measurements. The material barely covered half of her thighs, but no skin was bared, as the black boots traveled all the way up. Her dark hair was a mass of waves and curls, silver hung from her ears and throat, and full lips were painted a siren's red.

"I hope you don't dress like that when you slash your way through jungles," Paige said with a smirk on her face.

Lucia cocked her hip and held up one hand to study her nails, long and as red as her lips. "I dress according to the occasion." She lifted one side of her mouth. "And tonight we go hunting, no?"

"What are we hunting?" Viv asked.

Kylie strolled to a nearby table to pick up a small purse. "Don't you know? It's the only thing we don't have enough of on this island." She shared a knowing smile with Lucia before catching Shauni's eye and giving a wink. "Let's go find some men."

They all gathered below deck for the boat ride to the mainland. Joe Junior, as he was called, was on shift and stood happily behind the wheel. He was Joe's son and worked the late hours when his father was off. According to him, they liked to keep their duties "in the family." Like Mr. and Mrs. Attinger, the Joes had been working for Anna's family long enough to be considered relations themselves. Joe Jr. and Anna had actually toddled around the sand box together.

After suggesting a few places the women might like, he drove them downtown and reminded them he was only a call away. "Watch yourselves, now. A pack of lovely ladies is bound to catch the eye, and not every eye down here is friendly."

"We'll be careful," Shauni told the handsome young man. "Thanks for the ride."

Being a few blocks from the downtown area gave the women a chance to walk beneath the beautiful moss-draped trees. The night was moody and mystical in the dim light of the scattered lamp posts and half moon.

"Man there are oaks everywhere down here, and all so big, just reaching for the sky with their crooked arms," Kylie said in awe.

They passed buildings of various size and color, but all had one thing in common, architecture that dripped history and held echoes of the past. Wrought iron railings on balconies, streets still made of cobblestones, and Victorian homes with signs telling who the houses had originally been built for.

"There. I think that's the place Anna told me about." Viv lifted her chin to indicate a pub with glowing amber windows. An oval sign hung out front, black with gold trim and writing that told patrons its year of founding. Aged green columns stood on both sides of the door. "She said it's the oldest pub in Savannah."

"That sounds about right," Paige said. "If we want to learn more about our new town, we might as well start there." She smiled at Shauni. "How do you resist a place that's served beer for over a century?"

The sound of horns wailed into the night as they pulled open the door. It was a weeknight, so there were plenty of people inside but room enough to walk between the full tables. A few mingled around the bar, indicating the lack of seating there, too.

Kylie squared her shoulders. "I'll get us a table." And as only a college girl could, she narrowed her eyes at a couple of women hugging. "They're about to leave," she said before unapologetically sliding between them to get to the cushioned bench along the wall. Staking her claim, she waved the rest of them over with a wide grin.

"The table's not even clean, yet," Viv said, wrinkling her pert nose in distaste.

Lucia motioned for Shauni to take the seat by Kylie while she slid in after. "I want to be able to see the room," the Spanish bombshell explained, "but still be able to show my legs."

Paige and Viv sat in the two opposite chairs and crowded the remaining glasses together on the edge of the table.

Shauni looked up at the ivory ceiling, at the imprinted tin that was there as well as on the walls above rich wainscoting. "Claudia will be sorry she missed this place. I bet the ceiling's original."

"It is, I'm sure," Lucia agreed. "Look at the cracked tile on the floor and the wood partitions with stained glass. Those didn't come from a supply warehouse. Claudia would be on historical story time overload."

Shauni laughed. "You have a way of putting things." Looking at the stained glass, she asked, "You know antiques?"

Brushing a long, brown tendril away from her face, Lucia shrugged. "Many of the places I go are very, very old. It's easy to become fluent in the language of age."

Beside Shauni, Kylie leaned forward to look at the bar. "I'm just going to go get us some drinks. I haven't even seen a server yet."

"I'll go." Shauni motioned Lucia up to let her pass. "Kylie, you and Lucia keep the seat warm and continue to look beautiful. Paige, you want a beer, right?"

"Yeah, Guinness if they've got it."

Viv ordered an apple cider, and Lucia and Kylie wanted appletinis.

With a list in her head, Shauni made her way to the long, polished plank that was the bar and propped her elbows on it. She saw that the pub even had an antique cash register, ornate silver with old buttons. After a minute, she caught the eye of the bartender, a lean woman with brown hair in a short, spunky cut.

"What'll you have?"

After Shauni reeled off the drinks, the woman wrinkled her brow. "You at a table?"

"Yes, but we haven't been there long. One of my friends is impatient."

Looking toward their table and seeing the dirty glasses, the bartender frowned. "I'll get these out to you, and Claude will get those dirties out of your way. Sorry about that."

"It's really no problem," Shauni told her.

As she built the Guinness, the bartender asked, "You visiting? Because you don't sound local."

"Well, sort of. I just relocated from Colorado and don't know how long I'll be staying."

"Yep, I knew you talked too clean and crisp for a southerner. Down here we like a little sugar and whiskey on our words." She wiped her hands on a towel and extended one to Shauni. "I'm Jen. You need anything, just let me know."

"Thanks. I appreciate it." Shauni noted the bottles along the back side of the bar wall. "How much of the woodwork is original?"

"Just about all of it. Real source of pride to the owner and all of us. I've been here about five years now. Used to be a teacher but decided I'd rather live than tell about it."

"I get the feeling a lot of living goes on around here."

"You said it."

A customer from the other end yelled Jen's name and held up an empty glass, prompting the bartender to move his way.

Just as Shauni turned to go, she felt a tingle on the back of her neck. Whether it was intuition, imagination, or some newly tapped sixth sense, she was certain she was being watched.

Her green eyes scanned the room until she caught the open stare of a woman at a table near the back. Her skin was the color of coffee with just a touch of cream and her dark eyes were full of gleeful surprise. She had the look a child gets when planning something devious.

Waves of animosity rolled from the stranger, but Shauni chalked it up to alcohol or confusion. The woman couldn't possibly know her, since Shauni was sure she'd never seen her before in her life.

She must have stood looking back at the woman for longer than she'd realized, because the round of drinks was waiting on the newly cleaned table when she rejoined the others.

Kylie held up her apple drink. "A toast to us and those who couldn't join us. May we all find our inner strength and put the bad guys down when our time comes."

"To kicking ass," Paige added.

Viv smiled and shook off the last bit of rigid scientist for the night. "To new friends."

"*Hermanas*," Lucia rolled off her tongue through sexy red lips. "Sisters."

Feeling the need to add something, Shauni raised her own light beer and smiled at the four women. "Blessed be."

The clinking of glasses and happy laughs were interrupted by a voice that purred with wicked delight. "Well, look what we have here."

Shauni glanced up to see the woman from before, her straight brown hair now pulled into a tail. She had been right. This woman hated her for some reason. She hated them all.

The unwelcome guest put her hands on her hips and smiled smugly to a man standing beside her. "I think we've found some of Anna's little witches."

9

Paige sprung to a standing position, her fists clenched, face rigid. "Who the hell are you?"

The dark-skinned woman flicked hateful eyes at Paige then raked them over the rest of their group. Shauni could almost taste the revulsion she was sending out. "You should all run back to wherever you came from. Go back to your little covens. We're not dressing up and lighting candles down here. We're playing for keeps."

Shauni realized two things. Whoever this woman was, she didn't know they were all novices in the witch business. And even more obvious was her lack of respect for the craft.

"You never did say your name. We should at least know who's threatening us. How else are we supposed to avoid another chance encounter like this one?" Shauni was surprised to hear the thorns in her own voice as it flowed steadily through lips tight with anger.

The woman slammed her hand down on the table. Glasses jumped as she glared at Shauni and hissed, "Sylvie."

"Well, Sylvie," Paige stated quietly. Too quietly. "If you want to keep that manicure nice and neat I suggest you remove it from our table. And yourself from our presence."

As if taking a moment to decide if she'd rather have fish or chicken, Sylvie tilted her head with a blank look then popped a fake smile on her crimson lips. "Sure. No problem. We'll meet again. Why don't you go cry to Anna. Tell her all about the big, bad priestess that scared you."

"I'm not even going to ask," Viv mumbled, causing Kylie to stifle a giggle.

The man with Sylvie put a hand on her arm and pulled her through the crowd until they disappeared altogether. He had looked so young and innocent with sweet blue eyes and a head full of brown curls. Shauni wondered how well he knew Sylvie.

"*Mierda santa*," Lucia breathed before taking her appletini down in one slug.

"Ooh ooh. I know that one." Kylie translated the Spanish for the others. "Holy shit. Make that a double." And chugged her drink as well.

"Okay. I really hate to ask, but what storm just blew through here, and what did she mean by priestess?" Viv stroked her angled bangs out of eyes and frowned. "I just wanted them gone."

Loud conversations and music continued in the bar. No one else seemed aware of the confrontation. A long-legged blonde tossed her head back and laughed when a man in a business suit whispered in her ear.

"I don't know, but she was right about one thing. We need to tell Anna." Shauni set her beer aside, no longer in the mood. "How did she even know who we are? I saw her looking at me when I was ordering, but I blew it off. That doesn't explain how she knew about Anna or about *what* we are."

"Then let's go after them. Ask a few questions of our own." Still on her feet, Paige headed in the same direction as the couple.

"Wait," Viv called. When Paige charged on, the gorgeous Japanese woman in a borrowed party dress pushed back from the table and dashed after her.

Lucia edged out, tugging on Shauni's arm. "We can't let them go alone. That Sylvie looked a little *loca*."

As a trio, Shauni, Lucia, and Kylie tumbled out the doors and into the cool velvet of a southern spring night. Paige's boots gave her away as did the clicking of angry heels as Viv tried to keep up with her.

They all caught up when Paige stopped one block over and scowled at the busy streets. "I lost them. They were here a second ago, but I don't know which way they turned."

"Good," Viv said. "We have no business chasing after them. They've got the advantage. They know about us, and we're stabbing in the dark."

"They don't know we can't use our powers yet," Kylie pointed out.

So Shauni wasn't the only one that had noticed. The college girl wasn't as flighty as she liked to pretend.

"It's five to two, or maybe only one," Lucia chimed in. "And I don't like being told to go anywhere." She firmed her lips. "I'll find them." Holding out a hand, fingers straight up and palm forward, Lucia closed her eyes. She began slowly moving her hand back and forth.

Her eyes popped open, and she pointed. "That way."

"I don't like this," Shauni said, but went after the already moving Paige and Lucia.

Viv shook her head. "Neither do I."

Don't go, Shauni. You're not ready. None of you are. Cuileann's thoughts shot into Shauni's head like a bolt of lightning. The situation and Shauni's fear must have transmitted to the island and to her cat, who was now agitated and worried for all of them.

What did Cuileann know that Shauni didn't?

Hearing Paige's voice call out, "Hey!" jarred Shauni and had her running to stop the warrior-woman from getting them all into trouble.

It was too late. Trouble was striding toward them, right down the middle of the street.

Things were quieter here. Darker.

And Shauni realized the pair had been waiting for them.

A car on the next street gunned its engines to life, spilling earth pounding music into the night before falling quiet. Eerie gongs then rang out as if from massive bells and set an ominous tone. Soon Shauni heard music and realized the car was still nearby. It was playing "Hells Bells" by AC/DC.

At least it was fitting.

"You must be one of Ronja's groupies, since you know who we are," Paige told Sylvie as the woman came at them from the shadows.

"I object to the classification, but I'll be sure to pass it along to Ronja. She'll be entertained. Just as she'll enjoy hearing of the blood spilled in her name and how easily Anna's recruits were put down."

"The only blood staining these streets will be yours." Paige flicked a hand at the man still with Sylvie. "Why don't you send your date home? He probably didn't realize he was buying rotten fruit."

"Cute," Sylvie said with a laugh, then to the young man beside her, "R.J., honey. Why don't you tell 'em a thing or two?"

The young man nodded and focused on the women. He stared in silence.

Shauni looked around at the others when she heard one of them cry out. Viv and Kylie both put their hands to their foreheads while Paige shook her head as if trying to expel water from her ear. Lucia merely sank to her knees.

Something was pressing at Shauni's brain, a mental wasp beating at the glass that barred its entry. Only then did she understand what was happening to her friends.

R.J. was "telling 'em" something.

"Stop it," she shouted, but the man with the sweet blue eyes only grinned.

"I'm lost," Lucia cried, patting wildly on the pavement as if feeling her way. "I can't see anything."

Paige bent over, moaning and heaving. "I couldn't get there in time. I tried. I tried. It went off too fast."

Viv and Kylie were still standing together, hands clasped now and eyes shut tight. They weren't experiencing the amount of pain and disorientation, or whatever the hell was going on, as Paige and Lucia were.

Shauni ached to help her friends. She had to do something, but what? She didn't know how to call her power, and if she did, she wouldn't know what to do with it.

Again she screamed at the man to stop his assault. Sylvie laughed and clapped her hands slowly, enjoying the show.

A whimper from Kylie brought Shauni's eyes back to the young girl, still largely unaffected and still holding on to Viv.

Then it made sense. *Their hands are clasped. They're connected.*

In two running steps Shauni was standing behind them, her right hand on Kylie's shoulder, her left on Viv.

"Better. That's better," Viv said, letting go of her forehead and bringing her gaze up to search the area. "Don't let go," she told Shauni before raising her arm and twirling her free hand in two quick rotations. A traffic light on the corner started flashing a mad repetition of red, yellow, and green as its pole twisted in cement.

Viv slashed her hand, and the crunching sound of metal versus pavement turned into a wrenching scrape as the pole pulled free and fired toward R.J. and his invasive mind. He jumped, barely avoiding a collision of leg and streetlight, but the action was enough to break his hold.

Paige's head snapped up, but she still gasped for air.

"Dammit, R.J.," Sylvie said. Aiming both hands at the witches with fingers spread wide, she began to mumble unintelligibly.

Shauni couldn't make out the words and didn't know what to expect next, but knew they had to leave before R.J. tried to scramble their brains again.

Paige had fully recovered and was staring a hole through the pair of attackers. If Shauni had any doubt regarding the blonde woman's special gift, it was eradicated when she saw Paige move like a flash toward Sylvie. The malicious hands that had been thrust forward and shaking as if casting a spell were knocked down in a move literally too fast for the naked eye. In another blink, Sylvie was on her backside.

And Paige had moved on to R.J.

Sensing the lust for revenge in her friend, Shauni let go of Viv and Kylie, telling them, "Go to Lucia." She leaped forward. A blur of black and gray were all that gave away Paige's presence. "Paige, don't," Shauni called out. "Let's just go."

When the sound of bone meeting flesh continued, Shauni cried, "Lucia's sick. We have to get her out of here." Headlights flashed and grew larger in the distance. "Please."

The movement stopped to reveal Paige standing over a crumpled mass on the cobblestones. R.J.'s head lolled to the side, his face reminiscent of pizza with the topping ripped off. One of his legs was twisted under the other in an unnatural position.

Paige was backing away, breathing heavily. "Bastard. You bastard."

"Oh my God," Shauni said. "Is he dead?" She clapped a hand over her mouth then rubbed it nervously against her thigh. "Oh, Paige."

Wiping her hands on her gray pants as well, but in an effort to clean them of blood, Paige snapped, "He's not dead, and he won't die." She stalked past. "Come on. You said we need to go, so let's get the hell out of here. I have a few questions for Anna."

Fluid the color of wine spread from beneath R.J.'s head and ran between the stones. Sylvie was crawling over to him, but managed to throw an evil eye at Shauni. "You'll pay for this."

She lifted one hand with two fingers in a V shape but bent at the knuckles. "Ache. Cry. Bleed."

It was too much. They had come out to celebrate. Have a few drinks. And now Shauni stood in the shadows of hulking trees and watched as a human being leaked onto the dark street. More than human, she knew, but life just the same.

The majestic trees now seemed dangerous, the wind cold and cutting. Nothing here was as it appeared.

She checked back to see that the others were together.

Then without another thought for them or anything else, Shauni cast bleary eyes away from her friends. Away from her enemies.

And ran.

~

Time was fluid, and the moon seemed to hover in the same position. Shauni had no idea how long she'd wandered. A minute? Thirty? She was also good and lost.

Deciding to rest and clear her head, she veered into the nearest park. In the downtown area, there was a park every few blocks. A sign told her she was at Johnson Square. Here there were benches arranged at the edges of a clear area. The ground had long been covered by brick pavers, but lush vegetation still had a foothold. A fountain gushed in the center.

At the far end, she could see a couple walking and holding hands. Could they sense the corruption around them? Did some ancient part of them cringe when they passed a certain person on the street? Did they widen the berth between themselves and the stranger for reasons they couldn't explain?

Shauni had done no better. When Sylvie had first made eye contact, she should have known. Should have felt something. What the hell kind of witch was she if she couldn't recognize bloodlust when it was staring her down? As tests go, she scored herself a big negative for tonight. A failing grade that left her grateful no one had been injured or killed.

Well, except R.J., and he had provoked his own beating.

She had been unfair to Paige. If she and Viv hadn't acted, who knows what would have happened. If R.J. could tap into their heads so easily, who's to say he might not have eventually caused physical damage? Brain injury? Shauni couldn't judge the others' reactions honestly, since she had some innate defense against R.J.'s trick. She had to assume her telepathic abilities had something to do with it.

Paige had acted in self-defense and in defense of them all.

Shauni had only run.

Thank goodness you're safe. Come home now.

Shauni sighed and answered her cat. *I'll call Viv and find out where they are. And Cuileann...thanks for watching out for me.*

Always.

Opening the small, sparkling clutch for her phone, Shauni startled at the sound of her name. A male figure was rushing across the square before coming to a standstill in a patch of moonlight. Worried gray eyes searched her and the surrounding area as she sat in shock.

Michael.

Cuileann came back into play. *What's he doing there? Does he have a needle?*

Shush. Not now. Her cat was not in favor of having a vet in the family.

Shauni started to rise, to go to him, but found her legs unsteady and weak. "What are you doing here?" she asked him when he moved closer, wondering as much as Cuileann had. "How did you know where to find me?"

Michael breathed a sigh of annoyance and relief. How indeed? What was he supposed to tell her? That he could feel her? That the terror and revulsion she experienced earlier had covered him like a landslide? That he knew where she was by following the trail of her emotions? They had left a scar on the sidewalks she'd traveled, first a sickly greenish black that had changed to the flaxen gold of realization, then ended in a steely blue of remorse. The sad color that surrounded her now.

As a young boy, he'd found an injured bird, a fledgling, and had taken it to his grandmother for help. She had been blessed with certain gifts, and healing was one of them. Michael had bravely tried to staunch the tears when she'd told him the baby bird was out of her reach. He'd held it until the tiny chest stopped racing and its aura faded from pale pink to gray, then nothing.

She'd explained to him that he had abilities as well. He was what some called an empath. He picked up on the feelings of others as if they were broadcast in neon. She'd predicted he would use it for good.

And he hoped every day that she'd been right. That the animals that were brought to him received an extra gentle hand, a steady mind that saw them as more than servants of man. Michael Black knew beyond a shadow that animals felt joy, love, and grief as surely as their human counterparts.

Now he wanted to lend his healing hand to another cause. He wanted to extract the sorrow from Shauni's heart. No other woman had ever come into him with the clarity she had. He'd felt her pain as if it had been his own.

His grandmother, wise woman that she was, would tell him that meant something, and he'd be fool to let it pass without inspection. Just one more reason he looked at her sitting there and thought... *mine*.

"I was driving past and saw you." To inspect he needed to get close, and for now, a lie served him best. "What's wrong? I see it all over you." That much was true.

"Everything." Shauni ached to open up to Michael, to let him pull her head down to his strong shoulder and tell her it would be alright. But that was only a fantasy. She couldn't tell him what had happened. He was the rational sort, methodical and by the book.

He would call the police in a heartbeat.

A bird called from somewhere above, and to Shauni's ears, the rhythm of its song sounded as if it were repeating, "I need you. I need you." She winced and chose not to listen any closer. "I've had a rough night. Problems with friends, the project, and my part in it. It's not at all what I expected, and I'm afraid I won't be able to do what's...required of me." She pressed her fingers to her eyes. "We have some worrisome...competitors."

Michael recognized a partial truth and opted to follow the threads until he got to the whole of it. Deception was usually tied together with fact, and he would just have to sort the good from the ugly. "It's bad enough that you're in a park at night, and alone. Do you have a care at all for your own safety?"

"More than you know."

"What?"

Shauni shifted toward him as he sat on the bench beside her. "Never mind." She sagged a bit from the weight of it all and spoke with complete candor. "Seeing you twice in one day is a nice surprise."

Michael saw his hand rise as if of its own volition and cup her cheek. Her eyes shimmered, and though banked in shadow, he remembered their brilliant green and how they'd held his attention. Clouds whisked away, washing them in sudden light. He swore he could smell the moon on her skin, on the waterfall of midnight that spilled down her back.

His hands belonged there, in the cool black silk. And this time, he was in control as they eased back and fisted in her hair. As he pulled her quivering lips to his. Searching. Tasting.

Shauni let go and let Michael take. She leaned into the solid heat of his chest as the bird began its cry again. *I-need-you. I-need-you.*

Her body answered his, edging closer while her hands settled on his back, appreciating the hard muscles that moved under her palms as he shifted to hold her tighter. Need for his strength, the need for him, ached in her belly. It was raw and intense, like nothing she'd ever felt.

Lust rose from her core to claw its way into the simple kiss, and Shauni struggled to tamp it down. She was a psychological mess right now and didn't want to throw anything else on the fire. It was already on the verge of burning her for good, as she was sure she'd find out when she went home.

She pulled back but licked her bottom lip, savoring what was left of him there. "I should call my friends. Let them know where I am."

"Yeah. Good." Michael felt pole-axed, if the expression meant what he thought it did. He wasn't ready to let her out of his arms, much less out of his sight. The woman obviously needed a caretaker. "Tell them I'll take you home."

"Oh, well..." Shauni remembered the house on Skidaway. It would be a safe compromise. She couldn't afford to have Michael popping up on the island, finding out too much before she was ready. If he ever came to the mainland house, Joe or his son would be there. They would handle it and knew to be discreet. "Okay."

She called Viv and pretended to have a quick, polite exchange, giving her only the essentials, and clicked the phone closed as the voice on the other end escalated.

"Michael." Shauni turned to face him and took his hand. "Thank you. For stopping to check on me, and as crazy as this is going to sound," she placed her hand on the side of his neck, fingers playing in the hair that fell over his collar, "thank you for kissing me to distraction. I needed it."

Unable to resist, Michael angled his head to hers and grinned. Might as well get one more for the road. His breath mingled with hers before their mouths met, "Anytime."

~

Michael watched Shauni disappear behind the enormous yellow house. Whoever she and the other scientists were staying with had quite a spread. He wondered if the government was involved. That would account for the secrecy.

His phone jangled out the tune "Thank God I'm a Country Boy," the song his grandmother had insisted on being her ring tone. What was she doing up so late?

"Hey, Gran." He heard classic music in the background which meant she was cross-stitching.

"Are you okay? I felt a bad vibe." His grandmother didn't miss much. "And what about the girl?" she added. No, she didn't miss a thing.

"We're both fine. I was a little worried." He paused, wondering how much to say. "I sensed her stress, but it wasn't as bad as I thought it would be when I found her."

"Found her? Well, don't that beat all."

Michael knew what she was thinking. "Now, Gran, don't get any ideas."

"So what does she look like, this woman you're falling for? And don't try to hide it from me. You know I'll know anyway and would rather hear it from you."

Michael smiled in the darkness of his car as he slid out of the posh neighborhood and back toward home. "She's very pretty. Black hair. Like another beautiful woman I know."

She laughed appreciatively. "Save that sweet talk for her. I've been silver since your grandfather died. Now, what I really want to know is…what does she *look* like?"

Michael knew what his grandmother meant. She knew he could tell a lot about a person's nature if he spent enough time around them. If he had a chance to observe how their auras reacted to different situations. She also remembered how he'd ignored the warning signs in his last relationship. How that particular female had gone bright orange every time she saw something expensive.

"Shauni is a gentle soul. I'm sure of that." He thought of the rainbow she'd left behind as she meandered the city blocks. "But right now, she looks…" He searched for a word to sum up the mysterious woman who stirred him so. "She's conflicted… and extremely worried about something."

"Then you'd better find out what."

Staring out his front windshield as his headlights cut through the dark, Michael said, "I intend to."

10

Sparks were literally flying when Shauni crossed from the foyer into the grand hall. Her fellow witches were all in a tizzy, as her mother would say, and their newfound yet uncontrolled powers were creating the occasional pop and fizzle of light.

She noticed the cats were all wisely absent.

"What did I miss?" Shauni asked, risking the heat of Paige's wrath as that one was still furious.

Claudia lay on the green couch and lifted one lazy hand. "Just a recap of Tuesday night fights and what might have happened instead."

"You wouldn't be so blasé if you'd been there," Viv said, her own eyes flashing. "You didn't have some freak poking his way into your brain. It was the mother of all migraines for me and Kylie. I can't imagine what it was like for Paige and Lucia. They were isolated from us. He messed with their memories, their senses. Lucia went blind. I think that ranks some concern."

"I am concerned," Claudia told her with compassion. "I'm just trying to keep the balance."

Shauni puzzled over the words then looked to Anna, Hayden, and Willyn. The three of them were all calm. Too calm. They were carefully containing their responses and couldn't afford to let things get out of control. Shauni imagined the hum the nine created when they came together would quickly morph into explosive chaos if every witch were at full tilt.

Shauni felt responsible and guilty, so she did her best to match their serenity. She'd go a step further and attempt to quell the core of outrage.

"Paige," she said quietly, so that everyone dimmed their voices to hear, "I'm sorry for tonight. I reacted badly, and should never have left you. I deserted all of you."

"What do I care about that?" Paige said, wiping shaggy, white-blonde bangs from her eyes. "You didn't do us much good anyway, did you?"

"That's not fair," Kylie interrupted, but Paige waved her off.

"And to make matters worse, you looked at that rotten excuse for a man and let what I did to him make you sick. You felt pity for him and disgust for me." She shook her head. "Don't deny it. I saw it in your eyes."

Shauni took a deep breath. "I won't deny that I felt disgust, but not for you. Violence has never sat well with me, and it happened so fast. You were wiping blood on your pants, and I…it overwhelmed me. No. Wait," she said when Paige opened her mouth to retort. "I had a knee-jerk reaction, but I know you and Viv saved our lives." She walked over to Paige and saw the raw hurt in her sea-blue eyes. "You saved my life. So thank you."

"But it all started with you, Shauni." Kylie crossed her arms over her chest. "If you hadn't connected with Viv and me, Viv would never have been able to send that stoplight flying, which broke through slime-boy's concentration. That was what freed Paige, thereby allowing her to commence with the ass-kicking." She shot a defiant look to Paige. "You, Viv, *and* Shauni saved our lives tonight. So can we please move the hell on?"

"Well said." Claudia rolled her knees to her chest. "Let's not waste any more energy being angry with each other. I, for one, would like a cup of coffee now that our conjoined system can handle it." She rolled her eyes to Anna. "Then I want to know why we weren't prepared to expect this."

Anna knew when a dart had been thrown her way. "You're right. I haven't prepared you, and I take full responsibility for that. I underestimated them." She met Claudia's searching gaze. "It won't happen again."

"That's what I wanted to hear," Paige said. "Who were they? I mean, they're with Ronja, that's obvious, but how are we supposed to fight what we don't know exists? Do you have details on everyone in her group?"

Anna blew out a long breath. "Some. Ronja is sneaky and protective. If it weren't for the arrogance of some of her followers, I probably wouldn't even have that."

"Can't you see them? Psychically, I mean, like you see other things?" Hayden spoke for the first time, her caramel hair in a bun on the back of her head.

"Sometimes," Anna said. "It depends."

"Maybe I can help with that," Hayden added, rubbing her ear thoughtfully. She looked back to the group. "It's time we all came clean. I don't even know what some of you are capable of." She grinned at Paige. "But you can bet I'm taking you with me everywhere."

With the last of the feathers smoothed back into place, they all voted unanimously to relocate to the kitchen. The seating might not be as comfortable, but there was food, coffee, and wine, and it was going to be a long night.

Kylie's gift was thoroughly broken in by the time each of them had made a cup of coffee or tea. Brownies, cold pizza, scones, and cheese spread on crackers completed the feast. A fire burned in the kitchen fireplace, and Shauni was glad for it. Whether the hour of night or the upsetting events from before, something chilled the marrow of her bones.

"Okay, give," Paige said to Anna as she plunked herself on a stool next to her. The nine of them had pulled up extra seats so they all sat around the huge, crescent shaped island. "Who attacked us tonight?"

Anna sipped her Colombian Bold from a cobalt mug. "I'm not familiar with this R.J. you've described, but at least we're now aware of one of his abilities. You can count yourselves successful in more ways than one."

Paige cracked a wry smile. "We unintentionally gathered some intel, and what was the other thing? Oh, yeah...we lived."

"You told us it would be dangerous, but we never expected anything so fast," Viv said.

"Or so furious." Kylie munched a cracker, sipped her cola, and added, "We walked into the city completely unaware of what could happen. Really, in actuality, happen."

Anna grimaced. "And I'm sorry for that. I've lived my life with rules and guidelines and assumed Ronja had to do the same. I see now that she can do whatever she wants, or at least her disciples can. I didn't expect anything like this either, especially in the middle of a public place."

"Disciples," Willyn whispered then cleared her throat. "That scares me, makes me think of fanatics that will do anything for their cause or their leader."

"And they will. Ronja has promised them positions in the regime after they've won and their fiend has been loosed on the world. It won't come as a raging storm of evil, but more likely as a man. A young man who will find himself on the fast track to power and authority. What he'll do behind the scenes is unmentionable. Unimaginable." Anna clutched her drink, willing the warmth to seep into her fingers. "A demon who's successfully achieved corporeal form will be like Hitler without human limitations. It may one day decide to shed its human disguise and openly wreak destruction, to feed on our kind."

"How can this be real? And why has it never happened before?" Hayden asked.

"It has. There are a great many unsolved mysteries of the past. Many times the disappearance of people, either individuals or in large groups, has been swept aside. Men who ruled with bloody fists, who were either vanquished or changed forms. Most people don't feel comfortable with the unexplained, so they choose to turn away and ignore it."

"Or they try to dig deeper and someone or something removes them from the equation as well." Lucia looked solemn, more afraid than any of them had ever seen her look before, and Viv placed a hand on her before speaking.

"Then tell us about Sylvie. She called herself a priestess. Is she a witch?" Viv had her glasses on again and was decked out in lime green pajamas covered with strawberries.

"I would say she has some magic, which is vague, I know, but she's not necessarily a witch. You'll find that magic comes in a variety of shapes and sizes. Witches are often associated with Wicca or similar pagan beliefs, though the title has been grossly distorted throughout history. Wiccan witches avoid harming others, and adhere to the threefold law, meaning what you do will come back to you three times." Anna paused. "And three times stronger."

Shauni felt at odds with what she was hearing. "Then how can we do what we're doing? If we fight, it comes back on us?"

"There are exceptions. We are charged to defend the innocent, and that's priority. Besides," Anna set aside her coffee, "if it's pre-ordained, as our tasks have been, I think we get a pass. There is no guidebook, only the practices and beliefs that have been passed down over time. Each of us must follow our own moral code, and I believe it helps that we're not doing this for any personal gain."

"But Ronja is," Lucia pointed out. "And Sylvie. Are they both witches?"

"Sylvie is a practitioner of hoodoo, which finds its origins in Africa as a type of botanical based art of mysticism. Unlike voodoo, which is a religion, hoodoo refers to certain magical practices."

"I don't consider myself slow," Claudia said with the arch of one fiery brow, but could you go over the botanical mysticism part again?"

Anna laughed. "Sorry. So much of this is second nature to me."

"You're so lucky to have been raised knowing what you are," Kylie said wistfully before glancing around at the coven in their multitude of outfits from silk pajamas to street clothes. "We have so much to catch up on."

"True. But you also have the benefit of training and learning together. Even I have tapped into new capabilities since the rest of you have come to the island. Doors will open more quickly for you. Don't worry." Anna winked at the younger girl and held out her blue mug. "Would you make me another cup while I tell the rest?"

With Kylie popping a little container into the machine, Anna continued. "Historically, parts of Africa spawned tales of spirit guardians from the forest, azzizas, who helped hunters create medicines and potions. Sometimes poisons. It evolved over time and was carried to the Americas along with slavery. It very often exists within a Christian community, mostly in the Southeast."

"Sylvie doesn't sound like a Christian," Willyn ground out with heat in her words, surprising the others.

"She's not, I assure you, but as with most things, like draws to like. Ronja has twisted her powers for her own selfish desires, and whatever gifts Sylvie naturally possessed have been intensified through their association."

Claudia leaned onto the granite half-moon table. "You keep saying Ronja twisted herself or turned. You're implying she wasn't always a soldier for the dark side?"

"On the contrary," Anna replied. "Ronja was once a highly respected member of her society. She was a worker of magic, what was once called a *seior*."

"I've heard that before, I think." Claudia, the historian,

rolled the word off her tongue over and over. "But it's an older term."

Anna coughed and pursed her lips. "Ronja was a seior in Scandinavia." She stopped, held her breath. "Around ten-twenty."

"Excuse me," Shauni asked, "the year ten-twenty? She's over a thousand years old?" Shauni fought a wave of nausea. "You never told us she was immortal."

Having expected a negative reaction, Anna only nodded. "Bits and pieces. One bite at a time. None of you even knew what you were when you came here." She rubbed a hand across her face. "I'm sorry if I'm letting you down. I don't have a syllabus on how to train new witches. I have to find a spot somewhere between keeping you all informed and scaring you away. If any one of us breaks rank, we all fall."

In need of comfort, Shauni went to the far corner where Skid slept on a brown cushion that was optimistically large. The puppy was a little black kernel at its center. She stroked him and listened to the ensuing debate.

"You have to tell us everything, Anna. We can't go into this with anything less than full knowledge." Paige's voice, tight with anger.

"I agree," Hayden said in her perpetually mild tone. "You have to trust us. We've all committed ourselves, even those of us who were a bit shaky." She sat up taller. "We're not shaky anymore, at least in our resolve to do this. I can't say how I'll feel when it's my turn, but I won't falter or run."

"Fine. I can do that," Anna said, tapping her rosy, pink nails on the gray granite. "But understand that I only know so much. I can only see certain details when I'm allowed, and am still researching what's coming. Ronja didn't leave a clear trail, and she certainly isn't going to offer any help. I've told you about Bastraal, the demon. I do know he's the source of her immortality."

"How?" Viv asked.

"When Christianity came to Norway, Ronja and her kind were shunned, persecuted, tortured, and murdered. As many pagans were. In her thirst for revenge and will to survive, she somehow conjured this demon, and they were able to strike a bargain."

Shauni saw where the story was going. "He, or it, granted her immortality in exchange for her promise to help him."

"Yes. Demons are strong and devious but can do much worse when aided and channeled by humans, who already exist in physical form." Anna spread her hands. "Fate and the gods that be have an odd sense of humor. Now that we're all here and have accepted our destiny, the missing pieces should start coming together."

"Tell me what to do, Anna." Shauni stood and walked back to the group. "I feel like I'm wading around in mud, expecting something to come to me, but so far it hasn't. Other than the bird and the graveyard."

Anna held her tongue, not sure how much she should tell Shauni of what she'd seen. Since the arrival of the others, her psychic receptors had been going crazy. She got a lot of mixed signals and worried that revealing the wrong thing would alter the course. Her struggle was nothing new. Foresight and prophetic gifts were a tricky business. One wrong move to prevent or encourage a vision and an alternate future could be created.

"Hold it," Claudia spit out. "Bird and graveyard?"

Shauni glanced at Anna then told the others, "Sorry. I should have told all of you, but this day has been packed since sunrise and moved like a freight train." She took a deep breath and told them the story she'd already shared with Anna. They already knew about Anna's vision and the cryptic message about *the whisperer*.

"A graveyard, huh?" Hayden asked. "Given my ability, I

usually avoid them like the plague, but I can go back with you tomorrow." She smiled. "We can see if any ghosts are hanging around that can give us a clue."

A tiny seed of hope blossomed for Shauni, a sense of direction. "Good idea."

Anna still wasn't sure what to make of the whole thing and nodded her agreement with their plan. She smiled at Shauni. "See? Another stroke on the canvas."

"I thought I spoke in riddles," Claudia said, "but you have suspense down to an art form, Anna."

"Witches are supposed to be mysterious," Kylie joked, attempting to keep the mood light.

Paige wasn't quite ready for that. "Okay, so Ronja's immortal," she said, unwilling to let the subject drop until she was satisfied. "We know about R.J. and Sylvie. Who else?"

"I don't have an exact number yet. I'm afraid we'll have to wait and see. "Anna held up a hand. "But...she does have three that are closest to her. Her lover, Tyr, is a Native American man she found in this country in the mid eighteen-hundreds. He was a warrior with a gift Ronja had long desired for herself but could never achieve. Like myself, he is a prophet. A seer."

"He's immortal, too?" Lucia said, her accent thick with worry. "Are they all?"

"No. No. Only Ronja is truly immortal. She shares her reward with Tyr by allowing him to drink her blood when needed. And before you ask, no vamps, just some demon magic." Anna's grin turned wicked now. "Ronja's pride and lust for more will be part of her eventual downfall. She's always weaker after feeding Tyr, but the window of opportunity is short and uncertain."

"Who else?" Shauni sided with Paige on this. She didn't want to be caught unaware again.

"She has a human, a lawyer named Dalton Ellis. He protects her real world assets and her secrets. Other than being an unscrupulous man and legal genius, he's not a direct threat."

Anna frowned. "There's a woman. She's been with Ronja a very long time, I'm not really sure how long or what it means. She's a bit of a dark spot. I'm blocked from her, and that makes me both curious and wary. Her name is Scarlett."

"Then we need to hike our asses to witch's boot camp and learn as much as we can," Viv said. "Sylvie did us a favor tonight by telling us in no uncertain terms that their side came to play and play for keeps."

"Then we'll do the same," Shauni said. "I'm still afraid, I won't lie, and unsure how my gift will benefit me, us, before it's all over, but I want to try and find out."

Anna stood. "Good. We're all on the same page, so let's get some sleep." She looked squarely at Paige then shifted her blue eyes to Shauni. "We'll get started first thing in the morning."

~

Meanwhile, another was pondering the night's events and planning for the next day as well. Michael sat in his home office, staring blindly at an article on digital ultrasound in veterinary care, but his mind was on something else.

Black hair in the moonlight, full lips melding to his, and emeralds flashing with desire. He'd seen it on Shauni's face, felt it in the shift of her body toward his, before she'd put up her shields once again. The enigmatic woman had his full attention, and any qualms he still nurtured had been trampled by a raging need to be near her, to learn more about her.

For the first time in his life, Michael wanted to tell a woman everything. His hopes and dreams. Fears and secrets. The spark she'd kindled inside him grew stronger each time they met. And what about the sensation of her emotional state and the way her sadness or fury flooded his system from miles away? How could he explain that?

The resounding answer was he couldn't. Something was

burning for her, too. That same connection and yearning. But there was an obstacle in their way, and only she could show him what it was. He couldn't navigate without knowing what lay ahead, so he would keep hammering away at her resistance until she told him. Trusted him.

Maybe then he could trust her, too.

Michael closed the magazine and sat back in the chair, closing his eyes and recalling their kiss, her touch, his need.

And remembered the scent of Shauni in the dark.

11

Daffodils ran rampant in the grass behind the expansive house. Spreading their sunny cheer, birds twittered with glee, and the sun beating down was warm enough for shorts. Shauni was therefore beholden to wear some, along with a tee shirt, in the hope of soaking up some southern tan. Warm weather never came to Colorado this early.

The amazing day was one reason Anna requested they meet outside. The second was a desire to keep her home and belongings intact. Eight new witches practicing magic could be eventful.

In a variety of shorts, jeans, and sweatpants, the nine formed a circle and looked to Anna and the bag she had at her feet.

"Before we begin," she said, opening the tote, "I have something for you. An essential for any good witch." She pulled out two books. They appeared to be leather and embossed with Celtic braids, similar to the design of their medallions. She handed one of a brick color to Lucia and the other, sunshine yellow, to Kylie. Again, their signature hues were in play.

Shauni retrieved one of a mossy green before coral went to Claudia, and the rest of the women received theirs. Anna told them, "I've had a book of shadows most of my life but felt it was important to start a new one, along with my sisters. I still learn new tricks and especially now that you're all with me."

"I thought there was only one book of shadows. Like a myth,"

Hayden said.

"A book of shadows is where a witch keeps track of her spells, incantations, and even personal musings. The sharpest memory can't remember everything, so it's a sort of magic diary. I've already included the basic pagan rituals on the first pages."

"Thank you. They're beautiful," Shauni said. She pressed her own to her heart, touched to have another symbolic link with her coven.

"They're called grimoires as well, a European name," Claudia added.

"They can be," Anna said. "What you call it is up to you. The reference to a book of shadows is actually fairly new, part of what some refer to as neo-paganism. You can call it a cookbook if you like," she grinned, "because it will be full of recipes when we're done."

Paige raised a hand. "I'd like the one for putting bad guys on their backsides if you don't mind."

"I promise we'll touch on both defense and offense today, but first, let's focus on your personal strengths. Viv," Anna gestured to the Asian woman. "We all know you have an amazing ability to move inanimate objects, so stirring the air or calling fire should come easily to you."

"But I've never moved anything as big or heavy as that pole. I don't know how I did it."

"Think back to that moment. What were you thinking, feeling? My bet is a riotous mixture of fear and anger."

Viv nodded.

"Yet, you controlled it."

Shauni threw in some praise for her fellow witch. "Like a sharpshooter. Mind-bending boy almost had to limp home."

"I'm envious," Anna said. "Elemental manipulation is my weak spot." She moved toward Lucia. "So, we introduce new concepts while building on your inherent instincts. Lucia, where is your cat right now?"

Caught unaware, the exotic brunette fluttered her eyes but answered, "Sleeping on the Norman Rockwell book in the library."

"Hold on," Kylie interjected. "Can you hear her thoughts like Shauni?"

Lucia shook her head. "I...find things, and never get lost. The earth, it has a force inside it that has a direct link with my body." She looked to Viv, the physicist. "I've done some research on electromagnetic chips, how some animals use them, but that doesn't explain the rest. If I concentrate on a specific place or thing, I know where it is. Sometimes, like the other night, people leave marks. It's as if they alter the flow of particles and leave a wake behind."

"You, Viv, and Paige already called on your gifts to help you win out over members of the Amara. I have to believe we will all use our strengths in combination with the craft to complete the challenges." Anna turned her attention to Shauni. "Have you used yours, Shauni?"

"No, not against the Amara. I didn't think of it last night, but if I had, what could I have done? Used a bird to scout the area, maybe, but other than that, I don't know." Shauni rubbed her thumbs against fingers. She was only now getting used to the idea of battling evil herself. What could she do with the animals? She would never consider involving them or putting them in danger. Absolutely not.

Anna must mean something else.

"You should consider all your options," Anna said, letting her bright blue eyes lock with Shauni's before circling back around to stand beside Willyn. "Our sweet mother here can heal with a touch, which will undoubtedly come in handy, though I dread the idea of its necessity."

"I don't want to have to use it on any of you or myself." Willyn glanced quickly to where Tadd was playing and chasing something that hopped. The puppy, Skid, traipsed along with love in his eye for the small boy. She clenched inside, unable to imagine harm coming to her son.

She answered Anna, "But I would. No question."

"Even though it gives you pain," Anna said quietly.

Willyn's eyes widened. "How did you know?"

"I saw the briefest of tremors when you healed Quinn's bruise. I imagine a more serious injury would be another matter entirely."

"And you do it every day as a nurse, don't you?" Paige asked with admiration. She had new respect for the quiet woman with a gold cross hanging from her neck. The Christian was tougher than she looked.

Willyn shrugged it off then pointed at Kylie. "We know Anna can see things, the future, past, or the here and now, and Claudia can lay hands on an object and know its history, but what about you?

The college girl with the long curls rolled her eyes. "I have a crappy one, not nearly as exciting as the rest of you."

"Don't talk that way about yourself," Claudia scolded then smiled. "Picking out the perfect pair of shoes for any occasion is a tremendous talent."

"Yeah, yeah," Kylie laughed. "Other than my astounding fashion sense, I sort of communicate with electricity or something."

They all waited in silence, unsure what she meant. "Electronics or anything that uses energy, I speak their language. For example, my friend's phone glitches, I can touch it and know what's wrong. Usually fix it, too. But I haven't really done anything with it. I mean, sure I'd love to jack an ATM or something, but my conscience always gets in the way." She added as an afterthought, "Oh, but you should see what I can do in a thunderstorm."

"I knew I liked you for a reason," Viv teased.

Kylie put a hand on her hip and looked at Hayden. "And you really see ghosts?"

There was no way to dress it up with pretty words, and since she just couldn't pass up the opportunity, Hayden tossed up her hands and said, "I see dead people."

Kylie responded with a smile. "Can I just say...no way."

Hayden laughed. "Most assuredly...way. I have since I was little. They're usually benign, lost or needing to impart some crucial piece of information. I help when I can."

"Like that television show," Shauni put in. "I have to admit I love to watch, but it always makes me cry."

"Me, too," Hayden said. "Sometimes I cry when I do it in real life. It depends on the spirit and what they want. Unlike the show, I'm not always able to give them what they need."

"Well, tell us when you see any," Lucia said. "I don't want to pass through them or anything." She shivered.

"Now that we've gotten more on the table, let's start with a few protection spells." Anna flipped open the royal blue book that was her own book of shadows, or as she liked to think of it, her book of nine. She couldn't express to the others how her sensitivity and awareness had changed since they'd all come together. She felt like a lightning rod for every metaphysical phenomenon that floated past.

It was great.

"I've worked up a special one for the man we have affectionately named mind-bending-boy."

"What will it do?" Lucia asked, noticing that Paige was paying attention, too. Neither of them would speak of what happened or the pain and desolation R.J. had shoved into their heads. It had been a waking nightmare.

"If it works, the black magic he sends toward you will bounce back at him. He should experience the equivalent of a brain freeze by way of liquid nitrogen," Anna said with a wiggle of her brows. She and everyone else looked forward to a little payback.

"He was in pretty bad shape," Shauni said with a glance toward Paige. "How do we know he'll be back in the game anytime soon?"

"He had other magic," Paige said, then lifted one shoulder. "I could sense it every time I hit him."

"I've seen that as well. Last night, I used my gazing ball. I wanted to see if anything new had cropped up. Your contact with R.J. brought something back to us all. He's got power, but he wasn't born with it." Anna hated any referral to Satanism. It was a practice that painted many occult followers with a brush of hatred. Most people still associated the words pagan with the devil. *Hmph*, she thought, *as if there were only one.*

She continued. "R.J. was stolen as a child and raised with a Satanic cult. He learned everything he knows from some very malicious people. He traded his soul for access to magic when he was twelve years old and has only gotten stronger. We may yet see more from him."

"What did he do? When he was twelve?" Shauni asked, though she was afraid she already knew.

Anna blew a breath through her nose as if dispelling a foul odor. "Sacrifice is their exchange system, and the child that R.J. was chose to perform the ultimate. He offered a human."

They all responded with disgust and shock. Even Willyn looked ready to murder.

"Then let's have that spell," Claudia called out.

From inside the bag, Anna pulled violet material, already cut into pieces, and passed them around to the others. Upon inspection, Shauni saw the outline of what looked like a gingerbread man with the initials R.J. written in black. She took the pair of scissors handed over by Hayden and waited for instructions.

"We're going to make poppets, representations of the man we intend to block. Purple is for driving away evil or people who have influence over you." Anna held up a vial. "I took scrapings of the dried blood on Paige's clothes from last night. Once you stitch and stuff your poppets, you will sprinkle some of it inside."

"It's all his blood. Don't worry," Paige said. "You won't accidentally do anything to me.

"I'm not great with a needle," Viv complained.

Anna crossed to her. "It doesn't have to be pretty, but the magic will be stronger if made by your hands."

Sharing the scissors, they each took turns cutting out their own patterns and sewing them into the shape of a body before stuffing it with cotton. Last, they each sprinkled a bit of the blood inside and sealed their dolls tight.

Once the labor was complete, Anna said, "Now the part you've all been waiting for. I'll go first then we'll repeat the chant together three times while holding the poppets. Ready?"

Receiving no negative responses, Anna spoke. "Bar this man and his demon gift, his search a spiral into our rift, evil returns unto he, freezing pain three times three. Our minds are our own, reflect his deed, as we will, so mote it be."

They passed around a bottle. As Anna had explained, it contained a mix of oils that would aid with binding, and dropped three drops of it onto their little purple men.

With a smile both nervous and excited, Hayden caught Shauni's eye and gave her a thumbs-up. Remembering the night before and the torture her friends had endured, Shauni gripped her poppet and channeled every ounce of her will into the magic as the nine spoke together.

Words rang from a place deep within. Shauni's lips tingled as the strength of her enchantment rushed through. The air whipped around their circle and throbbed with energy as nine voices rose in unison.

When the third repetition came near its end, the circle and all inside were washed in white light. A brilliant surge of ecstasy accompanied the last as together they spoke, "As we will so mote it be."

And then the day fell back into normalcy.

Willyn's son and the puppy still chased through the flowers, unaware that magic had occurred. Birds flew and sun beamed.

Into the silence Viv said, "Now that was truly better than sex."

"Then you're not doing it right," Lucia quipped, sending them all into laughter.

"Okay," Anna said with a clap. "We've completed the defensive portion of today's exercise." She flicked her palm up where it glowed and burned. "Now how about a little fire?"

~

After a shower and some lunch, Shauni made her way through the library and out the French-paned double doors that opened into the solarium. This is where Mrs. Attinger suggested Anna might be found, and given the tropical surroundings and overwhelming peacefulness, Shauni could see why this was one of the head witch's favorite retreats. Sand-colored bricks formed circling paths and wound through vegetation. Bright flowers and thick palms flourished under the sun that filtered through a high glass roof.

Shauni found Anna sitting beneath a ridiculously large fern, on a wooden bench, with book in hand. She was intrigued to note the historical romance and said so. "I imagined you bent over an ancient tome, studying a new spell."

With a wiggle of her toes and stretch of her arms, Anna smiled. "We have to let our minds rest once in a while. A little escapism never hurts."

"My mother always told me that kind of book would give me fanciful ideas about what a man should be," Shauni said, sitting beside Anna. "And to read them often as a reminder not to settle for less."

"I agree. Why shouldn't we wait for sensitivity, brains, and brawn?"

"Don't forget the world-spinning sex," Shauni joked.

Closing the book and setting it aside, Anna settled patient eyes on Shauni. "But you didn't come to talk about romance books. You're confused, worried that you'll fail your challenge and thereby let us all down. Am I right?"

"That's the tip of it, yes."

"Only the tip? Perhaps you should fill me in."

Shauni pursed her lips. "What you said earlier worries me, about the animals. I've wracked my brain, but I just don't see how or why they need to be involved. I've only just accepted the fact that I will have to fight the Amara, sometimes physically, a practice that flies in the face of everything I was raised to believe in."

Anna absorbed the information and reflected for a moment before responding. "You are a biologist and are therefore very knowledgeable about the natural world. Add to that, you're a witch, even if you weren't aware, and so you are also in tune with the natural world and able to understand its inhabitants in a way most can't."

"Which makes it harder for me to use them or expose them to danger."

"Let me ask you this. A mother lion or bear, how do they respond if their young are threatened?"

Shauni raised a suspicious brow. "We both know the answer to that. It's where we get the expression, 'mama bear.' No one wants to cross an angry mother's path."

"Right. Even with your gifts, a grizzly would shred you if you came too close to her cubs," Anna said.

"But that's completely different. I would expect Willyn to become ferocious if anything threatened Tadd, but that's not what you're asking of me. I can't exploit innocent creatures for my own sake. I won't let them fight my fight. It's wrong, selfish, and cowardly."

"First," Anna raised a finger, "I'm not asking you to do anything but think about your gift and why it was given to you. To consider how you can use it to stop what's coming, because we will all have a role to play in this. Second, it is the same. That mama bear and Willyn would both be defending the innocent and the weak, because their babies were threatened by something larger and more powerful."

Shauni contemplated the rationale. "And our job is also to defend the innocents. The people who would be hurt if the demon is set free."

"And the animals," Anna said. "You don't think evil will ignore any life form it might benefit from using or manipulating, do you?"

Shauni felt the warmth of her blood turn a few degrees toward freezing, her breath catch in her chest with a tickle of dread. "No. He wouldn't. Why bother with them?"

Anna's features turned hard. "Because it is the darkness, and because it can." She stood, heaving an exasperated sigh. "You are the link to those that live in the forgotten places. Those with fur and scales that still live among magic. Just because humans have tossed aside fairy tales and charms, that doesn't mean they don't still exist. Would you abandon them when they need you most?"

"What? No. Never." Shauni shook her head fiercely. "I would protect them."

"Then don't make the same mistake I made. I wanted to protect all of you, and my ego almost got you killed. Or worse."

"What could be worse than death?"

Anna shuddered. "Just trust me on this one." She offered Shauni a look of consolation, because she knew the reality of what was happening had shattered her world of peace and gentleness. "They have the right to know what's coming. They have the right to fight alongside us."

"I need some time, and I need to talk to...well, my cat. I know that sounds odd," Shauni said lifting one side of her mouth in a half-hearted smile.

Anna patted Shauni's shoulder. "Consider who you're telling." She sat again. "There's more for you to think about, isn't there? I've seen some things, alternate possibilities, but I can't be sure what or who they're meant for."

"I don't understand."

"Phew...neither do I sometimes. Don't hold yourself back from joy, not now when it's most essential. You will need every source of strength you have." Picking up her romance novel again, Anna tapped the cover with its hulking male pirate and corset-clad damsel. "Part of our challenge is to become fulfilled. Only then can we unleash the mightiest of ourselves." She turned to Shauni. "I didn't come up with that, by the way. It's part of what's been handed down by the St. Germaine witches, my ancestors."

"Why didn't you tell us before?" Shauni asked.

"You're going to get sick of hearing this, but all things come in their time. I can only follow my instincts. It's all any of us can do."

Shauni heard Cuileann's voice in her head, telling her something in the cat's native language. Shauni repeated the word out loud. "*Iomlanaich.*"

Anna simply stared and waited.

"It's Cuileann. She's speaking to me, and that's what she said."

"It's Gaelic," Anna said.

Shauni ran a hand through her raven hair. "Yes, but I'm not familiar with it."

"I am." Anna grinned. "It means complete, or sometimes... fulfilled."

"Hmm. Now you're both ganging up on me," Shauni said

but with a laugh. "I think I'd better go have that talk sooner than later, and Anna," she locked eyes with the other woman, "thanks."

"Of course." Anna winked then opened her book to re-enter the world of undying love.

Churning the discussion over in her mind, Shauni left the enclosed garden to find her cat. Iomlanaich. Fulfilled. Complete.

Shauni wasn't sure how he fit, but Michael was definitely a piece of some puzzle that needed to be finished. She would follow Anna's lead and trust her instincts.

It was all any of them could do.

12

Days later, Shauni was happy to have followed her gut. She'd called Michael and let him suggest they have another date. Of course, she obliged, since it was what she'd hoped for all along. He'd picked her up at the house on Skidaway, promising to take her somewhere her parents would approve of.

And boy, her mother was probably somewhere dancing a jig right now.

Who would have ever guessed Savannah would have a St. Patrick's Day celebration such as this? Shauni was glad she'd worn the bright green tee shirt, or she might have stuck out in the crowd. The color was everywhere, as if the city had been invaded by chlorophyll.

There were bottle green sunglasses in the shape of shamrocks, hats of the same color, as well as beads, boas, and wigs. Any and everything that could be produced by mankind came in the emerald tone today.

Pets weren't spared either, she realized, as a dog strolled by wearing an outfit that looked like lime sherbet with frills. The animal was thinking about its owner's hamburger though, and seemed happy enough with its getup.

They passed a woman getting out of a black sports car in nothing but jade colored lingerie then a man in a top hat with green hair and a beard that was downright scary.

"Well," Shauni said, for lack of anything more intelligent.

"People are quite creative."

"Can be," Michael replied before taking her hand in his as they navigated the crowds. The strength in those hands was evident as he held on gently, and the contrast stirred something in Shauni's belly.

Because Shauni felt the color of the day was a good omen, she had chosen to wear her amulet on the outside of her clothing. Michael had complimented her on it but asked no probing questions, only running his finger over the intricate weave of the Celtic cross. Shauni would have sworn she felt the heat of his skin as if amplified by the necklace but chalked it up to her yearning for Michael to caress her body as lovingly as he did the piece of jewelry.

Before she could think on it too long, a band of drunken men barreled past them singing something about March seventeen and mothers, sons, and daughters dressed in green. The jubilant mood surrounded them and Shauni squeezed Michael's fingers to tell him she was hanging in with him as they waded in and out, looking for a good vantage point from which to watch the parade. He'd told her he knew a secret spot.

They veered into a mammoth building and were swallowed by blessedly cool shade. "A parking garage?" Shauni asked, with only a hint of skepticism.

"Great views, sun is optional, and you choose the height. So which will it be, one story up or bird's eye?"

"One story. I want to see the faces when the parade goes by."

They took the stairs and found a spot near the corner where cars slanted in their spaces were their only companions. The wind kicked up and sun streamed down. Despite the concrete décor, it was oddly romantic.

"I wanted to wait for this but don't think I can," Michael said.

Surveying the swarming streets below, Shauni asked absentmindedly, "Wait for what?"

Her answer was the touch of Michael's hand on her cheek as he angled her toward him and brought his mouth to hers. Soft. Sweet. Burning. The kiss was more familiar, steering them into uncharted territory, with a hint of what was to come simmering beneath the surface.

He nipped her bottom lip a final time before pulling back, gray eyes smoky and satisfied. "Now we can get on with things."

"Mmm...what?" Shauni shimmered inside.

"Our date." He leaned against the cement wall and squinted into the distance. "Good timing. Here it comes now."

Marveling at the man's ability to swing from casual outing to kissing her until the foundation swayed then back again, Shauni followed his line of sight and saw the spectacle heading their way. Bystanders cheered and waved their arms. Once the parade reached Shauni and Michael, she understood the outstretched hands were attempts to catch strings of beads as they flew from festive floats.

Twirling little girls in colorful dresses passed by next, their smiles and clothing equally bright and cheery. Close behind, a squad of young men in military garb marched along, a few of them carrying the nation's flag. Shauni noticed spots of pink and red on their faces. "What is that?" she asked.

"Just wait," he told her, then nudged her elbow as a teenage girl ran out into the street to throw a green necklace around one of the soldier's neck and plant a kiss on his cheek.

"It's a tradition to kiss the military men of all ages." He grinned wickedly. "I'm not the only one with the idea."

"No uniform here." Shauni held out her hands, giving him an eyeful of her form-fitting shirt and beige skirt that fell several inches above the knee. Though she wore flat, white tennis shoes, nothing could disguise the shapely length of her legs. There seemed to be miles of soft golden skin between shoe and clothing. Michael gave a grateful prayer to whoever invented mini-skirts.

"I'm an opportunist, but I'll cede your point. No more kissing until you're in full blues."

"Let's not overdo it." All joking aside, Shauni had been singed all the way down to her toes by his last kiss, and the promise of more made her tingle and throb. In the distraction department, Michael Black was top notch. She'd hardly thought about witchcraft or evil-doers all day.

"You know the legend of St. Patrick, I'm sure," Michael said, once again watching the parade as an impressive ship made of tissue paper sailed down the street.

"Drove the snakes out of Ireland? My mother is Irish, but my family made its own hodge-podge of tradition. Dad gave up haggus, thankfully, and Mom only told us Irish stories every other night. In between, there was pizza and The Goonies."

"All-American family?"

Shauni smiled as the gentle memories cascaded. "We were the proverbial melting pot, but Celtic through and through. They both speak Gaelic." So does my cat, she thought but refrained from saying it out loud. She didn't care to be abandoned in the middle of all this chaos due to the appearance of insanity.

"St. Patrick was the son of a Roman-British army officer, raised in privilege until he was kidnapped by pirates and sold into slavery in Ireland. He spent roughly six years imprisoned, and that's when he started hearing voices, specifically, the voice of God."

"When did he become a monk?" Shauni asked, as interested in watching Michael's full, firm lips move as she was in hearing the story. The wind played with his dark blonde hair.

"After he escaped, he ended up in France, joined a monastery then heard the people of Ireland calling to him to save their souls, or something like that."

"And the snakes were an analogy for pagans. His mission was to convert them to Christianity."

Michael nodded, his eyes darkening. "Some say the methods

used weren't always gentle and refuse to celebrate St. Patrick's Day. It's become its own tradition though, more about Irish heritage and pride."

"How does a vet know so much about history?" And pagans. Shauni would technically fall into that category, according to many. The words pagan and witch weren't synonymous, though. Pagans simply worshipped anything, gods or symbols, that fell outside of the Christian realm.

With the clean breeze whipping around them, Michael went with impulse and wrapped an arm around her shoulders. "My mother comes from a long line of Baptists, no dancing, hide your beer, the whole works. She did, however, fall in love with a guy from the open-minded side of the tracks."

"So we're both just a couple of mutts," Shauni said, leaning into his warmth.

Serious eyes roamed over her face. "I have a fondness for mutts."

She knew she was in trouble when being compared to a dog had her heart thumping wildly. Unless she wanted to end up rolling around with Michael under a big, muddy truck, she'd better act fast. Intelligent, funny, thoughtful, sexy, and a vet, a protector and healer of animals. That was the final nail in her libido's coffin.

"Does this outing include food?"

"Outing?" Michael whipped out his crooked smile. "I thought we were on a date. If that's the case, I always feed the other party."

With an ease she wouldn't have expected so soon, Shauni moved in and touched her lips softly to his. "Then it's definitely a date."

The crowd didn't dissipate just because the parade was over. Everyone around them seemed to be taking group pictures while holding plastic cups of beer aloft like conquering heroes thrusting victorious swords. It was the biggest, greenest party

Shauni had ever seen.

"It won't be any less crowded down here, but I've got an in with the bartender. We can get something pretty quick." Michael held Shauni's hand as they walked down treacherously steep steps that had to have been built centuries earlier. The stones were even a little crooked.

"Do you eat out that much? You know someone in every restaurant we go to," Shauni said, clutching the metal railing on one side, Michael on the other.

"Guilty. That and word gets out that I'm a sucker for the working man. I extend financing at the clinic to those who need it and pull the occasional string in return."

The ship docked at the riverwalk dwarfed the parade version they'd seen earlier. The sun was high in the sky, so Shauni held a hand over her eyes while she took in the wooden boat with its soaring masts and flags snapping in the wind. Here the streets were cobblestone again, and she winced to see women traversing the uneven ground in heels. She would break an ankle.

They wound between laughing crowds to the bar. A quick gesture had the man behind the taps nodding before he disappeared into the back. He returned with a white bag and two drinks which he handed to Michael.

Shauni waited until they were outside and searching for a place to sit before saying, "You do good work."

When he lifted out a veggie sub and handed it to her, she raised an appreciative brow. "Make that exceptional work." She smirked. "Wait. You told him beforehand didn't you?"

"Gotta' love texting."

"Too much trouble. I can call someone and say what I need before getting the first sentence typed." She bit into the sandwich and gave an inward sigh of delight at the taste of vinegar. Michael was a good guesser, too.

"Here." He patted a couple of pockets in search of something then settled on his rear before whipping out a phone and sliding its tiny keyboard from a hidden compartment. "Is yours like this?"

"Not even close."

Michael quirked one side of his mouth. "Then what kind do you have?"

"Um. The kind that dials a number."

He threw a hand over his heart, imitating a mortal wound. "I may have found your first flaw. Well, second, if I count how stunningly gorgeous you are."

Shauni stopped chewing and swallowed hard. "I...well, thanks, but you must be mistaken. I'm not the glitz and glamour type."

"It has nothing to do with the superficial. You're a natural beauty." He tilted his head to give her a dubious look. "Don't tell me you're not aware of your looks." Michael would have a hard time believing men hadn't always flocked to her.

"I've had a few relationships, but I would hardly say the turnstile moved very often." She stared hard at her wheat bread. "I'm just me. No bells and whistles, monthly manicures, or shopping sprees. I hope that's not a problem."

"Problem?" He took her hand. "Shauni, it's part of what makes you so appealing. You definitely seem to be low-maintenance." When she gave a short laugh and shook her head, he added, "That came out wrong."

"No. I actually take that as a compliment." She looked at him out of the corner of her eye. "I do have one weakness, though. I like things that smell good. Candles. Lotions, body sprays, the works."

His lids fell to half-mast as lust sparked again behind them. "I love the way you smell."

In dire need of salvation once again, Shauni pulled her hand free and said, "Tell me more about your family."

Michael paused and smiled, letting her know he was fully

aware of her game. "Which side first?"

~

After hours walking downtown, the crazy hordes of partiers, and a couple of beers down by the river, Shauni was exhausted and more than a little happy when the vet clinic came into sight. Michael's car was parked around back, and her tired feet gave a cheer.

"I just need to check in on my patients then we can go. Why don't you come in? It might be a few minutes." He unlocked the back door, and they entered through a storage area. Bags of pet food and other supplies were stocked on heavy-duty shelving.

"Do you mind if I check out your equipment?" Shauni asked when they passed the examination room. "I promise not to touch."

"Sure," he grinned. "Never had a woman ask so politely, but I can't say I don't want you to touch."

His meaning hit home, and Shauni laughed and shook her head before turning on her heel. Nothing broke through the jitters like a little alcohol, but Shauni was still surprised at how quickly she and Michael had grown comfortable enough to tease about such things.

But the innuendos were doing nothing to help the little problem of hers. The wanting to rip open his shirt and see just what was hiding beneath kind of problem. The good doctor kept himself in prime shape, and every inch of him was rock hard. The occasional caress or kiss had kept her stirred up the whole day, and she was about to boil over.

Maybe it was a good thing she was going home soon, since her ability to resist Michael was weakening. He hadn't shaved this morning, since it was his day off, and the afternoon stubble gave him a delicious ruggedness. Mmm.

Shauni shook herself. She wanted to go there, she did, but

she couldn't be intimate with a man she wasn't honest with. Yet how could she tell him about the insanity that was her life? Plus, she had a feeling he was onto her. The man was oddly perceptive, and more than once she'd caught him looking at her as if seeing something more than what was on the surface.

They both wanted the same thing, to fall into each other with abandon and see how well they truly fit, but Shauni couldn't afford to endanger their tenuous relationship. She would just have to keep the reins tight in her fist.

The real reason she'd had so few relationships was the inevitability of having to share her gift. She'd made the foolish mistake of telling a boy in college. He'd reacted badly then went on to make her life miserable for several months. He and his friends had hooted or growled every time they saw her. It had been humiliating, the stares and laughter, and knowing he'd told everyone what she'd claimed.

Shauni had trusted someone she thought she loved, and they'd turned and trampled her most protected secret.

She didn't feel the need to tell her life story to every man she went out with, but Michael was different. Special. She could feel it vibrate in the smallest part of her whenever they were together.

But she had to be cautious. She had even more secrets to guard these days.

She smelled the erotic scent of male and soap, then suddenly Michael was there, a strong arm circling her waist from behind as he moved in. His other hand brushed her hair aside, making way for his lips to find the sensitive spot on her neck. Shauni's knees went weak, so she leaned against the steel table in front of her for support.

So much for those reins.

Michael only took advantage and pressed himself against her, holding her with both arms and applying his skillful mouth to her skin. His hand rubbed across her stomach, lazy circles that fell lower and lower. The dual assault was more than she could bear, and a moan slipped past her lips. "Michael," she whispered. Half ecstasy, half plea.

He turned her to face him and backed her against the table, tongues tangling and hands roaming. His hips ground against hers, and the thickness of his erection was dangerously close to where she ultimately wanted him.

Her breathing grew more ragged when he angled himself between her legs, lifting her to sit on the cold metal before pulling her tight against him. "Tell me to stop. If you don't, I'll have you here and now." His hands gripped her hips. His eyes burned into hers. "You're all I think about. The enchantress with raven hair and eyes the color of green fire. I know what I'm after." He pushed against her. "But what do you want from me, Shauni?"

What did she want? She wanted to lap him up like a cat did its cream. And much, much more. It was the more part that really scared her.

As if splashed by cold water, her mind clamped down on the situation and his words. "I...I'm not sure." Her breath still tore at her throat. Blood still rushed. "I just know I think about you, too, but it's complicated."

"Why?" Michael brought his mouth to hers again. Then her cheek. The tenderness of the act almost swept her away again.

Instead of explaining, she said the one thing they both needed to hear. "Stop. It's not right. Not yet."

His shoulders fell in time with his sigh. "Why won't you talk to me? There's more for you to tell me. I know. Trust is not something I come easily to either, but I'd like to think we're building it. Together." He kissed her softly, his tongue taking a swift taste of her before he pulled away.

Shauni felt the world tilt, but not from the beer. Michael was more intoxicating than any drug, and she had to hold onto him for support. "I just can't keep up with it all. It's so fast. I never expected this. I never expected you."

Michael used his thumb to trace her collar bone through her shirt before sliding a finger underneath the material to do the same. Skin to skin. "You were quite a shock to my system. You still are, but we have time." He gave her a look that was half-frown half-smile. "And I guess I'll have to keep being a gentleman, as much as it kills me." He put his hands around her waist and squeezed. "But you know I want it, and I plan to take all I can from you. Hope that's alright."

With a small laugh, she nuzzled against him. Despite her own gift and the power within she had yet to yield, it was only here, in the arms of her veterinarian, that Shauni felt truly safe. That was something new. "I do have secrets, big ones, and I can't promise they'll come easily, but I will promise this." She lifted her head. "I won't lie to you."

He heard the hedge in her voice. "But you won't be forthcoming with any details, either."

"When I've got a handle on things, we'll talk, but there's too much churning inside me now." She rubbed her hand over his hard chest and sighed, "And you just keep notching it up a level or two every time I see you."

"Good. I expect you to be on even ground with me soon. Then we'll just see what happens." His eyes fired a lusty promise to her before he stepped back and held her hand to help her off the table. "Come on. I'll take you home."

"To the house on Skidaway," she said, then bit her lip and wished she could take it back.

His brows drew together, perplexed. "Of course. Where else?"

Shauni had just promised not to lie, so instead of saying anything, she simply shook her head and smiled.

13

Claudia entered the kitchen like a beam of light, a short sheath dress of quicksilver and her hair in a flaming braid down her back. "Morning, sisters."

"Morning," Shauni offered before continuing to brood over her coffee. She had hoped for some quiet to delve into the complications of her current life as she sipped on her java fix, but with nine witches, nine cats, a puppy, and one five-year old boy sharing the household, silence was a long-lost indulgence.

Paige cracked and plopped another egg into the blender before grunting and nodding in Claudia's direction. She added a banana, yogurt, and sliced kiwi then hit the button to create a concoction that resembled sludge of an unknown variety.

"Eww..." Claudia said with a wrinkle of her nose. "Don't you want to cook your eggs? Ever heard of salmonella?"

"Cooked eggs in a shake? That would be disgusting," Paige said, meeting Claudia's disapproving look with one of her own. "I haven't keeled over yet."

"Hmm." Claudia homed in on Shauni. "Hey, how'd it go with the vet? And don't try to wiggle out of giving the goods. You're the only one getting any action around here, and I want details."

"I was wrong before," Paige said, holding her glass of sludge just shy of her lips. "Vicarious sex is even more disgusting than lumpy shakes. Don't you have any pornos you can watch instead?"

Claudia gave her a quizzical look before her features settled into surprise and sympathy. "Paige, have you never had any girlfriends? Girl-talk?" She went to pour herself a mug of coffee. "I don't actually want physical details, just the romantic progression information."

Shauni groaned and put her head in her hands. "The progression is moving in leaps and bounds."

"Then why are you not glowing or something?" Paige asked. "You don't look like a woman who just got off."

Claudia held one hand up to resemble a crossing guard motioning for someone to stop. "Okay. Disgust-o-meter is now officially off the charts."

"Would you both please stop talking about my sex life?" Shauni huffed and crossed her arms. "Which is non-existent, by the way."

"Sexual frustration, huh?" Paige sipped and smiled. "Been there for sure."

"That's not it," Shauni snapped, but was too upset to allow guilt to peck its way in and make her apologize. "There's more at stake here than whether or not I get laid. I'm supposed to be preparing for my challenge, and I doubt my pitiful little fireball is going to do the trick."

Each witch had her strengths, as Anna was always reminding them, and so far Shauni's had not included manipulation of the elements. Lucia, Paige, and Kylie had no trouble tossing flames around like beach balls, but Shauni and Willyn had both remained in the baby pool. They could barely stir the air.

It didn't require many brain cells to make the connection. Strong personalities channeled emotion easily, and Shauni was just all dammed up.

"Well, whatever your problem is, don't bite my head off." It didn't take much to rile Paige, who was now frowning. She slammed her glass down on the counter. "Maybe you don't have any business seeing someone right now if you can't handle it. We need your head in the game, not daydreaming about picket fences."

"This is not a damn game. You can't begin to understand what I'm dealing with." Shauni pushed her stool back with a hair-raising screech of metal on flagstone. "It's so easy to sit back and criticize. You don't have to go first but have the luxury of learning from my mistakes."

"And you're giving me plenty of opportunities for that," Paige shot back, already in her battle stance. "You can't see past your own ideals to how bad things might be if you don't pull out your guns and fast."

Shauni smirked. "Oh, I see. Peace through superior witch power?"

Paige didn't return the smile. "Exactly. Why can't you …"

"Hold it!" They both turned to see Willyn in the doorway. The usually gentle blonde was scolding them with her eyes. A talent only mothers possessed. "We could hear you all the way upstairs."

And she had a child in the house. That's what she didn't say. She didn't have to. She shouldn't have to.

Shame rolled over Shauni until her face heated. "Sorry," she managed to tell her cup of coffee before looking at Paige. "I'm doing the best I can. If you have any useful suggestions, I'm listening."

With her jaw clenched hard enough to break nails, Paige waved a dismissive hand and walked out. She not only found anger easily, she clung to it.

Shauni realized the burgeoning sting in her gut was envy. Paige seemed so powerful, even if half of it was bluster, she still had the confidence and strength to back it up. The sting was growing, zipping around and bouncing off the bottom of her heart, a battle between disgrace and fury. She needed to ride the surge of anger fighting to find its way out, but that wasn't who she was.

Therein lay her problem.

"I was raised to respect life. To be a kind, peaceful person." She tapped a fist on her stomach. "Now I'm suddenly supposed to become a fighter?" She whirled to Claudia. "Oh, and let's not forget that I've become a liar, too. I had to come all the way to the East Coast to meet a man I just might be able to trust. Now, he'll never be able to trust me. Not when he finds out I've been deceiving him from the moment we met."

"Calm down. You're all twisted up," Claudia said, trying to soothe.

"You're damn right I am. Lives are at stake! Why did the magic gods, or beings, or whatever the hell is in control, think I would be the best first choice? Or any choice?" She sniffled and bit her bottom lip before adding in a pitiful voice. "And now I'm swearing."

"Honey. You need a break." Willyn still had her mom face on but was no longer angry. "You are worn out and tired. It's only natural to be upset, but I wish you could find a positive way to channel it."

"Like your fireballs," Claudia suggested, but scrunched her face when Shauni glared at the reminder. "Or something."

"I know what you need. You should write this all down in your book of shadows while you finish your coffee, then after our morning lesson, we can go have lunch somewhere." Willyn's eyes lit up. "Maybe do a little shopping."

Claudia spread her full lips like the cat who'd just spotted the canary. "I'm so in for that. Let's all get manis, too."

Shauni could do worse than spending the afternoon with women she trusted. Calm, logical women who were somewhat in her position. Anna was knowledgeable, but she'd been raised accepting her fate. Shauni and the others had been tossed in and spun around like Paige's gross milkshake.

And right now, Shauni felt as horrible as it had looked.

With the rage no longer controlling her, she was able to breathe the last of it out and smile at Claudia and Willyn. Brains and patience. Always an excellent combo.

Shauni looked at her ravaged fingernails. "Pedicures, too. And for once, I'm going with red."

~

Anna met with the other witches in the grand hall at the usual time, having decided they'd work on something a little different today. When she started down the stairs, she heard Kylie say in a loud voice, "Don't look now, but here comes Dumbledore."

The reference wasn't lost on Anna, and she laughed good-naturedly along with a few of the others. "Don't expect me to grow a beard or wear a wilted hat."

"Who's Dunbledorf?" Viv asked.

Kylie's hazel eyes widened. "Seriously, Viv? Seriously?"

"We have to further your education," Hayden said, tossing her caramel hair over her shoulder. She and the other women had taken to dressing in comfortable clothing for their lessons, as if they were exercising. Of course, after Kylie had burned a hole in her designer skirt and carried on for an hour, they were all a bit more cautious with their clothing choices.

Or anything flammable for that matter.

Anna teased Viv, too. "I've got all the movies on DVD. We can have a marathon sometime. But today," she said with wink for Shauni and Willyn, "I thought we'd veer away from battle maneuvers."

"We're still far from ready," Paige said immediately, always the soldier. "We should…"

"We should," Anna interrupted her, "learn to use every weapon at our disposal." She met Paige's challenging look with calm. "Don't you agree?"

Paige rocked on her booted heels. "Yeah."

"Glad we understand each other." Anna headed toward the kitchen with the others in tow and out the glass paned doors at the far end.

"The greenhouse?" Lucia asked. "What will we practice here?"

Anna rounded on the Spanish vixen with a mischievous grin. "You'd be surprised."

The air was heavy with warmth and moisture with sun lighting the area to a golden hue, paradise for any botanist. The plants obviously liked it as well, as they flourished and preened in their colorful glory. A row of well-used wooden tables ran down the center of the long room while shelves and more tables lined the walls. Pots and planters were marked with laminated cards in Anna's delicate script, the Latin names adding a hint of elegance and mystique.

"Over here we have full grown plants I use for potions, or cooking if I'm in need of a particular herb. There are the seedlings, not quite ready for picking, and the far end is where I do cuttings and plantings." Anna stopped in the middle and indicated the long tables. "They're clean, so you can write in your books here."

A motion in the periphery of Shauni's vision caught her attention, and she saw Paige stroking a mint colored frond lovingly. Of all the witches to go misty-eyed over flowers, Paige was the last anyone would have suspected.

"First the basics. If you don't have the proverbial green thumb...don't touch my babies." Anna lifted a finger. "Kidding. If any of you have a fondness for growing, you're welcome to work here."

"I should tell you up front that I killed a cactus," Kylie admitted. "It looked like it was rotting, so I kept watering it."

Anna's face contorted as if she were in pain.

"Don't feel bad," Viv said, "I once fed and watered an indoor tree for weeks before the telltale spot on the carpet made me realize it was fake."

"I've changed my mind," Anna said. "You two especially... don't touch my babies."

"But we'll all learn to use them for magic." This from Claudia who appeared eager to add spells to her leather book.

"Absolutely. Take this cinnamon, for example. It's the main ingredient in my own personal recipe for stimulating clairvoyance, but it also tastes wonderful. Most people, even talented cooks, are unaware that some of their favorite flavors could be used to calm their anger, open their minds while dreaming for improved clarity, or simply to help them sleep."

"Lavender. I use lavender quite often, and it does help stave off insomnia," Viv offered. "My mind tends to whir even when I tell it to go to bed."

Anna nodded. "It can also help you see ghosts."

Hayden barked a laugh. "Don't need any help there, thanks."

"What's this?" Paige asked, fingering a leaf. "*Symphytum officinale.*"

"Ah, commonly known as comfrey." Anna put her hands on blue-jeaned hips and smiled. "I keep that for when I travel, which I do fairly often under normal circumstances. A piece of comfrey root in my luggage ensures it will arrive at its intended destination when I do." She made a face. "The airlines were always losing my suitcases. A woman I met at a festival turned me on to it." She pointed at Lucia, another world traveler. "Haven't lost a piece since."

"*Si.* I might grow some for myself," Lucia replied. "Though I often serve as my own pilot."

"You can fly?" Kylie asked in awe.

"Sure. I'm parked in a hangar not too far from here." Lucia's brown eyes flashed with mischief. "I'll take you up sometime."

"Outstanding."

Shauni grinned at Kylie's choice of words. The college girl

always seemed to find new synonyms that were always just another version of her favorite, "cool."

Anna pushed up her sleeves and motioned for them to sit at the tables. She picked up a pot from several that appeared to have been selected for today's lesson. "Understand that our heightened powers will enable us to draw even more from our little green friends, so use caution, and don't overdo. This is anise, which might come in handy if you encounter Sylvie again. We'll take some seeds I have set aside and make pouches for you to carry at all times."

"How will that help with the priestess?" Viv asked. She was no fan of the cocoa-skinned, hoodoo hottie.

"Wards off the evil eye." Anna took in their doubtful stares. "I'm not just talking about a dirty look." She raised one brow and dared them to argue. "You'll carry the seeds."

"I'll buy a bigger purse if I have to," Shauni said. "Give me all you've got."

"Anything to avoid a fight?" Paige ran a hand through her pale blonde hair and looked away from Shauni, but her tone said she was still angry about their argument.

Shauni caught Willyn's meaningful shake of the head and bit back a retort. She needed to flush out more negativity. "Got anything to soothe the savage beast?" she asked Anna.

"Literally or metaphorically?"

Shauni glanced at Paige and clenched her fists under the table. "Both."

Reading the vibes that bounced between Paige and Shauni, Anna said, "I see we can use some purple loosestrife. I'll pull some out later and sprinkle it around the house. It will help stop arguments and restore harmony."

Another splash of regret hit Shauni in the face, but her mood was still too fragile and mercurial to address the issue between her and Paige. She stayed quiet.

After giving Shauni a long, cool look, Anna delved into her

assortment of herbs again and came back with a glass jar
filled halfway with a bright red powder or resin. "This is the
end product of harvesting, though not all will be in this form.
We'll get to the different ways of processing another day." She
hoisted the jar so they all could see. "This is dragon's blood.
Very helpful when added to incense or even your bath water.
Burn one while immersing in the other and you get a double
dose."

"What does it do?" Claudia asked, ready to scribble away in
her peach-colored book.

"It provides purification and protection from a multitude of
assaults, physical or mental." Anna set the jar down with a
thunk in front of Shauni and gave her a pretty good imitation of
the evil eye. Seems she had a point to make. "It also clears the
way for what's meant to be between two people when they're
blinded by pride or fear."

Shauni looked at her with panic. "What?"

Anna smiled and shoved the jar closer. "It helps with love."

Shauni stared at the red powder as if it truly were the
blood of a dragon and the scaly beast was breathing over her
shoulder, wanting it back.

She heard Paige grumble and Claudia laugh.

~

After showering and changing clothes, Shauni went back to
the cemetery with Hayden to further investigate the grounds.
They had hoped for a different sort of "spiritual" guidance
today, but the only ghost who made his presence known was a
confederate soldier searching for his brother.

Hayden had urged Shauni to leave ahead of her and meet
with Willyn and Claudia for their shopping trip. Hayden felt it
her duty to help the wayward man if she could, though how she
would do that for a man who'd been dead over a hundred years,

Shauni couldn't begin to guess.

The sunny weather held as Shauni made her way through town to meet the other women. Claudia and Willyn made good on their promise to take her out for lunch and feminine extravagance, and after a few hours they all had full bellies and sleek manicures. Shauni wiggled her bright red nails and admired them, happy to have her hands resemble a movie star's instead of sporting only a single coat of clear.

The sound of Claudia's gasp had them all stopping in their tracks on the sidewalk and peering into a store window. "Just look at all those antiques. And that side over there. They've got walls of ...honey."

"Antiques and honey?" Shauni asked.

Willyn looked down at the bags she carried, a dress and new shoes for herself, gardening gloves for Paige, who'd been so enthusiastic about the greenhouse, and books for Tadd. She still couldn't believe her baby was reading. "An antique store is probably like a fun park for Claudia. Just imagine all the stories she hears, or sees, however it works, when she picks something up. And the honey, well..." she lifted her bags. "You got me there, but it does sound appealing. A wall of honey."

"Since you put it that way." Shauni edged past Willyn but held the door open for her.

There were antiques, armoires, tables, and even a telephone chair mixed in with modern products. The walls were covered in wallpaper, wide cream and blue stripes, with a definite French feel to the place. Ivory lace covered tables that held all manner of knick knacks and household goods.

Claudia was already lost in a world of her own, smiling as she pressed the palm of her hand to the rosy silk of an old fainting couch. "This piece has seen a lot more action than swooning women in suffocating, whale-bone corsets."

Willyn fluttered her eyes in surprise. "You can pick up on things like that, too?"

"Oh, yeah. It's like they say in all the ghost movies. Any strong emotion will leave a mark." Claudia finally pulled her hand away. "If the husband of the woman who kept this sofa in her bedroom hadn't worked so many late hours or stayed out at the gentleman's club, he might have come home to quite a show."

Shauni picked up a silver picture frame holding a black and white photo of a bride and groom dancing on the beach. She had no business mooning over the happy couple and wishing it was her, but here she was, just like Paige had accused this morning. Dreaming of picket fences.

Damn. She was falling for the vet.

She rubbed the filigree, romanced by the old-fashioned design. "I wonder if there's a spell to slow down love as opposed to causing it."

Willyn pulled her attention from the phantom adultery tale Claudia was still telling. "For Michael? You think he's moving too fast?"

Shauni huffed. "No. For me. My heart is charging at a steady gallop, and I can't get it under control." She shrugged one shoulder. "I can't explain it. He touches me."

"I would certainly hope so," Claudia said, having picked up a blown-glass ornament to study the colorful swirls.

The red-head's dry tone forced a laugh from Shauni. "Maybe Paige had it right this morning. You have sex on the brain."

"Only speaks to my sanity."

Willyn rolled her eyes at that and moved to stand beside Shauni, angling her head and narrowing blue eyes as if probing silently for an answer. "According to Anna, you should be looking toward Michael, not scrambling back."

Pursing her lips, Shauni said, "And how exactly would she know what I need to do about him when I don't?"

"Uh, hello." Claudia set the globe back on a display table. "She's a seer. She has visions."

"But even she admits they don't always make sense at first. What if the Amara or their demon have conjured some spell and put Michael in my path to distract me? I'm the one that's supposed to be making the choices. If I follow Anna's lead like a puppy, it will be her passing the test, not me." Shauni threw an annoyed look at the wedding picture and put it back.

"Why are you making this so complicated?" Claudia asked. "You need to listen to what's inside you."

"All that's inside me is freaking out. It's not a very good advisor at the moment."

"Then talk to Cuileann," Willyn suggested. "She's known you longer than any of us."

"Take up yoga," Claudia said. "Learn to meditate."

Shauni let her head fall back and groaned. "I've never been this lost before. What do I do?"

"Have hot, sweaty sex with Michael."

Shauni's head snapped back up to look into Claudia's grinning eyes.

"I mean it," the professor said in her best lecture voice. "You need to blow off some steam, and you wouldn't be this stressed out about him if you didn't care, so what have you got to lose?"

"His respect."

"Because you strip down and do what you both want? This isn't eighteen-forty. Our kind have been liberated."

"Because he doesn't know you're a witch," Willyn said, placing a hand on Shauni's arm. "You feel like it would be wrong to be intimate without telling him everything first."

Shauni only stared for a minute. "It's freaky how you do that, Willyn. Sure you can't read minds?"

"Just maternal observation skills. I'm practicing for Tadd's teenage years. Way in advance."

Mulling over all they'd talked about in her mind, Shauni's gaze wandered until it fell on a set of wine glasses, green stems twisted haphazardly. They were unique, smart and modern.

She knew without a doubt Michael would like them.

She should buy them and take them to him. Along with a bottle of wine.

Claudia was right. What did she have to lose? As it stood now, she was only churning metal wheels on asphalt and burning herself up in the sparks. If she expected to find clarity, she had to clear away the smoldering heat from her brain that was all tangled up with nerves and lust.

Michael was a good man. Trustworthy. Her failure to share herself with him was her shortfall. Not his. He deserved a little more faith from her.

He'd asked her what she wanted from him, and the answer was more than she'd ever expected to find in a man. Going with the infamous gut feeling everyone seemed to be throwing in her face, she decided to get a full set. Maybe one day she and Michael would use them in their…No, one step at a time.

Hot, sweaty sex first.

She breezed past Willyn and Claudia to find someone to help her.

"We'll be outside." Willyn tugged on Shauni's elbow to get her attention as the sale was being rung up.

"Okay. Be right there."

A couple walked hand-in-hand past the window, wearing those lazy, I'm-so-in-love smiles as they leaned toward each other and laughed. He had his hand on the small of her back in a gently possessive way.

The stone that had been lodged in Shauni's chest all day crumbled away, leaving a light, airy feeling in its place. She felt better already.

The sales woman had packed the glasses in white tissue inside a white box for protection and bagged them up when Shauni first heard the buzzing. She flashed a quick thank-you smile to the lady before stepping out into the afternoon light to join Claudia and Willyn in the sweet, warm, magnolia air.

"All set?" Willyn asked.

"I'm not sure." Shauni let her eyes fall shut when the sound came again, crisper and more clearly enunciated. *I need you. They...*

"Headache? I have some..."

Shauni shook her hand to quiet Claudia and waited. A car passed and a mother pushed a stroller by with two crying twins, but Shauni shoved all her strength toward the pleading voice only she could hear. *Please come. They found me. They're here.*

"I have to go," she told them. "There's an animal in trouble. He's calling me. I think it has something to do with the Amara." Shauni looked to Willyn who'd driven them. "You can take me back to my car and go to the island. Tell Anna."

"Screw that," Claudia said, olive green eyes immovable and hard. "We go together."

"No, it's my..."

"Yeah, yeah, yeah. It's your challenge and all that, but there's a reason there are nine of us, and we at least are three, still a magical number."

Shauni stood her ground and muttered, "I won't have you hurt."

"And we won't have it for you, either." Claudia tapped her long bronze fingernails on Shauni's box. "It's not like you can get away from us."

Looking to Willyn for support, Shauni pleaded with her eyes. "I have to go. You two don't."

Willyn took a deep breath and glanced back and forth between the other two before shaking her head. "We go together." She pulled her keys from her bag. "And we're wasting time."

14

"Drive faster, Willyn. His voice is getting stronger." Shauni sat forward to peer out the front window, though her telepathic guide was more reliable than her eyesight. "We're close."

They'd crossed the Savannah River via the cable bridge minutes before and were already in the state of South Carolina. The charm of the city quickly fell away to swaying pine trees and picturesque rural life. The absence of life was overwhelmingly pleasant after the busy city streets where they'd shopped.

Blue like a robin's egg colored the heavens, dogwoods bloomed with innocence, and the sun sparkled on the hood of Willyn's white car, but a foreboding remained with Shauni. Something wasn't right, and she couldn't make out what had changed. The animal still cried out for rescue, but an unfamiliar timbre was imbued in the sound.

Interference by the Amara was a certainty, but she couldn't leave a helpless animal in their hands.

"It could be a trap," Claudia said from the back seat as if she'd read Shauni's mind. "They must know something about you, Shauni. They're using this poor animal to get to you." Her reflection in the rearview mirror bit her bottom lip. "Maybe we should get the others first."

Shauni hit the dashboard. "I knew you shouldn't have come. There's no time left, and now I've pulled you both in with me." She whipped her head to Willyn. "When we stop, I'm getting out alone."

"Negative," Claudia said.

"She's right, Shauni." Willyn stared ahead as she zipped along the road past yellow marshland, taking them deeper into the woods. "We knew what we were getting into. We'll just be cautious. R.J. shouldn't be able to get into our heads, if he's involved, and we've learned some defensive spells."

"And I have fire," Claudia joined in, reminding them that she had mastered the art of flame throwing, even if they hadn't. "Anna said evil things generally have an aversion to fire, particularly the white magic style of combustion."

"You have such a way with words." Willyn smiled into the rearview mirror, her gaze remaining locked with Claudia's for a moment. They were both prepared to back Shauni up. And they both knew there would be risk.

"Here." Shauni waved her hand. "Take this left turn."

They were enveloped by even more forest, thick underbrush and giant hardwoods that reduced the light to a dappled pattern on the dusty road ahead.

"Man, South Carolina can turn country quick," Claudia mused out loud.

"Pull over." Shauni was opening the door before the car had come to a complete stop. She jumped out and raced into the shadows.

"Shit." Claudia fought with the lever in an attempt to get out and follow. "Willyn. Child locks."

"Sorry," Willyn said. She hit a button and they were both out and running. Shauni would lose them fast out here. The topography was still of the pancake variety, but bushes and trees choked the immediate area, providing cover for anyone more than twenty feet away.

And Shauni might not be the only other one roaming around.

"That way," Claudia said. "I heard something. We could really use Lucia right about now and her internal GPS." They moved toward the thrashing sound and caught sight of Shauni. She was standing still, head cocked as if listening.

She turned to them as they approached and put a finger to her lips. "The animal's nearby, a dog. Someone else is here, too. It's one of the Amara, I'm certain, but I can't separate the two."

"Think whoever's out there is holding the dog as bait to lure you in?" Willyn asked, whispering like Shauni. Their hushed voices sounded eerie. Everything around them had fallen silent. The bird and forest creatures, even buzzing insects, had settled into hiding.

Nature in its goodness sensed a presence, an unnatural presence.

Help me.

Shauni responded to the voice in her head with a shudder. She would never forgive herself if she abandoned this poor dog. "This is it. Let's go." She flashed a look of warning to the others. "But be ready."

Spiky balls, fruit fallen from sweetgum trees, still littered the ground and were crunched beneath their feet as they crept along. Soon the path began to clear as they came to the edge of a swamp. The water was a murky brown, static and flat. Tree trunks split and curled downward to claw their way to the muddy bottom.

A dog sat on the bank. He whimpered and whined with heart-wrenching sadness in his big brown eyes. Small and shaggy, his white hair was matted with deep red stains. He looked pitiful.

"Oh, the poor thing," Willyn said, stepping forward.

Shauni's armed flashed out and caught Willyn across her mid-section. "Don't. This is not right. The dog...he's...wrong, somehow."

Now that she was close to the animal, Shauni was feeling nauseated. The dread that had grown stronger as they'd traveled here was now at full force, pulsing and spreading like an oily fungus. She closed her eyes and reached out for the dog with her mind.

An explosion of black tinged with crimson slapped back at her, followed by the sound of laughter. This was no dog, and Shauni understood why there had been a connection between the animal voice that called out for her and the sensation of danger. The dog wasn't being held by the Amara.

It was one of them.

She looked again when Claudia and Willyn both cried out.

"What is that? What's happening?" Claudia rasped, clutching her hand to her stomach as if she were being affected by the malevolence rolling off the dog.

But it wasn't a dog anymore. Its sides had split, opening into great holes that curved into stretching red crescents. In other places, the white fur bulged and thrashed. Shauni was afraid smaller beings would pop out at any minute.

The three women stumbled back when the writhing mass in front of them screamed. First a dog's whine that morphed into a long, low moan before becoming fully recognizable. A howl rose from the thick, black throat. A wolf's howl.

The creature standing before them now was twice the size of a normal wolf, and its eyes glowed with a devil's fury. Taking one step forward, it lowered its head and growled, thunderous and scratchy. Its jaws snapped in warning and promise.

It leveled its ferocious stare on Shauni. She could no longer hear words, but a string of unintelligible noises, guttural chanting in a language that sounded older than the earth. Demon speak.

Preparing herself to feel his fangs in her flesh, Shauni scouted the area telepathically. Only birds close by, and what could they do? A gator was resting in the depths of the marsh, but despite the threat of the wolf, she couldn't stomach the idea of pitting one animal against another.

He wasn't an animal. Not really, she told herself. So what

exactly were they dealing with? An earthbound demon? Could the one Ronja and her group intended to summon control life forms on earth? Whatever it was, the teeth were sharp, and they were bared.

"Start backing up slowly," she told Claudia and Willyn. "When you reach the cover of trees, run. Run to the car or split up. I don't know." She swallowed, and her throat felt like barbed wire wrapped in cotton. "Just run."

"Come with us," Willyn pleaded in a whisper, as if she hoped the wolf wouldn't hear or understand what she was saying.

"I will, but I need to know you're both safe and…"

Shauni broke off when the wolf lunged forward then leaped to latch onto her forearm when she threw it up in an instinctual response to protect her face. She felt unimaginable pain as the animal clamped down on her like a bear-trap and pulled her to the ground. Without releasing his hold, he looked into her eyes and screamed at her in the demon voice only she could hear. Then he threatened her, and she wished she didn't understand.

You'll die today, and the chain will be broken. The first link turns out to be the weakest. How nice for us. He shook his head and growled. *When he comes, Ronja will make Anna her bitch-slave. We'll fuck her in ways you wouldn't think possible, and your little healer will be around each time to bring her back for more.*

Shauni gritted her teeth against the pain, but her eyes fired daggers. *You're the one that's fucked.* She'd seen her friend move into position. "Claudia, now!"

Without question, Claudia aimed her freshly-manicured hand at the beast and released a stream of fire that branded his flank. A high-pitched yelp accompanied his jump away from the unseen attack, and Shauni rolled away from him. Willyn was beside her with healing hands before Shauni had a chance to stand. Claudia kept her arm pointed at the wolf.

The huge, black monster growled again but showed no sign

of re-engaging in the battle. He emitted a low howl, but the sound thinned and gargled as his dark coat began to shift again. Lifting his head to the sky, the wolf strained and grunted until his hair drew back into pores, and his torso shifted, limbs lengthening. The strange noises he made soon became a raspy laugh.

A naked man kneeled on the wet ground, his feet almost touching the still water behind him. So he was some kind of shapeshifter. "Nice return little bitches. I mean...witches." Insanity danced in eyes that were an unholy blue. "But what I said still goes." He snarled at Shauni. "You're the weakest link, and you'll never find what you're looking for."

The burial ground. The burial ground.

This voice came from another source, deeper and with more bass than the wolf's had. The shifter was speaking as a human now, so it definitely wasn't him. Shauni eased her eyes to where she sensed the source and spotted a large turtle sunning on a rock near the water's edge.

What are you telling me? she asked with her inner voice. *Is that what I'm looking for?* Then she thought about the bird. *Do you know what I seek?*

The turtle blinked slowly. *The burial ground. The burial ground.*

Shauni risked a glimpse back to the shifter who was giving her a quizzical look. *Where is it?* she asked the turtle.

The burial ground. The burial ground.

Frustrated, she said out loud, "Okay. I get it. The burial ground."

The shifter widened his eyes before realizing he was giving too much away. Then he curled his lip. "Doesn't matter. You still won't find it." He rubbed his hand across spiky hair, bleached to a blonde almost as white as Paige's then slapped his own face and spit at them. "Gotta' run. Company's coming." With that, he took a deep breath and seemed to suck himself into a tighter form, quickly changing into a black bird and lifting off.

As if suddenly realizing he was getting away, Claudia tried to throw another burning bullet his way but a single flicker speared forth then puffed out. "Damn. I wasn't paying attention. Lost my focus."

"You were amazing," Shauni told her. "You saved me." She looked at her arm where only ghosts of the puncture wounds remained, then up to Willyn who was panting a little. "You okay?"

"Fine. I got carried away. Healed you too fast, and I'm feeling the burn." She fell back on her rump. "I can't believe what we just saw. Even after witches, mind-benders, hoodoo, and demon worship, I can't believe what I just witnessed with my own eyes."

"Yeah," Claudia said with a shrug. "A naked guy. It's been a while."

Shauni couldn't believe the tickle in her chest was laughter waiting for release, but it climbed up and proved itself. She'd just been a wolf's appetizer, and here she was in the dirt laughing. "Wait 'til we tell the others."

Her skin ran cold and spiked with bumps at the sound of a bark coming from the woods, but she relaxed once she had her bearings. "Don't worry. That's a real dog."

"But what is it doing out here?" Willyn asked. She and Shauni stood together.

Claudia moved in to flank them, still a little on edge and in no mood for more canine teeth.

"Oh, no," Shauni said, and paled even more than she had while trapped in the wolf's vise-like bite. She could hear the dog mentally urging its master on. "It's Michael. I have no idea what he's doing here, but they're right on top of us." She looked at her arm then dashed to the water and frantically washed away the remaining blood, still wet but already thickening.

"He couldn't be with them, could he?" Claudia hated to ask,

but anything was possible. "The Amara?"

"No. Of course not."

"You sure?"

Shauni brushed the last drops off then wiped her arm on her pants. "I'm positive."

Joyful barks shot out of the brush like rapid-fire just ahead of a gorgeous golden retriever. He danced in a circle, barked once again, and smiled straight at Shauni. She, at least, recognized it as a smile.

"Fletcher," Michael's voice called. Footsteps pounded closer and Michael burst out of the forest. His eyes were wide as he scanned the vicinity. He took in the three women and his disobedient dog who was currently leaning full-body into Shauni's legs. "What happened?"

Shauni did her best to play dumb. "Nothing. We came out for a walk and to look around. What are you doing here?"

Michael firmed his brow. "You're lying." Guess he wasn't going easy on her this time.

Shauni decided to take a turn on the offensive for once. "What are you doing here anyway? Are you following me?"

"What?" He blew out a breath, disgusted by the idea she thought he would stalk her, but he wasn't going to spill everything here with his heart still beating painfully, and in front of strangers. The last twenty minutes had been agony, sensing Shauni's worry, fear, then incredible pain and the terror of death. "Fletcher led me to you."

Shauni gave him a look of disbelief and put a hand on her hip. "Oh? When did he learn to drive?"

Willyn jumped in. "It's so nice to meet you, Michael. We've heard a lot about you." After her awkward verbal rambling, she smiled and added more. "Skid is doing really well. His leg is healing quickly."

"Skid? Right, Puppy Miller." Manners ingrained since birth took over, and Michael inclined his head but didn't try to shake her hand. He was well aware that a man waited for the lady to offer. "Thank you. You're a friend of Shauni's, I take it."

"Oh, yes. I'm Willyn Brousseau," she walked over and held out her hand. "And Claudia Grant."

Claudia waved. "Dr. Black, I presume?"

Michael's shoulders unclenched, and he allowed a rough laugh to escape. Whatever had happened out here, the redhead's sense of humor was still intact. Shauni was apparently unharmed, and that was the most important thing. He wanted to have a few words with that particular female.

He shifted his eyes to find her glaring at him, now with both hands on her hips. The conversation they were destined for was going to be a blowout, because man, was she pissed.

Good, he thought angrily, maybe a little of her annoyance would push her to lose control of that unflappable calm, and she'd finally come clean with him. Though from the look of things, it might be brutal honesty.

"We need to talk," he said, his gray eyes as frigid and unmoving as a glacier.

"And then some," Shauni replied in a voice of sugared acid.

"Well, we need to get going and, Michael," Willyn put a soft hand on Michael's arm but sent him a meaningful message with her eyes. "You *will* see Shauni home safely?"

"Don't worry, Ms. Brousseau. She'll be in good hands." He forced a reassuring smile, but it fell away quickly beneath the weight of his aggravation with Shauni and impatience to be alone with her.

"That's exactly what we wanted to hear," Claudia said. She pulled Willyn with her and started back toward the car. "Give us a call later, Shauni."

When her friends were out of earshot, Shauni told Michael, "I want to know what the hell is going on." She was on her third strike for the day as far as temper management went, but she figured she might as well take it for all it was worth. Something strange was happening with Michael. Stumbling across her in the park that night was believable. Barely. But finding her way out here? They were in South Carolina, for Jude's sake.

"I could say the same to you. Why is there blood on your pants, and why would women be out in the swamp in dresses and sandals?"

"I'm dressed appropriately." She indicated her gray capris and modest shirt, though the black flats were pushing it.

"Your friends weren't, and regardless, I know you were in danger out here." He crossed the clearing in two great strides to grip her upper arms. "I want to know what you're not telling me." Because he was torn between shaking sense into Shauni or kissing her to the ground, Michael clamped his hand on hers and dragged her behind him. "But we need to clear out of here before the gnats set in."

Jerking her hand away, Shauni grumbled, "Don't treat me like a child," but continued walking. She felt and heard him fall in behind her. "Just take me home," she said, on the verge of a colossal pout. This day had gone from bad to hellacious.

"I will...eventually."

When she stopped and spun around, their chests collided and his arms went around her waist. His mouth naturally followed, but the kiss was heated and forceful. She could feel his passion and anger boiling just beneath the surface as his hands razed over her curves and settled on her hips. It was a volatile mix.

She knew, because she was churning inside with the same emotions.

Michael broke away with a growl similar to the one she'd heard not so long ago. "But first, you're coming home with me."

15

Neither Michael nor Shauni spoke the entire ride, both too afraid they would unleash terrible words and leave scars on a relationship still struggling to exist. Michael glanced one more time at the blood on her pants and swore a blue streak to himself. What the hell was she involved in? He doubted the three women had been so far out of the city working on anything to do with animal behavior. They'd carried no instruments or notebooks.

The redhead had been wearing a short silver dress. Definitely not biologist threads.

Michael gripped the steering wheel and looked up at the skies that darkened to suit his mood. Black clouds roiled above like a poisonous witch's brew, and fat raindrops began their assault on the windshield.

He slid into his parking spot in the alley behind his home as the skies opened up and doused the city of Savannah with an angry torrent. "I've got an umb..." Michael started, but Shauni was out and dashing for his back stoop. "Dammit," he muttered and ran behind her.

They fell into the brick townhouse and Michael disappeared upstairs before returning with a dark brown towel. "You didn't have to get wet, but I guess foolish behavior is your MO these days." He cut stormy gray eyes over to her. "Or has it always been your way, and I'm just finding out?"

Michael opened the stainless steel refrigerator and grabbed two waters, offering one to Shauni with a quick jerk of his arm. She tossed back her hair, rubbing it with the towel, and said, "Let's just get this over with. You and I both have things to tell the other, and since you obviously know more about me than I do you, you can go first."

Forcing the last gulp of cold water down, Michael set the bottle aside and stared hard. "I know you? Is that what you just said?" He ground his teeth. "I don't know what keeps me coming back to you when all I get is another lie or evasion."

"I haven't lied, and I told you I was maintaining the right to keep secrets," she shot back furiously. A boom of thunder outside only added to the tumultuous argument, but Shauni ignored the symbolism. Chaos in nature. Chaos between Michael and her. Would they come out unscathed?

He threw the empty plastic bottle into the metal sink, the action and resulting noise both startling Shauni. "You're going to stand there and tell me you and your friends were out walking? You said that before." He stepped toward her. "Now say it again." There was steel in the depths of his eyes, daring her to repeat what they both knew to be a falsehood.

"I was there to help an animal, but things were not what I expected. That is the truth." Shauni's voice was calmer, the level of discord between the two of them finally taking its toll. She was confused and bone tired. Her skin chilled from her wet clothes, and she hugged herself to drive away the shivers.

She raised emerald eyes to Michael. "Your turn. If you weren't following me, tell me how you found us out there."

Shauni's skin was so pale against the black of her shirt, her hair fell in heavy, wet ropes, and her lips were tinged blue from being cold. Michael thought she was the sexiest woman he'd ever seen. He could smell her mysterious scent through the damp clothing.

"Because I felt you." His voice sounded and felt thick, with longing and hunger. He needed her in every way a man could need a woman. He stalked to her and slid a hand behind her neck. "I'll always feel you, no matter where you go."

He captured her mouth with his and let his other hand roam where it would. He would stop if she asked, but please, he begged higher sources, don't let her.

Shauni didn't pull away, but held herself stiff, as if unsure how to respond. When Michael's thumb found her hardened nipple beneath the wet fabric, she moaned and collapsed into him. She clung to his shirt and kissed him back with a vengeance. They'd opened the dam and no force on earth could stop what was flowing between them.

Sense reared its head for a split second, and Shauni clamped her hands to Michael's wide shoulders, her head resting on his chest while she gathered her thoughts. "Michael, I have to tell you something."

"Forget that," he said. "It can wait."

Shauni felt herself being lifted and carried. With impatience riding him, Michael made it as far as a long couch in the next room before lowering her to it and plundering her lips again. He stopped only long enough to rip his shirt over his head, but it allowed Shauni an answer to at least one question. His chest and arms were thick with muscles while his stomach was tight and lean.

And smooth. He was smooth and golden all over, except for a triangle of blonde hair on his chest. He was a Nordic god bearing down on her for retribution, and she would willingly take her punishment.

His hands were pulling on her shirt now, and she found herself helping him pull it off. Her amulet fell onto her bare chest, the silver cool and smooth. Her pants were next to go, and she rolled seductively side to side as he pulled them down slowly, worshipping her long legs and placing a gentle kiss behind one knee as he went.

If she thought his eyes had been smoky before, they all but went up in flames as he studied her lacy black bra and panties. She gave silent thanks for her habit of matching lingerie to whatever she wore.

"I hope you'll wear these for me again some time," Michael said in a husky voice.

Shauni smiled, enjoying the effect she was having on him. "What's wrong with now?'

His hands moved to his belt. "I'm not going to be able to give you the proper undressing you deserve, but maybe we can put them back on when we're done and try again."

When his jeans fell to the floor, the sight of his erection caused a liquid pool of heat to circle and squeeze in Shauni's core. He was more beautiful than she could have imagined.

And he was all hers.

His hands were suddenly everywhere, pulling off her bra and tossing it aside, before he settled himself on top of her again and plunged a hand beneath the lace between her legs. Shauni jolted at the contact, her already sensitive tissue throbbing and tightening as his fingers worked to bring her closer to the brink. He pressed and stroked as if he knew her body by heart, finding the exact spot she wanted him to.

Michael watched her when her eyes went hazy and rapture took over, indulging in the pleasure of feeling her warmth squeeze around his hand as she came. Shauni gasped his name one time before melting into the sofa, her lids heavy and a lazy smile on her face.

"Mmm," was all she could muster.

"Hold that thought," Michael said, finding her tongue with his and molding his firm body to her soft curves from head to toe, working her into a heated frenzy all over again. This time, it wasn't his hand pushing for entry into her depths, and the velvet head brought her quickly back to the edge of climax.

"Please, Michael." She had no more pride. It lay in shreds

beneath the magic of his touch and the power he held over her. "Now. I need you now." Her eyes burned with demand. "I have to feel you."

With one stroke he filled her then held himself still for a moment to savor. Shauni, he thought in triumph. Finally.

Urging him to move against her, Shauni's hips undulated as tiny cries and gasps passed between lips still swollen from his kisses. He wanted to join with her there again as they broke through the last barrier and took her mouth as they moved together, building the tension until it was wonderfully unbearable.

Shauni's nails found his backside to pull him closer as the world shattered around them, and she moaned into his mouth. After spilling himself into her, Michael collapsed again, panting near her neck and saying her name only once.

Hearts thudded and breathing gradually slowed as they lay in the darkness of his home. Thunder and lightning still raged outside, but neither paid any mind. They were both wrecked by the intensity of what they'd made together. It had been quick and ravenous, but no one was complaining.

She sighed while gazing at the flashing window, no longer afraid of the tempest. "I'm completely…no…wait. What's more than completely?" She stretched her lips into a feline grin. "I'm ubercompletely satiated."

Michael only grunted in agreement.

Trailing a hand down the curve of his back, Shauni luxuriated in Michael's male perfection. She placed a soft, exhausted kiss on his shoulder, then another closer in, trailing bit by bit up his neck until her whisper found his ear. "I think I'll take that water now."

~

Sharing a drink and entwined beneath a velour throw for

warmth, Shauni and Michael took turns glancing at each other. Michael leaned over and raked the back of his knuckles across her chest. Smiling, Shauni took another sip and stopped him just short of pushing the blanket below her cleavage.

"Oh, no you don't," she said with a shake of her finger. "I'm not being derailed again."

"What?" His gaze lingered on her shoulders and the curve of her neck. He wasn't halfway finished with her yet. "Yeah. You were going to tell me something."

"Now you're catching on. And you were going to tell me how you found me out in those woods." She looked at the large golden lump of dog snoring in the foyer. "And don't tell me it was all him."

Michael felt his previous mellow aura zipping up tight. She'd relaxed him to the point of pre-catatonia, then after one look at her, he'd been aroused again and gunning for round two.

Now he felt neither level of satisfaction. He was back to agonizing over how she would react to his dirty little secret. Hell, she might consider it a breach of privacy, the way he perceived what people were feeling, especially his ability to tune in to her so well. It was like he had a direct line to channel Shauni. All day. All night.

So he did what any fearless man would do. "You go first."

"Well," she lifted one raven brow. "Only because I had planned to seduce you later tonight anyway..."

"Hold it." He thumped her thigh playfully. "Rewind for a second."

Rolling her eyes, Shauni heaved a great sigh and told him about the wine glasses and her plan to come over, have a serious talk, and jump his bones. "Since we've already accomplished the jumping part, we can now have said serious discussion."

"Where are my glasses? And the wine? I feel gypped."

"Still in Willyn's car, I imagine, though she probably took all the bags in. Regardless," her face settled into somber lines. "I have to…no, I need to tell you about me."

Michael mentally readied himself. What could warrant such anxiety? Would she tell him she was married or that she had a child? No…he didn't sense that. Whatever was coming, her body was clenched and trembling as if she were about to receive a blow.

"Hey," he rubbed her bare arm, languorously kneading her soft skin. "Relax. It can't be that bad."

Oh, Michael, she thought. It can be that weird. She licked her lips. "Remember when I brought the puppy in, and I knew which leg was hurt? Well, I didn't see him favor it like I told you."

"So?"

"I knew for another reason. In another way." She pulled in the bottom lip she'd just licked and held it under her top teeth.

Michael braced himself. If she told him that she had been the one to hurt the puppy…well, that was something he couldn't abide. Everything he felt for her would be destroyed.

Michael looked into the fearful green eyes, and he just couldn't picture that scenario. She loved animals, he was sure. "Then how did you know, because I have to tell you, you're not making any sense."

"The thing is. I have sort of a gift. I have ever since I was a child. Animals naturally flocked to me, no pun intended, and they did so for good cause." Shauni took a much longer slug of the water. "I can communicate with animals."

Michael laughed, relief flooding through him. "Well, sure. I can, too. I'm not exactly a dog whisperer, but some people seem to be. You have a special touch."

"No. No. That's not it. I can talk to animals, as in, I hear their thoughts and understand them." She pulled the cover closer and shook her head. This was not going well. "And they understand me."

Shauni hazarded a peek to see his reaction and was disturbed to see the intense speculation there. She'd seen it before, and it only ever meant one thing.

He thought she was nuts.

"Don't say a word." She stood, taking the throw and wrapping it around her, leaving Michael bare-assed in the process.

He didn't seem to mind but carefully moved a pillow to his lap.

"I'll prove it."

A wrinkle formed between his eyes. "You're going to prove it," he said flatly.

With her makeshift, velour robe, Shauni padded across the hardwood floor to where the dog slept and nudged it with her foot. It only rolled on its back and snored.

"Come on, Fletcher. Work with me." Another nudge and he opened one deep brown eye. "Fletcher, I'm going to ask you a question so that Michael will hear, and I want you to tell me the answer, okay? You don't even have to get up."

She faced Michael. "What's something he would know that I couldn't possibly?"

Michael stared slack-jawed for a few more seconds before rubbing a hand over his face and through his hair. "Um, sure. I'll play." He tossed a hand up, letting it slap back down on his leg. "Ask him what he got in trouble for this morning before we went to the clinic."

Michael almost hated to give her the rope to hang herself. There was no way she could know or guess the answer, and then he'd have to deal with a whole new reality. Shauni was either insane, or she was a compulsive liar.

She looked down at Fletcher then smiled triumphantly at Michael. "Ouch. I'd have threatened to have him shaved, too."

The first tendrils of unease trickled through Michael's veins. He had told the dog that almost verbatim when he found him…

"…dropping your glasses in the toilet. That's what he was doing when you walked in and caught him," Shauni finished his very thought.

"No...that's just..."Michael stood, dropping the pillow and catching Shauni's eye. "That is not possible. There's no way he told you that. Specifically word for word. No. Uh-uh." Michael bent to pick up his discarded pants and jerked them on, one long leg at a time. "What are you doing, Shauni?"

He didn't believe her. After what they'd just shared, because she knew he'd felt it, too, and after the proof she just gave him, he was actually angry. He patted the pockets of his jeans, and when unsuccessful, he scanned the room for his shirt, hoping his glasses were with it.

"See? That's why he drops your glasses in the toilet. You always lose them, so when he finds them, he puts them somewhere you can't miss them. His heart's in the right place." The tightness in Shauni's voice was only an attempt to cover the hurt stabbing into her lungs. She'd shared herself with him, body and soul, and he still thought she was deceiving him.

"I'm sorry, Shauni." Michael let his arms fall to his sides. "This is not anywhere near what I expected to hear. Not in the same ball park. Hell, not in the same universe." He brushed past her and headed up the stairs. "I need to take a shower," he said over his shoulder, not even bothering to look at her. "Then we can talk or...I don't know what we'll do."

The frigid resentment he left in his wake froze Shauni in place. The room closed in on her, and she could barely hear her own mind over the rush of static in her ears. Her heart hurt. It actually seemed to be caving in on itself, and she was having trouble drawing a breath.

Only then did she understand what she'd so foolishly denied all along.

She'd fallen hard for Michael. His gorgeous heart, sharp as a razor wit, his intelligence and casual humor. Everything he was, she loved, and the knowledge had come too late.

Stupid. Stupid.

He was done with her. Any woman who'd stood where she was now would recognize the signs, and Shauni had been here before. She'd seen the looks of pity or disgust, though she'd only risked herself with a select few in the past.

But none of them had been Michael.

Still numb, Shauni found her clothes and put them on as quickly as possible. Tears burned in her eyes as she fumbled for the doorknob in a house that had turned very dark.

Very black.

She had her phone, and planned to call Joe or his son for a ride, whoever was working at the house tonight. But first she had to get out, away from the revulsion Michael had thrown at her after they'd found each other only moments before.

Slipping out into the night, Shauni didn't look for Michael or listen for his footsteps. She couldn't bear the thought of facing him again, and her stomach knotted with the realization that the time they'd had tonight was all she would ever have.

A fierce gust slammed the door shut, but she was already moving down the steps, running up the street, and into the chaos of the storm. The sky cracked and roared while threatening clouds continued to drench the city.

Shauni viewed the rain as a friend, a kind of shelter. Because with the cool wetness rolling down her face, she could pretend she wasn't crying.

16

Michael's tension drained away as if carried along with the hot soapy water and the haze clouding his vision cleared as he soaked. After taking time to reassess what Shauni had told him and putting some distance between himself and her injured, accusing eyes, he was able to view his actions for what they were. An overreaction.

How could anyone who read the auras of others like a color wheel balk at the idea of telepathy? He'd always considered himself an open-minded sort, especially with his grandmother's influence keeping the doors spread wide. Maybe it had been the added quirk of interspecies communication, or that he hadn't been expecting Shauni to reveal anything of the paranormal.

Drying off and wrapping the towel around his waist, Michael raked a hand across the steamed mirror and scrutinized himself. *Admit it, Black. You acted like a damn hypocrite.*

At least he'd told her he needed a shower to rehash everything. He'd go down and sit with her, show her the respect she deserved, and listen to her this time. Just listen.

Then he would share some paranormal psychoses of his own.

In a fresh pair of jeans and loose gray shirt detailing the tour dates for Train, Michael came to a stop at the bottom of the stairs and listened. Too quiet, and the air had lost the sweet apple scent and pleasant green light he associated with Shauni.

She was gone.

Another flash and monstrous drum roll drew his attention to the tropical storm that beat at the earth and showed no signs of waning. "She left in this?" On the floor, Fletcher snorted in answer before rolling over and dozing off again. "Too bad I can't hear what you think," Michael said, kneeling to rub the white belly displayed to the world.

"But if I have my way, someone who can is going to be spending a whole lot more time with us, so be prepared to give up all the loot you've stashed around the house." Fletcher moaned, and for the first time, Michael considered the animal might understand every word. Maybe he always had. Oops.

"You stay here and hold the floor down, Fletcher. I know where she is, and I'm going to bring her back."

The city had been ravaged by brutal winds and relentless rainfall. Streets were littered with debris and miniature floods ran along each side of the road. No one should be out driving in this, but a craving to erase the pain he'd caused drove Michael on through the storm.

He pulled up to the large yellow house, jumping out to dash through the rain without protection, but discomfort was an insignificant detail in comparison to his need to apologize to Shauni. He'd been the one to reserve trust, keeping his own skeletons bound in the closet, then had stomped all over her guileless attempt to share herself with him.

A woman he judged to be in her forties answered the door, smiling hesitantly to reveal one dimple in her lovely, dark face. "Yes?" She looked behind him at the squall. "Bad night to be out. You lost?"

"No, Ma'am. I'm here to see Shauni Miller. It's very important," he added in case she hesitated.

Her eyes took on the familiar glint of one woman watching out for another. Damn female solidarity. "You must be Michael, but you just missed her, I'm afraid."

"Missed her? Where did she go?"

"Out to the island, of course. Joe and I, that's my husband, we tried to talk her out of it with the weather and all, but she said she would drive herself if she had to." The woman frowned. "I've never seen her so upset. Mighty big change in that sweet girl."

A boulder landed in the bottom of Michael's stomach. "How do I get to this island? It can't wait. I have to see her tonight."

"Well..." her eyes told him she was deliberating.

"I can take you," a male voice called from inside, just before a younger black man came from around the corner. "I'm just coming on duty anyway. Never have a good reason to drive through a fury like this one's turned out to be. The waves are awesome."

"Joe Jr." The woman had warning in her tone. "You just wait until your father gets back, and he'll decide."

"Please," Michael said. "I have to talk to her."

Joe Jr. smiled at the woman, his mother Michael assumed, with a mischievous and determined grin.

The woman threw up her hands, relaxing both her manner and her speech. "I know better than to argue with two bull-headed men when they get together on a thing." She waved them toward the back. "G'wan now, before I change my mind."

After refusing a towel and grudgingly putting on the neon orange life vest, Michael settled into a seat. The speed boat offered no shelter from the pelting rain that would feel more like bullets once they shifted into high gear, but again, he told himself, none of that mattered.

He had to get to Shauni.

Why would she take a boat to an island at a time like this? What was out there?

He threw a look to Joe Jr. who was squinting as they blasted over choppy waters. "Thanks for this," he yelled to be heard.

"No problem, man. You ask me, we need a little shaking up around here occasionally."

They made up some time in the faster boat, and Michael saw the other craft still docked when the island materialized through the sheets of falling water. Its white hull stood out in the dark, bobbing in the wrathful tide. Two people were hurrying toward the woods, one holding an umbrella over the other.

Michael stood precariously. "Shauni!"

His voice was battered down by the gale and pounding ocean. She couldn't hear him.

"Thanks again," he yelled before jumping onto the dock. Joe Jr. waved him to go and catch the girl. Michael saw a warm color around the younger man, as if he knew exactly what was going on between the blonde stranger and Shauni. And he approved of the match.

The colossal trees waved their branches in the night as if battling the invading storm. Michael felt sure they would remain standing as they had for a hundred years. The path Shauni and the man had taken was visible, and Michael darted into the dense foliage, intent on catching up with her.

Soon he came out of the forest and into a clearing. A grand stone mansion rose from the earth, windows warm and yellow against the night. Searching the area, he located the front porch and the door as it swung open.

His world imploded and a frozen hand squeezed his thumping heart.

There was Shauni.

Falling into the arms of another man.

~

Dripping despite the umbrella and feeling like a drowned cat, Shauni took one look at Quinn's sympathetic face and collapsed against him.

"Hey now. You're safe," he crooned, pulling her into the

house. He led her into the grand hall where Anna and Willyn were once again bonding over a romantic comedy. "Are you hurt? Was it the Amara?"

"No." Shauni shook her head, embarrassment painting her face. "I'm fine," she said aloud for everyone's benefit. "I'm upset, but no black magic involved. Just my own form of self-flagellation rearing its ugly head again. Trusting a man."

Quinn lifted his hands away, effectively turning the crisis over to his sister. "That's my cue to leave."

Anna's bright blue eyes softened with understanding. "You told Michael, didn't you?"

Swiping at her tears as if they were the enemy, Shauni moved to the comfy, green couch and plopped down. "I thought he was different. More than that, I felt it inside. We had a connection, a warm sizzle that always seemed to be pulling us closer."

"I know that sizzle," Willyn said. "I had it with Mason, and he turned out to be my soul mate." Sadness and remembrance crossed her face but was pushed aside when she focused on Shauni. "Start from the beginning and don't leave anything out."

"None of the lead-up matters." Shauni looked to the large flat screen where a man and woman kissed in the middle of swelling music. Her heart broke a little bit more. "He didn't believe me. Open and shut."

"About being a witch?" Anna asked, still standing and hoping her vision had been right. This had to turn itself around.

"Ha. I never got that far. Thought I'd ease him into animal speak first." She slapped her hand on her thigh. "I even proved it by telling him why his dog drops his glasses in the toilet, and he had the nerve to get angry."

Claudia walked in then. "Who drops glasses in toilets?"

No one got the chance to explain. Banging on the front door interrupted the flow of conversation, and Claudia flinched at the sound. "Somebody must be getting rained on," she said, walking through the foyer.

She returned quickly, but on the heels of Michael, who stalked into the room ahead of her, clothes soaked and face a mask of loathing. His eyes were molten silver and settled on Shauni immediately. "Why the hell did you even bother?"

A whirl of emotions swamped Shauni at the sight of him, but confusion took the lead. "Bother with what?" She stayed seated, unsure what he was talking about and wishing they didn't have an audience.

"The whole thing, Shauni. Me, us. Being so torn up about sharing your big secret when you were coming home to someone else the whole time." His eyes cut to Quinn then back. "I should have gone with my gut when I first met you. I know beautiful women can be devious, but I never took you for a slut."

A general cry of outrage went up in the room, and Shauni sucked in a painful breath as the words cut deep. Quinn took a step forward, and the motion severed the thin string of control holding Michael back.

In one smooth movement, Michael pivoted and swung, catching Quinn on the jaw and sending him reeling backward. He stood waiting for Quinn to come back at him, though his words belied his readiness to fight. "You can have her."

"Michael!" Shauni sprung to her feet. "That's enough. You don't know what you're talking about."

She moved between him and Quinn, who was rubbing his jaw but keeping quiet. His blue eyes blazed, but he held his tongue, considering the picture he and Shauni had made on the front porch when he'd held her. This guy had only been a minute behind. Probably saw the embrace and ran with it. Because of that, and what he knew of Anna's vision, he would reserve judgment and a response.

But he wasn't about to get punched again.

"Nice right hook for a vet," Quinn said, making Shauni's jaw fall slack and Anna's lips spread into a smile.

"Quinn. I'm sorry," Shauni started, but he waved her off.

The ache and turmoil that had been brewing inside Shauni sparked and ignited into something bigger. A sizzle coursed through her veins like nothing she'd felt before, or been able to summon before. She was brimming with outrage, and it wanted out.

Michael had doubted her and that hurt. He'd struck one of her friends over his own twisted misinterpretation of what he'd seen, casting not only doubt on her again, but shame as well.

And he'd called her a slut.

"Quinn is Anna's brother, Michael, and he just happened to be the one opening the door in time to witness me losing it. I hugged him because I was a mess. Crying over you, if you want to know all the dirty details. And you do, don't you?" Shauni took two deep breaths, her chest heaving as she worked herself up.

"Here it is. I talk to animals, and I don't really give a damn if you believe that or not. It's who I am, with or without your consent."

Michael felt the first inkling of guilt, worse even than what had assaulted him before. On top of it was a raking fear that he'd probably ruined any chance of a relationship with Shauni, and because of his own distrustful nature.

He'd barged into the place and pounded on a man she considered a friend. And in front of others. He knew what she thought of violence, and all he could do was stand here and take his medicine.

And he had to do it while trying not to notice how gorgeous Shauni was as her aura burned brighter and brighter with wrath. It just didn't seem right to be so turned on by a woman who was probably about to let him have it.

"Now you want the big one?" Shauni asked in a low, breathy voice that chilled him as much as it aroused him. "My talking to animals is only a side effect of the fact that I'm a natural-born witch."

Shauni's shoulder felt as if lava had found its way inside, but there was no pain. It coursed down her arm, past the elbow and gathered in the center of her palm, which she lifted to show to Michael. Here was what she had so unsuccessfully attempted to make before. All she'd needed was to have her heart plucked out and dissected on a platter, her pride serving as dessert.

Fire undulated and danced in her hand, but she held it back.

She heard Willyn gasp and mutter under her breath, "Oh. Not inside the house."

"This is just one thing I can do," Shauni told Michael, "and I'm honing my skills every day. I'm a witch, and this is where I really live, with my coven." She snapped her fingers into a tight ball, extinguishing the flame. "So maybe you should take some more time and decide if you can live with that, because it's part and parcel, Dr. Black."

Turning on her heel, Shauni stalked across the room and out toward the solarium. She needed to be immersed in the green and find a way back to herself. She would forge a path through the anger and hurt, because she still had a job to do. If Michael ended up being collateral damage then it was meant to be.

Maybe this was what Anna had foreseen? Had it always been Shauni's fate to be devastated by the only man she'd ever truly loved? If that was the catalyst she needed to fulfill her part of the prophecy, so be it.

She found the bench she'd shared with Anna that day, when Anna had told her to go after pleasure if she had the chance. To find fulfillment.

Shauni had found it, if only for a moment, and now the sinkhole left by the removal of Michael and the pleasure he'd brought her felt huge and gaping. Large enough to swallow her very existence.

~

Michael was unsure what to do. He wanted to go after Shauni, but he felt it prudent to assess this new and disturbing situation. If what she'd said was true, he'd just stepped in it big time.

"So, you're all witches?" he asked of Anna, Willyn, and Claudia.

They all nodded, but the deep voice from across the room was what worried him. "So am I," Quinn said with a quirk of one dark brow. "But don't concern yourself. We vow to harm none." He crossed his arms over his wide chest. "With magic, anyway."

Clearing his throat, Michael held his ground but offered an apology. "Sorry about before. I was upset and couldn't make out anything through the red curtain that had come down over my eyes."

Quinn laughed. "It's all done now. Besides, Willyn can pat my cheek and put me to rights."

"Excuse me?" Michael asked with a cock of his head.

"Never mind that," Anna put in. "All in good time."

"You love saying stuff like that, don't you?" Claudia said to Anna before pointing a finger at Michael. "Look, buddy. Three strikes and you're out. Now get it together before you go to her. You don't want to mess it up for good." She relaxed and offered him a smile. "I'm on your side. Honestly."

Michael let his shoulders drop, feeling more at ease. That was quite a feat, considering he was surrounded by witches, but he also had the added benefit of seeing the bluish-green radiance around each of them.

That meant no one wanted to kill him.

"I'm not screwing up again, and I appreciate the cheering section." Michael looked to Anna. Something told him she was the one giving out the hall passes. "Do you mind if I..."

"Please," she said with a sweep of her arm in the direction Shauni had taken. She moved in and placed a feather-light touch on Michael's arm. "In fact, I'm counting on you."

Nodding slowly, Michael didn't ask for an explanation. Frankly, he was full up for the night.

He made his way out of the room, praying to himself that he could repair the damage he'd done, and went in search of Shauni.

17

Shauni had her nose buried in a golden flower when Michael walked into the solarium. Her eyes were closed, and the glow surrounding her had faded from murderous crimson to merely an irritated umber. The clean, fruity smell of whatever was blooming carried to Michael, so he assumed she was in the process of some sort of aromatherapy.

The heart-shaped curve of her face conjured images of angels, or in her current state, goddess of the hunt. Whether vengeful or blissful, Shauni was right at home in the flora. He assumed they were almost as much a part of her as the animals were.

Michael frowned. He seriously hoped she couldn't talk to plants or the one in his study would accuse him of neglect and murder.

It was then, as he stood staring, that Shauni looked up, but instead of seeing a return of her previous ire, Michael saw something else. And it wrenched his soul. If he had to guess, he would say he just saw her aura wilt, as if struck by intolerable suffering.

And he was the cause.

Crossing to her with the caution of a child facing a principal, Michael stopped only when Shauni let out a tremulous breath and sucked it back in as if she were trying not to cry. She thrust out an arm, clenching the extended hand into a fist then releasing again in a signal for him to halt in his tracks.

"Don't…" she swallowed. "If you have any…" Shauni clamped her mouth down tight when her voice wavered. "If you plan to say anything argumentative or hurtful, don't. Just leave, because I can't take anymore tonight."

Michael risked another step. "You won't have to. I'm not here to cause you any more distress."

Shauni gave a dark laugh. "Distress? Is that doctor talk for making me feel like something you'd rather toss back and forget about? For coming here and attacking an innocent bystander?" She let go of the plant she'd clung to and rubbed her hands on her thighs. "If all of that was distressing, then I don't want to know how far you think you need to go before causing any actual pain."

Michael saw her fidgeting and jerky movements for what they were. Her defenses were worn out, but she was still expecting to be attacked. He'd done that to her. He'd put the shadow in her eyes. He alone had left the bruises on her once glorious color.

"You're right. I've been nothing but an ass." He sat on the bench, leaving her in the advantageous position and hoping to draw her closer.

She only gaped.

"Thought I'd cut to the chase," he explained. "I'll say I'm sorry, because I am, sorrier than I can put into words, but first I want you to know that everything that went wrong tonight falls squarely on my shoulders." Solemn gray eyes held hers. "You did nothing wrong, Shauni." He held out a hand. "And there's nothing wrong with you."

His quiet gesture rocked Shauni to the core as a warm current rolled through her, making her light-headed. He was saying he accepted her as she was. Parlor tricks and all.

With a quick shake of her head, she put her fingers to the place on her chest where something foreign and light fluttered. The spot where she had stored the weight of remorse and anguish. The lies she'd carried around with her just for Michael.

They were gone.

The new sensation growing there was breezy and effervescent. Michael knew everything about her now, and he was still here. He still wanted her. More than that, he was actually asking her forgiveness.

The smile that struggled to form fell back into a doubtful frown when she remembered the rest. "Isn't there something else you want to add?"

"I..uh…" he wanted to say the words. Was that what she was asking? How could she know he loved her when he'd only just ended up on that road himself? Would she laugh in his face?

"About how you found us today," Shauni said.

Oh, that. Michael wasn't sure if he felt relieved or frustrated. He'd been so close.

But they wouldn't be able to move forward until every last contaminant was purged, and the ability he kept hidden from the world was a single drop in the storm compared to what Shauni had revealed.

He opened his mouth to give her the extended version of how his grandmother first recognized his gift along with a few anecdotes from his younger years, but realized he would have to make it short and sweet. "I can sense emotions. Most people wear them like an outer shield, for me anyway." He stood and walked to her, glancing over her shoulder to make sure he wasn't imagining things. "I have a deeper connection to you. For some reason, I can tell where you are, within reason, and literally feel you."

"Like you said before," Shauni whispered. She'd hoped at the time he meant he felt her on another level. Like two people who were meant to be together. Except, he'd been speaking literally.

So much for romantic notions.

Noticing his furtive looks behind her and the concern marring his face, Shauni asked, "Michael, what's wrong?"

"I'd planned to do my story better justice, but we don't have time for that." He gave a quick jerk of his head, indicating the wide window patterned with French panes. "Someone is outside. Two people are headed this way."

He grabbed her hand and pulled her behind him. "And their colors are all wrong."

~

"The Amara are here," Shauni called out to Anna and Willyn who had burrowed back into the couch to finish their movie. Claudia and Quinn were both gone.

Jumping up and clicking off the DVD, Anna shifted into witch mode, her face a thundercloud that gave Shauni pause, even though they were on the same side. "I didn't see them coming. They found a way to block me," she said, throwing the remote control onto the green velvet cushions. "Well, not on my own land they won't."

Moving with the determination of a general rallying her troops, Anna stopped at the bottom of the stairs and yelled for her brother. "Quinn!" He appeared as swiftly as a wraith. "We've got company," she told him.

Quinn's brow furrowed and his fists clenched. "How many?"

"Two." This from Michael, who surprised Shauni by moving in front of her, blocking her from the discussion in a protective fashion.

"Michael. You don't know what's happening. Please just stay in the house while we handle this." Shauni tugged on his arm, ignoring the luscious feel of the thick, hard bicep. "I have to go outside."

He whirled on her. "I go where you go."

Shauni felt the tightening in her belly that was becoming much too familiar for her taste. Anger seemed to be her new best friend, and it was not welcome. "I know you want to do the manly thing, but..."

Shauni was interrupted as Quinn swept past them. "Save the lover's spat for later. We have worse problems."

"Shauni, stay with me," Anna said. "They shouldn't be able to work any magic on this island, but as we've already seen, they evidently have their own rule book."

As a unit, Quinn, Anna, and Shauni went to the foyer, Quinn bracing his hand on the doorknob and looking to Anna for consent. At her nod, he threw open the massive wood barrier and marched out. The storm was still battering the land, rain dipping and spiraling with the vicious wind as its dance partner.

Shauni felt Michael beside her, his hand on the small of her back, and knew there was no shaking him. She gripped his hand and cast pleading eyes at him. "Please, don't interfere."

He returned a haphazard smile, one that would shame the devil. "You think I don't recognize black magic when I see it?"

"I'm beginning to think you see a whole lot more than I gave you credit for, but that's a discussion for another time."

"We'll be having it tonight, regardless of what your uninvited guests have to say." He let go of her hand and looked ahead.

Shauni saw Anna's intention and intercepted her, forcing her to fall in behind. "They came to see me, Anna. You know they did."

"Then they'll be getting two white mages for the price of one," Anna said with a glint in her eye.

Quinn stopped on the porch, tossing a dry comment over his shoulder even as he scanned the yard. "What does that make me, then?"

"That makes you the eye candy warrior who's going to protect his three white mages." Kylie bounded out of the house to join them. "Why didn't you call us, Anna? I came down for coffee and just happened to see you going out. I could tell by your posture something was wrong."

"We've got this one, blondie," Quinn growled. He wasn't sure whether he was more disturbed by the younger woman's presence in the face of danger or that she'd referred to him as "eye candy." Probably just a silly college girl thing. She needed to carry her ass back inside. "Let the adults deal with this."

Kylie crossed her arms and cocked a hip. "Deal with what, oh surly one?"

"Hey, hey. We've got a welcoming party, Sylvie." The shifter that had gotten his fangs into Shauni emerged from the darkness and strolled into the light.

Tensing, Shauni lifted her head and glared down at him from her position at the top of the stone steps. "So you're not hiding behind your wolf's clothing tonight? Did you find the bravery to face me as yourself?"

The man changed faster than the lightning streaking across the sky behind him, his lip curling in a snarl. "I'll rip your neck out with my own teeth."

"Calm down, Ross," the black woman said in a quick but harsh rebuke. "Not here."

Shauni realized then that they knew they would be outmatched on the island, and right in the middle of Anna's ancestral home. The heart of the coven's power. "What do you want?" Shauni asked, striding ahead to stand with Quinn and ignoring the oath Michael muttered when she left him.

"A rumble in the jungle," the bleached-blonde shifter said. His name was Ross. One more they could add to the Amara roster.

"You can't hurt us," Sylvie said, directing the statement to Anna. "We mean no harm tonight, so you can't strike."

Anna made a sound of annoyance. "I see. We follow the guidelines and adhere to magic's decree, but you and Ronja don't have to?" She put her hands on her hips. "How convenient."

"Come on over to the dark side, baby." Ross rubbed a hand over his crotch. "Then you can break the rules, too."

Quinn took a menacing step toward the crazed man, but stopped when Shauni's voice whipped out. "State what you came for or leave. You won't be allowed to stand here and insult her or any of us." She looked at Sylvie. "What does Ronja want, because I know she sent you."

Sylvie licked her lips and all but purred. "Tomorrow. We'll meet and give you a chance to pass your test." She lifted a condescending brow. "Or are you afraid, little animal lover? I know there's not much fight in you, so why not get it over with and end the suspense?"

"When and where?" Shauni snapped.

Demented laughter burst from Ross as he shook and punched his fist into the palm of his other hand. Shauni had serious doubts about his sanity, but that made him even more of a threat.

"We'll let you know, sugar. And if I were you, I wouldn't stand us up. You've already agreed." Sylvie sent one last withering look toward Anna, then Kylie, before rolling her shoulders and turning away to disappear into the trees.

"What did she mean?" Kylie asked. "Did what Shauni said really count? Is she like, bound to the challenge tomorrow or something?"

Quinn brushed past the group to head back inside. "We have to perform with honor if we want to beat them and prevent the return. So essentially, yeah, Shauni's duty-bound to meet them." He looked at Kylie. "Like, totally."

The sarcasm wasn't lost on any of them, but Kylie decided to take the high road, her concern for Shauni outweighing her aversion to Quinn. How did a sweetheart like Anna end up with such an irritating brother?

"You're not going," Michael said in the firm, even tone parents used with willful teenagers.

Shauni stayed where she was, in the rain, as the others left her and Michael alone to finish what they'd started before.

"I am. There are obligations here that you don't understand, Michael. Besides, you heard Quinn. I have to."

"What I know," he shot back, taking the steps two at a time to grab her arm and haul her onto the porch. "Is that you don't have sense to come in from the rain." Michael had about all he could take of secrets, lies, and half-stories. "I'm not letting you out of my sight until I know you'll be safe from…whatever those people are."

Dragging a disdainful eye up and down his wet clothing, Shauni smirked. "Look who's talking. And again, don't think you can stop something bigger and more powerful than you. There are more lives at stake in your precious Savannah than just mine."

He moved closer, capturing her face in his hand before smashing furious lips onto hers and forcing his way in. Talking with the woman was getting him nowhere, so he'd go back to the form of communication that worked best for them.

Once she'd relaxed against him and aligned her body with his in a way that invited him to take more, Michael used the advantage and pulled back. He left her panting and irked by the sudden departure. "You keep telling me I don't know anything."

He rubbed his thumb over her bottom lip then stroked it down her throat to the cleft between her breasts. "I think it's time you filled me in."

18

Shoes off, lying stretched across her quilt of icy mint green, Shauni rolled her eyes as if seeking celestial guidance while Michael continued to pace. She was sure his running shoes were wearing a path in the floorboards. Feeling a chill, she pulled the crocheted ivory throw from the bottom of the bed and covered her bare legs.

"So you're saying you only found out you were a witch after you came to Savannah, guided by an unseen force that you can't describe, and were magically chosen to be the first to face a series of challenges." He drilled serious gray eyes at her. "And any one of these face-offs with the…what are they called again?"

"The Amara," Shauni supplied in a flat tone.

"Right. Any conflict with them could be dangerous if not lethal." He gave his glasses a hard push into place. "Tell me again why I shouldn't be worried."

"Because it's destiny. A prophecy to be fulfilled, and I have to do what I can to make it come out the right way. If I don't, they will succeed in calling forth their demon who will wreak bloody devastation on the world. Or at least the nearest part of it, for starters."

"Savannah."

"At least."

Struggling with more occult activity than even he was used

to, Michael attacked the issue the way he did any problem. Knowledge and preparation. "Tell me more about this demon."

"I can't. I only know the basics." Shauni plucked at the crocheted wool, amazed that the complicated design had been done by hand over a hundred years ago.

"Would you at least pretend to be focused?" he asked. "I have to come to grips with this before tomorrow, and you're not giving me a whole hell of a lot to work with."

Green eyes flashed at him. "I'm giving you what I've got, and you don't really have anything to do with this." She saw his jaw clench. "I don't say that to offend you or your male sensibilities. If you hadn't come out here tonight, I would still be going to battle the Amara tomorrow. Your presence changes nothing."

"I'm not so sure." Michael raked a hand through his blonde hair and stared off into the air.

Shauni pressed her lips together. She knew that look. "What's that supposed to mean?"

"You were the one who said everything happened for a reason." He pulled his gaze away from wherever his mind had wandered and crossed to sit beside her on the bed. "What if I'm part of your test?"

Shauni shook her head and let out a breath of exasperation. "That makes no sense."

"Hear me out. You said you found Skid because he sent vibes to you, and that doesn't happen with all animals, only the ones that you think are supposed to be in your life for some reason."

"Yes, and now I have an adorable puppy as a source of entertainment during the turmoil." She looked at the little black bundle in the corner of the room, then over to Cuileann who was pretending to be asleep but was listening to every word Shauni and Michael said. The cat had already voiced strong objections to sharing space with a veterinarian, sworn enemy of all domesticated animals.

"What if that's not all?" Michael stroked Shauni's leg under the wool. "What if he was meant to bring you to me?"

"Fine. Suppose he was. How does that help with the Amara?"

Michael leaned over and buried his face in her hair, breathing in the natural scent of her and wishing he knew the answers. "I don't know, but I have to keep trying to find a way to help you. If you won't take my protection or my offer to steal you away, you have to at least let me help."

Leaning closer to him, Shauni closed her eyes and let him comfort her. Tonight might be their last moments together, and so far they'd only had a small taste of each other. She felt in her heart there was something strong between Michael and her, and she wanted the chance to discover it all.

Outside the roiling storm had finally given way to steady rain that pattered against the window. The sound was soothing and brought with it the promise of new life as it soaked into the earth. Shauni should be here when the cycle continued. She had an urge to see the famed wisteria that hung in lilac bunches, blooming in only a snapshot of time.

Skid would come out of his cast and grow into a fine healthy dog. Cuileann had many years left in her short feline life. Shauni couldn't leave them behind.

And the coven. What would happen to them if she failed tomorrow? Would the ugly threats Ross had told her in the woods come true? What would they do to Anna if she fell into Ronja's hands?

Shauni shivered, and Michael held her tighter, his large, warm hand circling over her back. She couldn't bear the thought of losing him. Not now.

Shauni didn't want to fail. She didn't want to die.

"Stay with me," she whispered, turning her head toward his and resting against his cheek.

"Nowhere else," he said before finding her lips even as they quivered with fear.

Before there had been a heated urgency and impatience,

but what buzzed between them now was easy and quiet. It encompassed Shauni's entire body at once. The power of their bond was still as strong, but there was a surprising new current flowing underneath.

If Shauni didn't know any better, she might think it was love, but the way they were feeding off each other would require the same depth of emotion on both parts.

She couldn't be sure how Michael really felt and was too afraid to ask. Instead, she would drink in the lovely feeling of his mouth whispering over her skin, and the way he would pull back and devour her with his eyes as if he were utterly fascinated by her.

One of his hands cupped her breast through the thin cotton nightshirt she'd changed into, causing her body to shake with the need that shot from her hardened nipple all the way to her womanhood. She was instantly prepared and throbbing for him. She stretched in languor and lifted her hips slowly.

Groaning in response to her fluid, erotic movements on the bed, Michael sat up to slip off his glasses and the shirt he'd borrowed from Quinn. "If you don't stop that, this is going to happen faster than I'd planned."

"That's what the second round is for," Shauni said with a lick of her lips. "We've got all night, and I intend to put every minute to good use." She basked in the glory of the pure lust she drew from him, apparent in the hard shaft beneath his jeans.

"Then we're wasting time," he said in a low voice before spreading her thighs with a quick thrust and positioning himself between her knees. Long, firm fingers danced up her legs until they hooked beneath the waistband of her shorts and panties. Michael pulled them down but did so at a leisurely pace, kissing every new inch he exposed and paying special attention to the sweet spot on her hip.

As if suddenly overcome, he whisked the clothing away and

fell to his chest, turning his face to nuzzle the inside of her thigh.

Shauni almost shot off the bed. His hot breath so close to her core sent juices flowing, but she had only just recovered when the heat of his mouth found her sensitive flesh and went to work. "Michael," she gasped.

He hummed in response, treating her to a new level of stimulation. She sensed a quickening deep inside, a jolt that foretold of blooming pleasure.

Reaching around with one hand, Michael cupped her backside and held her in place while he used his other to fill her, stroking gently. The combination was more than Shauni could take. The orgasm rose up like a tidal wave and broke over her again and again, with her lover's mouth and hands taking her as far as she could go.

Only when she collapsed and whispered his name in reverence did Michael slide himself up against her to remove her remaining shirt. He had no intention of giving her much of a recovery period, and stood to let his blue jeans drop to the floor.

One look at his fierce erection and Shauni was ready for more. She reached out to feel its velvet heat, but her hand was grasped by Michael's. "I can't wait any longer. I have to be inside you."

Before lowering himself to Shauni, he raked a molten gaze over her from head to toe, and she swore she felt it burn her skin. When his quicksilver eyes met hers, a thread of tension formed between them, and she held out her hand for his.

A shock ran up to her elbow when they touched, like it had on the day they met, only this time it was stronger.

Michael felt it, too, and put a name to it as he joined her on the bed. "We make magic together, Shauni. Like nothing I've ever felt."

Her throat thick with emotion, Shauni only nodded as love

poured out of her soul and ran through the length of her. It seemed to meld with Michael and spark a supernatural glow that shimmered over their skin as they came together. The thrill of making love to him was heightened by the enchantment of their union, and they caressed each other everywhere, awed by the miracle and the sensuality of simply lying together.

When Michael kissed her lips, she knew they were about to meet each other truly for the first time. She sighed his name when he pressed himself against her sex and slid inside slowly, stretching and filling her until he was buried to the hilt. Their eyes, bodies, and souls locked together to produce an eruption that rocked them both.

Then Michael smiled and began to move.

Other, more natural sensations threaded through Shauni as she anticipated an eruption of another kind. Michael fit her perfectly, rubbing against every sensitive spot she possessed.

He gripped her hip with one hand as the other slithered up to bury in her hair. He thrust hard against her and growled, "This night can't last long enough."

Smiling as he lowered his mouth to hers, Shauni roved along his tight stomach and broad chest, flexing and twisting to take as much of him as possible.

No. It can't, she thought, squeezing his shoulders and holding on for life. *No it can't*.

~

Michael's eyes opened to a blurry world, his lids as heavy as hunks of lead. Brushing fingers through his hair, he coughed and tried to clear his groggy head.

He remembered the cool lemon light of early morning when he'd woken to the ringing of a phone. Not much later, Shauni had been at his side, offering him a sleepy, rumpled smile along with a steaming cup of coffee.

That's the last he remembered.

Jerking upright, he studied the brazen sunbeam that filled most of the room and spilled across to the far wall. It was at least eleven o'clock. The woman who'd whispered hot, sweet words in his ear all night had taken a different turn this morning.

Shauni had drugged him.

Launching himself out of bed, Michael pulled on the jeans still lying in the floor and quickly found his shoes and socks, both still a little damp. Running out the door and down the hallway to the stairs, he pulled on the borrowed shirt.

After calling Shauni's name in vain, he paused in the center of the grand hall on the floor below and listened. The house was silent. They had all gone, leaving him to sleep away the day while the woman he loved faced down evil that meant to end her life.

Not if he had anything to say about it.

Michael had a few tricks up his sleeve and was grateful the night's downpour didn't affect aura trails like they would physical evidence. Racing into the yard, he searched for traces of the witches, Shauni in particular.

Damn it. Shauni had done something to cover her path, no doubt expecting him to follow. He could locate her as soon as she felt any intense emotion like fear, pain, or grief, but couldn't risk waiting. By the time she felt any of those things, it might be too late.

Like a smudge on the day's beauty, an oily black mark drew his eye to where the two representatives of the Amara had stood the night before. Two iridescent lines, faint but still effective, meandered across the grass and into the woods.

Shauni had forgotten about them.

Michael knew he would lose the trail at the water's edge, but felt certain he would have no trouble picking it back up. There was an unpleasant tingle as he came up on the markings left by the two corrupted souls, so all he would have to do is get close enough to sense it on the other side of the ocean.

The second problem hit him in the gut, and he sprinted through the woods, praying to a plethora of gods that he was wrong.

When he saw the white boat tied to the dock and Joe Jr. lounging in the sun, Michael's breath rushed out in relief. He wouldn't have been able to make the swim to the mainland.

"I was just about to come wake you," Joe Jr. said, raising a bottle of soda in salute. "The ladies have been gone a good hour already, and they gave me strict instructions to wait here and not disturb you."

"But you were going to anyway?" Michael asked as he untied the closest rope.

Joe Jr. gave him a devious smile. "You're not gonna' report me, are you?"

Waiting for the younger man to climb in and rev up the speed boat, Michael shot back a smile of his own, full of appreciation and male understanding. "You know, Joe Jr., when this over, I'm going to take you out for a beer."

Joe Jr. hit the throttle and shouted, "And I'll let you."

19

"Where does this road lead?" Shauni asked as she and the rest of her coven emerged from the two vehicles, a black Range Rover driven by Joe and a Kiwi green Escape with Quinn behind the wheel. Anna liked variety, even in her cars.

"It looks like it's straight out of one of those old southern epic dramas," Kylie said, winding her multitude of blonde curls into a heavy braid. She stared down the curvature lined with sentinels in the form of giant live oaks. "Bet there's a plantation out there, or the ruins of one."

"Or a ghost for Hayden," Lucia chimed in, her dark eyes teasing the caramel-haired medium.

Hayden's lips lifted slightly in a quiet smile. "They'll have to wait. We'll be busy today." She glanced at Shauni, unable to hide the worry she was feeling about what they might find around the bend.

"There is a plantation at the end of this road, abandoned by the family some years back," Anna said. She let her eyes close and held her head up as if sensing the wind and whatever tales it carried to her clairvoyant mind. "Ronja's recently bought the land. She plans to rebuild, making this her…base of operations, for lack of a better description."

"So we're walking right into the spider's web," Viv said, her long gray eyes narrowed as if the enemy were already in sight.

"I wonder if the burial ground is out here," Willyn interjected.

"Maybe Shauni's supposed to find it today." Shauni had filled them all in this morning, while Michael lay drugged in her room, and she had been preparing for a death match.

"I don't think so," Anna answered, looking to Shauni for confirmation.

Shauni shook her head. "No. Something tells me I followed that thread as far as I was supposed to." She hoped that was the only role her special gift was meant to play, the animals sending messages from the spirit world and starting her down the right path to whatever she and the coven were supposed to find. She prayed that was all. "It's a start, I think, and we obviously have to find it, but..."

"But your part in it is done," Anna added. "I agree. You did what you were supposed to do by leading us in a direction we didn't even know we were supposed to take."

"First you will lead us," Hayden said, remembering Anna's vision and message for Shauni. "And you did."

Shauni stared thoughtfully into her friend's golden eyes. "I guess I did, but it seems so simple." Now she was focused on the rest of Anna's little info packet. Shauni still had to go through the dark, and she had a feeling she was about to be entrenched in plenty of that. "We'll just have to figure the rest out." She looked back down the road. "Later."

A very disgruntled Quinn slammed a car door closed and marched over to his sister. "Anna, I know I can't interfere, but if it goes wrong and there's no saving it," he tossed an apologetic look at Shauni for considering the possibility she might not succeed, "call for me, and we'll get you out of there."

Anna patted his cheek, "Not to worry brother. I have every confidence in our little whisperer." She winked at Shauni.

Quinn moved to give Shauni a hug and a chuck on her chin. "So do I. Takes balls to be the first."

A full laugh bubbled from Shauni. "Why Quinn, that's about the nicest thing you could have said."

"Just kick some ass, okay, and don't hold back." With one last frown for Anna and all the women he'd come to care about, Quinn moved to stand beside Joe. The older black man raised his hand to Shauni as if sending her any good energy he possessed.

The kind gesture from the only one of them without power reminded Shauni why they were here. Why she was here. "I'm ready, Anna." She walked ahead of the others, her hiking boots sending up tufts of dust from the dirt road. She was dressed in her usual uniform as far as the shoes and her black cargo pants, but a mischievous voice inside had made her choose one of Claudia's shirts, sleeveless black with lace that hugged her lithe form. The outfit represented both sides of Shauni. Naturalist meets demon-killer witch.

She would need to embrace both if she wanted to come out with her skin intact, of that much she was sure.

And from her neck hung the amulet, created for her hundreds of years ago, on an island three witches had made their home after defeating the demon once before. The vibrant green stone in the middle marked Shauni's character as much as her own name did, and she promised the spirits of those three women that she wouldn't let them down.

Silently, the coven filed in behind her.

Anna and Kylie, the eldest and youngest of them all, paired up to watch Shauni's back. After them, Viv, Claudia, Hayden, and Lucia joined the ranks, also wary and mindful of any disturbing sights or sounds.

Finally, Paige and Willyn, the one who dealt the damage and the one who healed it, both ready to do whatever was necessary to aid their sister of the heart.

As the sun sank lower in the sky, threatening to burn the horizon, something moved in the bushes then darted away, rustling leaves as it went. The area beyond the road's edges had been allowed to run rampant, growing into a thick morass of foliage, but Shauni had no fear of the southern jungle. Only friends resided there.

The same couldn't be said of the great plantation-style house that emerged as they rounded the last curve. Cracked and stained, the once white home was now a broken down version of its past splendor. Its color and gaps were similar to those of a tooth left to decay and crumble. How could anyone let it fall into such disrepair? Shauni had only a moment to wonder over the previous owners before she came to a dead halt, startling the others into doing the same.

Something was moving inside the house, and a surge of evil emanated from the building as if it contained something rotten.

"Is anyone else feeling that?" Claudia asked. She too had prepared for the unexpected, wearing a pale blue terry set and her long red hair in a braid. The goddess turned warrior princess.

"It's like our hum," Paige said with a frown," only it's a bad vibration. I can almost taste it."

Anna clenched her fists and spoke with a barely controlled fervor. "She's almost there. She has all of them." She shook her head, loose sable hair falling over her shoulders. "No, there are seven, but there will be another before it's done."

Shauni turned around, hearing the flatness in Anna's voice. Her blue eyes were dazed, as if she were in a trance brought on by one of her visions. "Anna," Shauni whispered. This was no time to lose their leader. "Snap out of it."

Grimacing and putting a hand to her temple, Anna exhaled a breath like blowing through a straw. "Oh, that hurts. It's stronger here, my gift, but also more dangerous." She continued to rub her head. "It sucked me in so quickly, and I didn't see it coming."

"Then no more looking while we're here. Not even a peek," Shauni said, sending a fiercely worried look to Anna. "I need you." She knew Anna couldn't help her outright, not in any way that would help Shauni pass her test. That would be cheating. Still, she wanted Anna around, and preferably conscious, if only for a moral boost.

"Don't worry. I'll keep my mind to myself. I've never had a vision come with claws before."

Paige was beside them then, nodding in the direction of the house. "Here they come." The beautiful priestess with cocoa skin was walking down the front porch steps with the air of a debutante, as if the wooden steps weren't creaking and groaning beneath her feet. She wore black from head to toe, tight and stretchy material, telling Shauni the witches weren't the only ones who'd come for a fight.

The crazy Ross appeared next, his eerie blue eyes squinted with hate. He was flanked by two ridiculously beautiful women, one blonde and wild looking, the other a sleek brunette. Shauni wondered if a one-way ticket to the dark side came complete with a mystical makeover. They too came outside and down the steps, moving onto the overgrown lawn.

Viv made a grunt from somewhere behind as R.J. sauntered out in a black leather jacket with studs over a white tee shirt. He was channeling a greaser from the fifties, despite the brown curls still gracing his head. He smiled and winked before flicking a finger to point at Paige, and the threat was clear. He hadn't forgotten the beating she'd given him, and today was all about payback.

Shauni shuddered, his cheerful attitude somehow more frightening than Ross's obvious dislike. A chill raced through her nervous system.

We're here. An alien voice shot out from a nearby bush. From the raspy edge to its signal, Shauni knew it was some type of reptile. *I won't use you. I won't. I can't sacrifice the innocent, even to save the innocent,* Shauni sent back.

Odd how even telepathic voices were affected by species. Scientists would be fascinated to learn how much was actually encoded in the nucleotide pattern of DNA, but she dared not wave that flag. She was happy enough that Michael accepted her for who she was.

At the thought of him, Shauni flushed throughout. She imagined gray eyes twinkling as one side of his dimpled smile lifted, laughing at something shared between lovers. The safety she'd found in his strong arms.

Then she remembered a declaration of love that had almost spilled from her lips as they climbed together into the light, body to body and soul to soul. Regardless of his feelings, she needed to tell him. She wished she had, in case there was never another chance.

A bright red flash pulled her back to the current mess she was in. A woman, who absolutely had to be the infamous Scarlett, judging by her curly red hair, strolled out with a wiry, black-headed woman who looked like the equivalent of a human alley cat. The ebony topped vixen was tight and mean, obviously having been around much more than the block a few times. Where Scarlett was decked out in a frilly white shirt and high-waisted navy pants, the second was perfectly outfitted for a night out to an acid rock concert. Chains and all.

Willyn edged up to the front with Anna, Shauni, and Paige. "Good Lord. How many are there?"

"More than us," Anna said with no sugar to coat her words. "But they still don't have what we do."

"Since it's not strength in numbers," Lucia interjected, "what exactly is it that we have?"

Kylie crossed her arms over her chest. "We're the good guys. And the previous witches who foretold the prophecy were our forebears. All we have to do is what we're supposed to do." She shrugged. "And we win."

"That simple, huh?" Viv asked with a doubtful tilt of her head.

Anna nodded to Kylie then turned back to Shauni with a

radiant smile. "Actually, it is. The only trick is knowing what right is. The correct choices and actions can only be felt by whoever's up to bat."

"Well, here I am, coach, and I'm still not sure." Shauni glanced back at the gathering of Amara, wondering what would set them off and when they would go into action. Or was that supposed to be her call? If she struck first, would that be what the fates wanted from her?

She could use a how-to-pass-mystical-trials crib sheet right about now. The classroom door was shut, and she was staring at a blank sheet of paper. No one left to help her.

All of the Amara shifted their focus back to the door of the house. They were waiting, and their expectant body language caused warning signals to fire in Shauni's gut. She had a feeling they were about to meet the queen of the damned.

She was right.

Ronja appeared, sailing smoothly through the decrepit door frame, and for a woman who was almost a thousand years old, beautiful was an understatement. Her features were classic, milky skin with royal bone structure, gently sloping nose and a wide mouth. Her stony-blue eyes were set off by arching brows and gently lifted cheekbones. Hair the color of pale morning light streamed freely with long bangs angled across her forehead and in waves down the side.

Shauni met the challenge in the woman's cold eyes, the smile that promised nothing but pain and death for the coven and all that they loved. Here was the immortal who would call forth a demon if given the chance.

Shauni had every intention of making sure that didn't happen.

Striding forward as if the area weren't littered with people who would slit her throat in a second, Shauni left the safety of her coven and moved to meet the opposing side or their representative. Why she still expected them to play fair was a mystery, but she refused to lower herself to their tactics by punching out at them with her power.

Like Kylie said, they were the good guys, and that position came with unfortunate requirements.

"What is it you want, Ronja?" Shauni called out. "Your sidekicks have failed twice, so you decided you'd need the home field advantage?" She felt her lip curl of its own accord, a derisive message she sent straight to Ross. "What happened to my being the weak link, wolfie?"

The shifter tensed and started to waver.

"Hold!" Ronja spat at him, her face a sudden mask of anger. Either Shauni's taunts or Ross's impulsiveness had shaken her icy exterior. She flicked a disgusted look back to Shauni. "Why you were chosen as the first remains an enigma. A devastating mistake for you, and her," Ronja said, indicating Anna, "but that's not my problem."

The smile oozed back across the frosty blonde's lips. "I'm simply impatient. Tired of waiting." She took two steps down and stopped before throwing up her hand. "I'm ready to have you dead, so I can receive my prize."

Overhead, ominous clouds rushed across the sky, having materialized from another dimension. The clear afternoon transformed into a luminescent twilight, with otherworldly shades of greenish gray creating a veil that prevented any of them from escaping to the real world.

The smell of sulfur and festering evil filled the air, and Ronja laughed wickedly. Her enjoyment of the disgusting changes were in stark contrast to her angelic looks. The long silk dress she wore changed from gray to blood-red, and Shauni clenched her eyes to clear them, sure she was hallucinating.

Everything she felt, saw, and smelled was genuine and had been called forth by Ronja. The extent of the black seior's power shocked Shauni into action. If this was it, she wouldn't be struck down while she stood with her mouth hanging open.

One at a time. Shauni heard Cuileann's calm advice and was grateful her beloved cat was far from harm. She'd wanted to come with Shauni but had remained behind with the other animals on the safety of the island. It was only the strong bond between Shauni and her familiar that allowed the communication over such distance.

"Okay," Shauni said aloud. "You've never steered me wrong before." Then she sought out R.J. who stood at the ready, hoping for a chance to inflict mental anguish on Shauni or any of her friends. The witches all had their poppets pinned inside their clothing. Time to see how they worked.

"Hey, R.J. Paige said she's fought girls who stood up to her better than you did. Maybe you should concentrate on improving your muscle over your mind for a while."

The cocky grin fell away, and the cherubic man flashed to fury, similar to his friend Ross. Without waiting for approval from Ronja, R.J. thrust an electric wave of distortion at the coven. Shauni could feel the fluttering around her head like the last time, but it was weaker, more like a breeze than a tapping at her mind. Casting a look around to the others, she saw Viv, Paige, and the others smiling broadly. They were completely unaffected.

The spell was working, and a shriek from the other side of the yard had Shauni jerking back to see R.J. with his hands clasped to the sides of his head and falling to his knees.

"It's freezing!" he cried, practically sobbing as he sank to the ground.

"You bitch!" Sylvie shouted to Shauni, obviously angry at seeing her partner in pain. *Good. Now the next. Shake them up*, Cuileann said. Shauni wondered why her cat was suddenly so chatty and forthcoming with battle tactics. Why had she waited until now? *Because it just came to me*, the cat whispered.

She was on the right track. Shauni could feel the knowledge singing its way into her as if it had been waiting for this moment. And for the first time, she truly believed she might do it. She might beat the Amara and sail through her test with flying colors.

Sylvie was mumbling her unintelligible hoodoo language with her fingers twisted into strange shapes. Some bad hex was about to be unleashed, and Shauni wasn't sure what to do. She instinctually raised her hand to use the only weapon she had, and her fireball missed the chanting priestess by a hair.

Sylvie opened her mouth to either mock Shauni's aim or to laugh, but was brought up short when a second stream of fire not only landed dead center but continued to flow, engulfing her until she broke her stance and jumped to the side to roll across the grass.

Following the streaks of fire back to their origin, Shauni saw Claudia right behind her to the left and smiled at the history teacher turned flamethrower. "Showoff," she muttered, but was glad to have the backup.

She should never have turned away and only realized her mistake when a *whoosh* sounded from the Amara camp and bursts of light blinded her as something hard hit her in the side of the face. Dazed, Shauni shook her head and discovered herself on the ground, flat on her back. She forced her eyes to open wide and saw two versions of the little black-haired woman who'd come out with Scarlett.

How had she moved so fast? Before Shauni's vision cleared, she sensed a white blur launching itself over her prone body. *Paige*. The coven's warrior finally had a worthy adversary, and she was sparring and twisting with the acid rock brunette, an occasional grunt emitting from the tangle of bodies when one of them landed a hit.

Anna's voice was closer now, calling out across the clearing. "Don't do it, Scarlett. Step out of line, and you'll be dealing with me."

As Willyn and Lucia hauled Shauni back to her feet, she saw

the redhead toss up her hands and twirl one arm in a mocking bow. She evidently felt they would still win, even without whatever low blow she had been about to deal Shauni.

"We won't have to lay a hand on your girl," Ronja said with too much gaiety for Shauni's liking. She had something up her sneaky sleeve. "We'll steal the breath from her without ever making contact."

Shauni nodded when the others asked if she was alright, but her eyes followed every movement Ronja made. The diabolical woman called over her shoulder to someone inside the house. Curses and bumps carried out on the foul wind, and Shauni felt his presence before he was shoved out the door.

Something sharp and piercing stabbed inside her chest as Michael stumbled out, his arms secured behind his back and blood smeared on his face. "No. Oh no," a trembling voice moaned, then Shauni realized it was hers. This was what she'd tried so hard to avoid. How had he gotten here? Surely the Amara hadn't been able to go to the island and break through the protective spell Anna had cast.

She wanted to weep, to break down and beg for his life. When she opened her mouth to do just that, Michael whipped his head up and pinned her with turbulent eyes. He was furious and was telling her to do the very opposite of what she had started to do. He didn't want her to grovel or plead, even for him.

He wanted her to fight.

20

"You have no respect for the standards laid down for our kind, Ronja," Anna cried, holding Shauni in place with a tight grip. "You've brought an innocent into this, so you'll reap the return of your actions. Three times three."

Ronja spread her arms and shouted her laughter. "Bring on your pathetic rules, Anna. They don't apply to me anymore. I've moved far beyond the bindings of any witch's decree. Bastraal is greater than a legion of your kind, and he is who I serve."

"Then your soul is void," Anna returned, lowering her face to peer at the other woman from beneath furrowed brows. "And it will burn alongside your demon when we send him into oblivion." Releasing Shauni, Anna stepped away from her and motioned for the others to do the same.

"We can't leave her alone," Claudia said, refusing to leave Shauni's side.

"You're not," Shauni told her friend. She understood that Anna wasn't abandoning her, but was giving her the final shove toward victory. "You're not leaving me, you're just giving me room to work."

With a rage like she'd never known exploding from her depths, Shauni focused her wrath on those that had Michael in their grip. She didn't recognize the man, but his Native American features and dress made her reasonably sure he was Ronja's lover.

Good, Shauni thought. *Quid pro quo*.

Recalling the words sent to her from the snake, Shauni let go and allowed the authority she'd been born with to have its way. The animals were her friends, to be cherished and respected, but they had made it clear that they were also her allies.

Today, they were brothers in arms. *We're here*, she heard whispered from a thousand voices, and knew they needed no protection from her. All they needed, all they wanted... was to be unleashed.

A single command flashed through her head, and the snake that had found its way to the shadows on the porch struck the leg of the dark-haired man holding Michael. The man jumped and yelled an oath, sending Michael plunging down the steps as he retreated from the strikes. Shauni saw that it was a rattler going after the man, and realized it had gone against its own instincts. There had been no warning rattle for its victim. Only a surprise attack.

The Amara all jumped to the defensive when the commotion erupted, except R.J. who was lying motionless on the ground and the black-haired woman who was still squaring off with Paige. Ronja's eyes blazed red, as did Ross's who howled to the sky. Though still in human form, the shifter eagerly charged Michael as he was trying to stand. With his arms still tied, Michael was easily taken down, and Shauni swore to herself she would have some of Ross's blood before it was over.

Scarlett stayed rooted next to Ronja's side, but shouted to the blonde with the long, wild hair who looked like she'd just come from the jungle. The woman was tall and lean, but well-muscled. She let loose a battle cry in a foreign language and came toward Shauni at a run.

She never saw the dogs coming.

It was as if a telegraph had been transmitted through some underground network Shauni never knew existed. She could feel the presence of more animals, and the number was growing. The coven and the Amara may have been trapped inside the mystic curtain Ronja had created, but the wildlife was having no trouble getting through.

The expression on the Amazonian blonde's face was almost comical as a German shepherd and another large black dog knocked her to the ground. They didn't rip her to shreds, as even they had more compassion than the human clamped in their jaws, but the growls they made were warning enough. She stayed put, terrified eyes darting around in search of help.

"This has gone on long enough," Ronja shouted over the cacophony. She pointed a long, black fingernail toward Michael and directed Ross to finish the job. "Kill him now!"

"No," Shauni screamed, panicking at the thought and losing control for only a moment.

Anna ran several steps ahead and made a slicing motion with her hands as she called out a spell. The ropes fell away from Michael's arms as if they'd been cut. Anna had attempted to give him a chance, but Sylvie was back in action, seething over her burned skin and clothing. She lunged at Michael, holding onto him as Ross started to quiver and bulge.

Shauni realized Ross was going to shift. He would be fighting her army with a creature of his own, and she dreaded what he might become.

An alligator slunk around the corner of the house, as if he'd just made it to the scene, and more dogs stood at the edge of the lawn. Birds of various types swooped and darted in a threatening manner, so many the sky grew even darker as hundreds of bodies circled above. All of them were waiting on Shauni.

And she was waiting to see what form Ross would chose to take Michael's life.

Ross's body stretched and grew, his voice changing from his usual insane laugh to a growl, a scream, and then a roar that deepened as his shape expanded. Taller and taller he grew until he towered at least seven feet above Michael who still struggled with Sylvie. The priestess was abnormally strong.

Claws lengthened from the tips of Ross's fingers, from a monstrous paw covered with brown hair and glinting copper streaks. The animal's head was huge, its mouth spread wide as saliva dripped from deadly teeth before spraying when it gave another murderous roar. The grizzly was almost complete, and its sights were set on Michael. There was no more time.

Shauni closed her eyes and called out with her mind. She felt the wind lift a body from beyond the tops of the trees. A glorious cry ripped across the sky, and the cluster of birds parted to make way for an avenging angel.

He had traveled far, like Shauni, to do his part for salvation of the innocents. Like Shauni.

The golden eagle's wings spanned at least six feet, his brown and gold body streamlined as he homed in on the target. It was no small prey he was after now, and the bear might easily end him, but Shauni felt the bird's determination as surely as she did her own.

She would give him help, a backup team like her own coven.

She cried out to Ross this time, with her voice as well as her telepathy, "You won't touch him!" And in unison the gathered animals turned toward the bear who was now raising his great paw to swipe. The razor-sharp claws would cut through Michael's throat in one clean slice, but as the grizzly reared, the eagle landed.

Sinking its talons into the bear's face, the immense, golden bird clutched the neck and face of its prey and continued to beat its wings as if it might fly away with Ross's head for a trophy. The grizzly gave a higher-pitched roar this time, and swung a brutish arm at the eagle, glancing off its body but leaving three bloody marks behind.

Before the bear could take another swipe, the rattler had returned from its chase of the Native-American man and was viciously biting at the bears legs. At the sight of the striking serpent, Sylvie screeched but didn't let go of Michael. Instead she clung harder, using him as a shield from the relentless snake.

The dogs were in on the fight now, leaping and snarling at the bear. Ross began to twist and turn in his grizzly form, trying to dislodge the many assailants that were pulling and ripping at his skin. After an agonized howl, he began to shift, shrinking quickly with a wet sucking noise as he imploded into the form of small bird. Once released from the eagle's grasp, he wasted no time before zipping past Ronja's startled face and into the safety of the plantation home.

Paige and the brunette stopped sparring and stumbled away from each other, both gasping after their exertions.

Shauni silently pushed an order toward the animals to cease and await her command. "Unless you want to find yourself covered with snakes, Sylvie, I'd let him go," Shauni said in a menacing voice as she strode toward the hoodoo priestess now wrapped around Michael like a drowning woman on a buoy. "On second thought. That gator hasn't gotten any action yet, and he looks pretty hungry."

Glancing around to see she was alone, and that Shauni was still advancing, Sylvie scrambled away from Michael, making a wide circle to avoid the rattler before climbing up the side of the porch to leap over its rotting banister.

Shauni found it laughable that the sadistic Amara woman was afraid of snakes.

Michael crossed to Shauni and swept her up in his arms, temporarily forgetting everything except his fear for her. "Don't ever do that again," he grumbled against her neck as he held her close, breathing the clean, apple smell of her hair.

"What," she asked innocently. "Save your life?"

Michael let go of her and turned toward the house as if suddenly remembering where they were. "You know what

I'm talking about." He squeezed her hand and began moving backwards, pulling her along. "Don't ever leave me again."

Shauni kept her eyes on Ronja, who looked as if she were about to detonate. "Never again." She let the love she felt for Michael run through her body and glow from every living part of her. "I've got something I want to tell you," she added. "Later."

"You don't have to," Michael said in a satisfied male voice. "You're aura just changed." He stopped when they got far enough away from the house and pulled Shauni to him. Wrapping his arms around her waist and pressing his chest to her back, he whispered in her ear. "And I love you, too."

The amulet on Shauni's chest began to warm against her skin, but it took her a moment to notice, since she was still wrapped up in the wonder of Michael's words. It all made sense to her now. *Iomlanaich*. She was complete.

And she had passed her trial.

A cry of outrage burst from Ronja's lips, her lovely mouth twisted in fury. With a swing of her arm lightning arced through the sky to land near Shauni and Michael, blackening the ground and leaving little doubt of the Amara leader's ability.

"You're too late, Ronja," Anna cried out. She raised one finger while holding Ronja's eyes locked with her own. "Listen."

At first it was a high, thin wail, like a finger encircling a shiny, crystal glass. It slowly grew, becoming more glorious with each passing second, a sound like none Shauni had ever heard. It was beauty and light in a gentle, lilting harmony.

It was coming from Shauni's necklace. If there had been any doubt regarding Shauni's feat, there was none remaining as the amulet sang of her triumph.

Anna stepped in front of Shauni and Michael. "It's done, Ronja. Over. If you strike her now, you will forfeit, and even your demon won't be able to repair the damage."

Like a curtain dropped after the final act, Ronja's face collapsed into a calm but aggravated look of defeat. "You don't need to educate me on the prophecy, Anna. You're a child, a novice compared to me." She turned a scathing look on Shauni that would have flayed her skin had it been a physical blow. "Enjoy your period of protection." Ronja smiled. "It won't last long."

With a dismissive toss of her head, the queen of the damned turned and stalked back into the old mansion. Her parting words had been unsettling, reminding the coven that the war was far from over.

Still gripping Michael's hand, Shauni faced her coven. "Let's go home."

~

Candles flickered and incense permeated the air with the thick, spicy scent of exotic flowers. A dark blue globe rested on the wooden table that stretched along the wall of Anna's sitting room, under double windows thrown open to the night sky. The salty breeze from the ocean carried in to blend with the perfumed incense, enveloping Anna in a haven of pleasure.

It was always easier to see things when her body was relaxed, and aroma therapy was a well-known friend.

Downstairs, the witches were rehashing the events of the day, relieved and thrilled by Shauni's victory. Anna had left them in the midst of an impromptu party around Kylie's magic coffee machine. With complete confidence in her young charges, Ms. Attinger, along with Joe's wife, Claire, had prepared a celebratory feast, complete with a multitude of vegetarian dishes in deference to their guest of honor.

Anna had enjoyed the meal and shared in the revelry but had slipped away to her quarters, bringing with her a cup of coffee to sip while making preparations. Her gift was sporadic at times, showing her things she hadn't known to expect, but she still had the power to call forth what she needed to see.

If the spirit world was agreeable.

It was a blessing for her to receive information that would aid the coven in their quest to fulfill the prophecy, but it was also a frustration that the invisible forces expected her to work with patchwork bits of information. With Shauni, she'd revealed only portions of what she knew for fear of interpreting the messages incorrectly and sending her fellow witch down the wrong path.

When she was given a clear and whole picture, she knew it was for the benefit of the coven as much as herself, and she felt a tingle in the wind that told her tonight would be a good time to commune with the secrets of the universe.

After the abrupt vision at the Amara plantation, as she now thought of it, Anna knew there was something she was supposed to discover. She needed to take a look at what might come, now that she was sure another Amara member had yet to be recruited.

One that would be vital to the fulfillment of the prophecy.

She sat on the dressing table bench of red velvet, the perfect height for looking into her globe. She refused to call it a crystal ball. In fact, it was a only a decorative garden globe, but any reflective surface would serve, and the deep blue iridescence helped soothe her into the right state of mind.

Glancing up, she saw distant clouds wisp away to reveal the new moon. Another good sign. This phase of the moon was connected to the Dark Mother, the Wise One who controlled cosmic energies. It was the perfect night for meditations and achieving spiritual knowledge.

Anna's lids closed gently as a continuous breath eased from her lungs, taking the last of any remaining tension with it. Her vision remained misty behind her closed eyes for only a moment before the image came upon her again, swiftly, like before, but with none of the pain she'd felt. She made the quick realization that opening her mind around the Amara, particularly Ronja, had been a mistake, but didn't have a chance to dwell on the insight.

Her third eye had been drawn to a room, or rather a place. She was in a magical forest, with pristine red apples and golden pears hanging in the surrounding trees. A woman with long white hair stood beside a portable chalkboard, no a whiteboard. Even her visions were adjusting to modern times.

Was the woman real, the representative of an actual soul that had crossed over? Or was she a symbol? Age was often equated with wisdom.

The older woman brought her hand up to write on the board, her silver robe swinging and shimmering with the movement. She began to draw a large circle, leaving blank spots in places, then crossing them with short lines. Another arc and a few more connections made it clear she was creating a labyrinth.

Then the woman made a small dot on the outside of the maze and pointed to Anna.

"That's me," Anna said, receiving a nod for her correct answer.

Arm lifting in a silver flash, the woman made another mark at the center of the labyrinth, a question mark, and turned back to Anna for a response.

"I don't understand. Am I supposed to go to a labyrinth?" As with all riddles, Anna knew to ask short, simple questions. If she asked two in one, and only part of it was correct, the vision's answer of yes or no would still be ambivalent.

The woman shook her head in the negative.

"Should I build a labyrinth?"

Still no.

"The labyrinth is a symbol?"

A nod for yes from the old woman.

Anna pondered and chose the most inclusive word. "It

symbolizes finding something."

"Yes."

When the woman spoke, Anna knew she was getting close, and the urgency in the vision's voice alarmed her. She was about to lose it. "Is it an object?" Anna asked quickly.

A shake of the head.

"A person."

"Yes."

There was so much more she needed and not enough time. Frustrated, Anna blurted out, "How am I supposed to know who to find? I need more."

"That you need to find them is the answer."

With a rush of air and floral spice, Anna found herself back in her room with nothing but burning candles and a spring night's chorus of frogs serenading the island.

21

"Well, it makes perfect sense to me," Claudia said over her steaming cup of French vanilla coffee.

Anna had returned to the kitchen, bringing the riddle to the others as soon as she'd finished her trip to the alternate dimension. The message was for all of them, she was sure, and their input was crucial.

"It *would* make perfect sense to you," Paige chided, sweeping her white-blonde hair out of her eyes. "You always speak in riddles. They're practically your second language." The teasing was good-natured, though, as they were all feeling pretty happy. They had been dragged into roles of serious consequence, to protect those who didn't even know they were in danger, and they had all come into this as strangers.

Now they were family.

"So share with us, Teach," Kylie said, hoisting herself onto the granite countertop and looking more youthful than ever with the action. Even she and Quinn were getting along tonight. Whatever grudges those two bore each other had been put aside so they could enjoy the festivities.

"What is any person that has to be found?" Claudia asked the room at large.

"They're lost," Michael volunteered, then looked around as if concerned he'd crossed into something he shouldn't have. He'd been welcomed by everyone, especially after his horrifying initiation into the club, so to speak, but wasn't sure if he was supposed to be participating in "coven business."

Anna's crinkling eyes and easy smile relieved him of that notion. "That's exactly right. We need to find the one that's lost."

Wearing her glasses as she often did when in thinking mode, Viv gave a double blink with her gorgeous Asian eyes. "Sorry, but did I miss the description of said lost person? I still don't know who we're looking for. Anything you need to look for is lost by definition." She crinkled her nose. "I just repeated the riddle, sort of. I'm confusing myself."

"Yeah, stick to the easy stuff like your quantum physics," Shauni said with a grin before throwing a carrot stick at Viv.

Hayden snatched it out of the air to swipe it through veggie dip and plunk it in her mouth.

"You said you felt the need to meditate tonight, because you thought you were supposed to see something," Willyn said in her calm voice. Tadd had already been put to bed with Skid after the two had eaten too much cake. Her son and Shauni's puppy had bonded, and she would swear they were bad influences on each other. She'd have to remember to ask Shauni what she heard in that little dog's head.

Looking at Anna she added, "So what were you thinking about before you had the vision tonight?"

Anna nodded slowly then with more enthusiasm. "I was considering what I had learned earlier, about the addition of a new person to the Amara. I think that person will be significant, either by helping fulfill the prophecy or de-railing it."

"You think that's who we're supposed to find?" Lucia asked. She was spooning in another bite of the *Tortilla de patatas*, or potato omelet, Claire had cooked. It reminded her of home and the housekeeper who'd been like a mother to her, in the absence of the woman who'd actually given birth to her.

"I do." Anna looked more closely at what Lucia was eating. "I don't think I've had any of that. Looks good."

"So we're supposed to find a person and a burial place? Or will the person be in the burial place? Maybe the person is dead," Kylie said, dragging out the last word in a horror movie voice.

"I don't think so," Anna and Shauni said in unison before grinning at each other. Then Anna added, "I think I have an idea on that, but let's leave it for tomorrow, shall we? I'm bushed, not to mention starving." She reached for a plate.

"Wait." All heads turned to Hayden, normally the quiet one, at least compared to the others. The serious tone had gotten everyone's attention. "When will we find out who's next?"

"I don't honestly know," Anna answered. "I hate to sound like a broken record..."

"A what?" Kylie asked.

"Tell me it isn't so," Viv said, rolling her head back. "No one can be that young."

"Get with it, sister," Claudia said, offering Viv a piece of chocolate cake in sympathy. "We're the last of a dying breed. We didn't grow up speaking with our thumbs."

"Hey," Kylie said the word with three extra syllables.

"Anyway," Anna said, "back to your question, Hayden." She lifted one shoulder. "We'll know when we're supposed to."

Hayden frowned and replied, "Cryptic."

"Welcome to my world." Anna eyed the Spanish dish again. "Now, do I need to warm that up?"

And as easily as that, they returned to everyday small talk and filling their bellies with food, the mystery of the riddle solved, to a degree, and plenty of dessert left to be consumed. The choosing of the next to face her challenge would have to be left in the hands of fate, or magic, as Anna would say.

Another hour and a half was all Shauni could wait before she slipped out of the kitchen and into the grand hall with Michael. They made it as far as the second floor before falling into each other, their searching hands and mouths worshipping and seeking assurance that they were both alive and well. The day had been difficult, to say the least.

Though Michael had been the one restrained and abused by the Amara thugs, he'd still felt his blood drain straight out of his body and into the ground when he saw Shauni standing in the yard, alone with no weapon or any type of protection.

He'd underestimated her influence over the animals, or really, their connection with her. Respect? Kinship? Maybe even love. They had essentially offered themselves as sacrifice when Shauni needed them. When he had needed them as well.

And Shauni. His sweet little pacifist had surged toward the fiendish group with hell in her eye. Forget a woman scorned. He would forever remember a witch riled, ebony hair tossed about in the wind and brilliant green eyes aflame with promised restitution.

She had been magnificent.

He was getting turned on just thinking about it. That and whatever she was doing with her tongue.

Ending the kiss abruptly to regain his senses, Michael retreated and motioned for Shauni to come with him.

"But..." she said in a take-me-to-bed voice, sending a look of longing toward her bedroom.

"I know." Michael drew a deep breath then expelled it, looking over the black lace top and practical cargo pants. He knew what was hidden beneath the clothing. "Believe me. I know. If we go in there now, we'll never get this done."

"Get what done?" she asked with an irritated look, having no choice but to go after him as he headed back downstairs and toward the solarium.

Michael kept walking but tossed over his shoulder, "The talk."

"No. You're not serious," Shauni said with a droop of her shoulders. Reluctantly she followed after him, and mumbled beneath her breath, "I'd rather we had the sex."

Either he hadn't heard or was ignoring the comment, as he continued on, stopping only when he was deep in the foliage of the solarium, facing toward the window he'd been looking out the night before when he'd spotted the approaching invaders. With his hands on his waist and legs spread in a stance, Michael appeared to be deep in thought over a troubling matter.

Shauni came to a stop behind him and waited in silence, more than willing to allow him the floor. Eventually he turned, and the stern expression was not that of a man inflamed by passion.

"You still have something to say to me. Out loud and while looking me in the eye this time," he told her.

Michael pulled his glasses out of his pocket and put them on. The first time Shauni had ever seen him find them on the first try. Uh-oh. This was serious.

"But let me lay down something now, before we go any further." With the muscles flexing in his jaw, Michael penetrated her with a hard stare, virtually gluing her to the spot where she stood. "No more deceit. Of any kind."

Shauni swallowed past the lump in her throat. "I thought we already covered that."

"Funny. I thought we did, too. Then I was drugged and left to wonder if the woman I loved was being violated or mutilated while I lounged in the sheets where we'd just shared magic. Literally magic, because I felt it, too."

His face had grown red at the edges, and one temple pulsed so hard Shauni could see it. He was well and truly pissed.

"It was just a little belladonna," she said. "I was only protecting you."

That did it.

Michael made it to her in two large steps. "Don't do it again. Not that way. If I can't trust you, Shauni," he gripped her arms, "really trust you, then we're going nowhere. I won't be with someone who lies to me, for any reason." He let her go and stepped away. "Even you." The words seemed to cut him open as they left his mouth, but Michael couldn't be with Shauni again, couldn't let her in any more than he already had if she wouldn't stand with him on even ground.

With hot tears trapped inside a pounding head and her throat clogged with anguish, Shauni could only nod.

"You think I don't realize what you're involved in? How could I not, after today?" Michael paced the tiled floor in an attempt to vent some of his irritation. The more he thought of his panic and fear from this morning, the more upset he became. "I can't live every day wondering if you're sneaking off for some covert operation or to go up against them alone." He stopped, brows slashed together. "Because right now, I wouldn't put it past you."

Clearing her throat, Shauni lifted apologetic eyes, glimmering green from the unspent fear that she might have pushed him too far. "You're absolutely right. One-hundred percent. I've lied and tricked you at every turn, and originally I was protecting myself, because I've been burned a few times after telling a man my secret." She was the one who stepped forward now, holding up a hand to silence him before he could respond. "Let me finish." She smiled. "Please."

The large peace lily that bloomed to the side suddenly became an item of interest to Shauni. More like a diversion, but she stroked its dark, shiny leaves anyway and found the courage to forge ahead. "You're not like them. I know that... now. But at first, how could I? In addition to myself, I felt it was my obligation to protect the existence of the coven as well. I'd only just met Anna and the others. What kind of person would I have been to spout off about them to some guy I'd just started dating?"

"Some guy," Michael said incredulously.

"You know you're more than that, but at the time, that's how it would have been. One should guard the secrets of others as veraciously as they would their own. Maybe more. So that's what I did, and honestly, I wouldn't change anything in that regard." Easing over to him to place a hand on his chest, Shauni said, "And I wanted you to stay here, safe on the island, when I faced my trial. I was afraid you'd get hurt, true, but I was also afraid you might be a distraction, and I had others to think about."

Lifting one onyx bow, Shauni said, "If you'd been a little more cooperative, I might not have used such drastic measures."

"I won't be any better in the future, that I can tell you." Michael's gray eyes held hers. "Don't you know I need to take care of you, too? The thought of losing you guts me. It's not a pleasant feeling."

His statement made Shauni deliriously happy and her smile bloomed. "I know. It was the same for me when they brought you out of that house. Which reminds me, how did they get to you?"

Michael glanced over her shoulder then back with a chagrined look on his face. "I sort of found them. Followed their murky trail all the way to the plantation." He shrugged unapologetically. "I thought you were in there, and that's all that registered, not the fact that there were about a hundred of them and they weren't exactly friendly. I had to find you."

"I'm so sorry." Shauni cupped his cheek. "From now on, we'll make decisions together. The ones that only concern us, anyway. I can't tell you the coven's decisions will be put aside if you don't agree with what path we choose, but I can promise you'll be my partner, in all things."

"That's all I ask." He pulled her close to lose himself in her soft warmth, the sexy smell of her that fired his need to fill her in every conceivable way and be overtaken by her in return. He felt her nestle closer and sigh against his neck. Right where he wanted her. "Don't you have something to tell me?" he asked.

Shauni didn't open her heart to him as she'd said she would, but countered instead. "Are you sure you can you still love me after what I did?" Her voice was faint, as if she were uncertain she really wanted an answer.

"What are you talking about?"

"For becoming so angry and violent. For using the animals that way." She shuddered. "Don't get me wrong. I know it was necessary, but it was just so unlike me or what I thought was me. I've changed, Michael. I understand what you mean now. That it's sometimes necessary to do something that goes against our very makeup, if it's for a greater cause." She bit her lip. "Still..."

Michael lifted her face when she let it fall, his gaze steady and full of the honesty they both needed. "I love you more for it. Going against your beliefs to save someone else, that wasn't wrong, it was completely selfless. You saved my life, Shauni." He grinned wickedly. "But next time it's my turn."

Placing her open palm against the purple bruise growing on the side of his face, Shauni was well aware of his bravery. Reckless or not, he'd gone up against black magic for her, unsure of what he would be facing.

Fools rush in. Cuileann said from somewhere in the house, and Shauni knew the cat had given her blessing.

Even though the man Shauni had chosen was a vet. With needles.

"I love you, Michael, and I'm going to spend every day for the rest of our lives showing you just how much." A deliciously warm sensation filled Shauni and glowed even brighter when she put her lips to his to seal the vow.

"Now," Michael sighed when they broke apart. "Now let's go have the sex."

Shauni laughed out loud, realizing he'd heard her after all. "And tonight, we'll let the animals sleep somewhere else. Don't want to leave them scarred for life."

Michael's eyes lit up. "Sounds like a plan."

Together they weaved their way back through the lush plants and fragrant flowers, back into the grand hall, and straight up the stairs.

Shauni was already sending signals to Cuileann to make herself scarce and to take the puppy with her.

Michael was watching Shauni as they made their way through the majestic island home, testing the soreness that lingered in his ribs and determining himself fit enough, thankfully, for whatever she had planned.

Alive and well and with the woman he loved, Michael knew her special gifts would never be an issue. Her powers complemented her. Completed her. They were her crowning jewels.

And he was one man who would forever be grateful that Shauni Miller could talk to animals.

Suza Kates writes both paranormal romance and suspense. She lives in Savannah, Georgia with her family and five ridiculously spoiled cats.

For more on Suza and her books visit

www.suzakates.com